Something hot...

Faith wanted to respond, but she was afraid. He held her forearms tightly and shook her.

"I am not one of your cats," he said.

"I know."

"I don't think you do."

"Why does it matter?" she asked desperately.

"What are you hiding from?"

Part of her noted he hadn't answered her question, so she wouldn't answer his. She knew exactly what she was hiding from. Him. Pretending he was just like one of the cats made him safe. It was dangerous to think of Cort as a man, because he tempted Faith. He made her think of family and forever, and she'd learned long ago that she didn't have what it took to inspire a man to want either.

His grip on her loosened, and she jerked away. She thrust a bandage at him. "Here. Finish it yourself." Then she fled the room.

Dear Reader,

It's March, and spring is just around the corner. To help you through the last of the chilly days and nights, we've got another lineup of terrific books just waiting to be read. Our American Hero this month is Linda Turner's *Cooper,* the next hot hero in her miniseries called "The Wild West." He's a man you won't want to miss.

The rest of the month is equally irresistible. Justine Davi is back with *Wicked Secrets,* a tale every bit as enticing as its title implies. Lee Magner's *Banished* makes it worth the wait since this talented author's last appearance. And then you'll find Beverly Barton's *Lover and Deceiver,* Cathryn Clare's *Sun and Shadow,* and Susan Mallery's debut for the line, *Tempting Faith.* Each one will have you turning the pages eagerly; this really is what romance is all about.

And in coming months, keep looking to Silhouette Intimate Moments for all the passion, all the excitement and all the reading pleasure you're seeking, because it's our promise to you that you'll find all that—and more—in our pages every month of the year.

Yours,

Leslie Wainger
Senior Editor and Editorial Coordinator

Please address questions and book requests to:
Reader Service
U.S.: P.O. Box 1325, Buffalo, NY 14269
Canadian: P.O. Box 1050, Niagara Falls, Ont. L2E 7G7

TEMPTING

FAITH

Susan Mallery

Silhouette®

INTIMATE MOMENTS®

Published by Silhouette Books New York

America's Publisher of Contemporary Romance

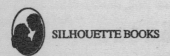 SILHOUETTE BOOKS

ISBN 0-373-07554-5

TEMPTING FAITH

Books by Susan Mallery

Silhouette Intimate Moments

Tempting Faith #554

Silhouette Special Edition

Tender Loving Care #717
More Than Friends #802
A Dad for Billie #834

SUSAN MALLERY

has always been an incurable romantic. Growing up, she spent long hours weaving complicated fantasies about dashing heroes and witty heroines. She was shocked to discover not everyone carried around this sort of magical world. Taking a chance, she gave up a promising career in accounting to devote herself to writing full-time. She lives in Southern California with her husband—"the most wonderful man in the world. You can ask my critique group." Susan also writes historical romances under the name Susan Macias. She loves to hear from readers, and you can write to her at P.O. Box 801913, Santa Clarita, CA 91380-1913.

To Stephanie, without whom a chair would have no emotional significance and "putting a finer point" on something would simply mean sharpening a pencil. Your instincts and insight have added clarity and depth to my writing, while your humor, intelligence and sensitivity have greatly enriched my life. Here's to all the good things to come.

Chapter 1

"**Y**ou need the extra security."

Faith Newlin shook her head and smiled. "Are you trying to convince me or yourself?"

"Maybe both."

"I'm already convinced. If you think I need the protection—" She shrugged. "I'm hardly going to argue. After all, you're the expert. What did that last promotion make you? Head spy?"

Jeff Markum, the chief of a division in an agency whose name Faith had never been told, grinned. "That's *Mr.* Head Spy to you."

"Give a man a promotion and it goes straight to his—" she paused for effect "—head."

"Watch it, Faith." He pointed at the badge hanging from a chain around her neck. "I could have your security clearance pulled in a second. Then where would you be?"

"Back home where I belong." She laughed. "Don't try threatening me, Jeff. You're the one who arranged for me to be here today. I'm pleased to know your agency trusts me, but if you want me to go back home, I'd be happy to." She grabbed the ID badge and started to release the chain.

"Don't leave yet." He pushed off the wall of the small observation room. "Let me go explain the situation to him."

Faith raised one hand and touched the two-way glass that allowed her to see into a hospital room, but didn't allow the patient to see her. "He doesn't know?"

Jeff shook his head. "Even though you need the extra protection, I was afraid you would fight me on this." He held up his hand to stop her interruption. "I know you think I'm overreacting. Maybe you're right. But there's this knot in my gut. I have a bad feeling about the whole thing. I want to keep you safe."

She looked up at the man towering over her. He had the easy good looks of a California surfer, but behind his deep blue eyes lurked the mind of a computer and the temper of an injured panther. Faith knew she should be intimidated by Jeff, but she'd known him too long. She trusted him— *and* the knot in his gut.

"It's your call," she said.

She turned back to the two-way mirror. This was no ordinary hospital. No mothers-to-be came here to give birth, no child had broken bones set. This secret facility, concealed behind high fences and guards with dogs that attacked on command, catered to those without identities. Shadowy figures who lived in the dark, who disappeared at will and carried out elaborate operations in places with names she couldn't pronounce.

"He's not like one of those wounded strays you take in, Faith. He's the best I've got, but he's damned dangerous, too. Be careful."

Faith glanced at her companion. "Because he knows fifty ways to kill me with his bare hands? Give me a break, Jeff. Use the scare tactics on your green recruits. They'll impress easier."

"You think you're so tough." His good humor faded into regret. "I wish we had time for dinner."

"I'll take a rain check. Next time I'll pack something nice to wear and you can take me to an expensive restaurant."

"You're on." He squeezed her arm and left the room.

Faith stared after him. He'd already forgotten her, except as she related to his operative. She smiled to herself. *Operative.* She was starting to talk like them. She fingered the tag at the end of the chain. Jeff saw her for what she was: a nice person, competent at her job. She sighed. At one time she'd hoped for something more than friendship, but it wasn't going to happen. No great surprise. Her luck with men had never been the best. But there were compensations, she told herself. She had a fine life, a career she loved. She didn't need anything else to feel fulfilled. Yeah, right, she thought. Now who was trying to convince whom?

She turned her attention back to the two-way mirror and the man on the other side, in the hospital room. He stood next to his window, the one that looked out over the grounds. Instead of a hospital gown, he wore a T-shirt and jeans cut off on one leg to accommodate the thick bandage around his calf. There was something tense and watchful in his pose. Ever alert, he scanned the open area. Perhaps it was the set of his head, or the way he kept glancing over his shoulder toward the mirror, as if he sensed someone watched from the other side, but he intrigued her. He reminded her of Sparky. She smiled, wondering if he would care for the comparison to her favorite cat.

His lips moved, but the two-way glass didn't allow her to hear his words. With a quick twisting motion, he picked up the crutches that rested next to the window and slipped them under his arms. Despite the bandage on his leg, and the crutches, he shifted his weight with graceful ease and began to pace the room. From end to end he moved, swinging his useless leg along, mumbling phrases she couldn't make out.

On his third pass, he paused, then turned toward the mirror. He looked directly at her. She knew he couldn't see her, but she backed up instinctively, as if he'd threatened her.

Light hit him full in the face, sharpening already gaunt features. Was the thinness the result of his injuries or the mission he'd been on? The cut on his chin looked raw. Tiny stitches held the skin together. Fading bruises darkened his left cheek. Tawny hair, more gold than blond, fell over his forehead. But it was his eyes that captured her attention and held her immobile.

Dark brown irises glittered with suppressed rage. A trapped animal. The predator had been captured and wounded. Jeff was right: this man *was* dangerous. Without thinking, she rubbed her right hand against her upper arm. It wasn't until her fingers felt the ridges of the four long scars there that she realized what she was doing. Marks left by another predator, the four-legged kind.

The man blinked and turned away. She followed the movement and saw that the door to his room had opened. Jeff appeared and spoke to the man. Faith stared at their mouths, trying to lip-read, but it wasn't any use. From their angry gestures, she knew they were arguing. The injured man stood eye to eye with Jeff, and neither gave an inch. Jeff wore a suit, but he still looked muscular and dangerous. Two lions fighting for their pride. If the stranger weren't injured, it would have been an even match.

For the second time, he glanced at the two-way glass. Faith felt a flash of guilt. Eavesdropping, even without sound, wasn't her style. She turned and walked out of the observation room. It was almost eleven in the morning. She had a six-hour drive ahead of her, plus supplies to pick up. She was leaving within the hour, with or without Jeff's wounded man.

"I need to know, dammit." Cort Hollenbeck grabbed the crutches and leaned on them. "And you're going to tell me."

His boss sat on a corner of the hospital bed. "The doctor said—"

"The doctor can shove his advice." Cort swung around on the crutches and glared. "There are things I can't remember. I spent three weeks in South America on a mission. I don't know what happened there." Sweat popped out on his back. His leg throbbed from the surgery two days before and his head pounded. "For all I know, I went on a killing spree and shot up an entire town. So you're going to tell me what the hell happened down there!" He raised his voice until he shouted the last few words.

Jeff didn't look the least bit intimidated. He crossed his arms over his chest. "No."

Cort tightened his hands on the crutches. He wanted to force Jeff to answer. Not a chance of that. Between his bum leg and his aching head, he would barely get off the first punch before Jeff nailed him. He swung the crutches forward and eased himself into the plastic chair in front of the window.

"The doctor said you would remember on your own." Jeff leaned forward. "I understand what you're going through."

"Like hell you do."

Jeff ignored him. "And I sympathize."

"I liked you better before your promotion," Cort snarled.

"I didn't think you admitted to liking anyone," Jeff said calmly. "Professionals don't get involved. Aren't you the one always preaching that?"

Cort didn't bother answering. He dropped the crutches onto the ground and leaned his head back in the chair. As hard as he tried, he couldn't remember. There were bits and pieces of conversation. A word or two in Spanish and Portuguese. The flash of a face, then nothing. Three weeks of his life gone. He remembered leaving the States on a private plane. He remembered waking up in the same craft, only with the mission over, and he didn't have a clue what had happened. He fingered the cut on his chin. Bullet to the leg and a slight concussion. So much for bringing back souvenirs.

"You'll remember in time," Jeff said. "Don't push it."

"That's easy for you to say. You're not the one—" Cort bit back the words. God, he had to know. "Is he dead?"

Jeff didn't answer.

Cort sprang to his feet and almost fell when his bad leg gave out. Instantly Jeff was at his side, supporting him. Cort grabbed the other man's suit jacket. "Is he?"

Jeff stared at him. His mouth tightened. "I'm not going to fight you."

Cort released his grip on the jacket and slumped back in the seat. "Only because you know I'd beat the crap out of you."

"I'm shaking with fear." Jeff stared down at him. "So you remember that much?"

"Dan, you mean?"

Jeff nodded.

"Yeah. I remember I was meeting Dan. I don't know why, or if I did."

"And you think he might be dead?"

Cort closed his eyes and rubbed his thumb and forefinger over the bridge of his nose. No, he thought. I think *I* killed him. But he couldn't say that. No matter how much he thought it, he couldn't say those words.

"Is he?" he asked.

"Yes."

Cort snapped his head up. "You're sure?"

"We have a witness."

The pain in Cort's leg intensified. He thought of the dead man. They'd met in training, almost fifteen years ago. They'd worked together countless times. Had he killed his friend? Jeff was right, it wasn't supposed to matter. But, dammit, it did. It mattered a lot.

"Don't push it," Jeff told him. "It'll come to you." He returned to the hospital bed and perched on the corner. The morning sun flooded the small room, highlighting the institutional furniture and scarred green linoleum. "And while you're getting your memory back, I have an assignment."

Cort raised his injured leg. "Aren't I on medical leave?"

"Yes."

"Then I'm going home."

Jeff stood up and shoved his hands in his pockets. "I need you to do something for me."

"But you said—"

"Unofficially." Jeff walked over to the window and stared out. "I can't assign anybody through regular channels. I don't have specifics, just a gut feeling."

"Which is?"

"There's going to be trouble." Jeff looked at him. "I need you to look after a friend of mine. Provide a little security. Nothing high tech. She's located—"

"She?"

"Her name is Faith. She lives up in the mountains. Runs a way station. I left a package in her care. The men we took it from might want it back. I want you to be there to stop them. If there's any trouble, I'll have the proof I need to officially provide backup. I know it's asking a lot. I wouldn't, if I had another option. You up to it?"

Cort thought about his small one-bedroom apartment in D.C. It was late spring. The tourists would be flocking into the city, and the temperature would be rising. Last time he'd stayed at the apartment, the air-conditioning had given out twice in three days. He thought about the time he and Jeff had spent in Iraq. On more than one occasion, the other man had been there to save his skin. This favor sounded like a way to even the score.

Cort grabbed the crutches and used them to help him stand. "I'm up to it."

"Thanks, Cort." Jeff collected the duffel bag from the locker against the far wall. "The place isn't fancy, but I think you'll like it. Plan on staying a few weeks. Two months at the outside."

"Who's this woman? Agency?"

"Private. A friend. You can trust her."

Cort was doubtful. Trust wasn't something that came easily to him. "She know what I'm there for?"

"She understands that there might be some problems and is willing to take precautions." He pointed at the bandage around Cort's calf. "She's great with wounds."

"Sounds like you speak from personal experience."

Jeff's blue eyes grew stark. "She took care of me after Lebanon."

Cort moved into the small rest room and collected his belongings. He worked slowly, giving Jeff time to put the past in its place. His boss had almost died in Lebanon, but that wasn't what caused his expression to grow bleak. He'd also lost his wife and young son to terrorists.

Cort zipped the shaving kit and hobbled over to the bed. He dropped the case into the open duffel bag. "Seems like I'll be gone long enough to get back to a hundred percent. You didn't happen to plan that, did you, boss?"

Jeff shrugged. "It works for both of us."

"What about South America? What if I don't remember?"

Jeff pulled the duffel bag shut and slung it over one shoulder. "If you don't remember by the time you're healed, you can read the file, and to hell with what the doctor says. You have my word."

Cort nodded. It was something to hang on to. But he knew the price of Jeff's offer. If he hadn't recovered his memory, he wouldn't be coming back. The agency didn't have a place for someone who couldn't remember whether or not he'd killed a fellow operative.

"Thanks," he said. He shrugged into a dark blue jacket, then slipped the crutches in place. "If I have a choice, I won't be taking you up on your offer. I'll be at work instead."

"Good." Jeff walked to the door and held it open. "I want you back. You're my best man."

"You always say that," Cort grumbled. "I heard you were telling John the same thing. We can't both be the best."

Jeff grinned but didn't answer.

Cort followed his boss into the hall of the hospital. Several medical personnel nodded as he passed them. They wore ID tags with photos and numbers, but no names. At the end of the corridor, Jeff turned left. Cort hobbled along behind. He scanned the smooth floor, the walls, the doorways they passed, instinctively looking for escape routes. It wasn't necessary; he was safe here. Old habits, he thought grimly. In his current condition he would get about ten yards before being taken down. He needed time to heal...and to remember.

A woman stood in the waiting room. As Jeff entered, she smiled her greeting. They spoke softly, but her eyes strayed past her companion. Cort paused in the doorway and met her gaze.

Blue eyes, he catalogued, taking in the flicker of guilt that told him she'd watched him through the two-way glass in his hospital room. Hair: brown, nondescript, long. Medium height for a woman. Work shirt, jeans, boots. Instinctively, he calculated an approximate weight, made a mental note of her straight posture, evidence of physical confidence, and guessed she was in reasonably good shape. Ordinary.

No danger, unless she came armed. His gaze moved back to her face. Mid- to late twenties, he thought, then dismissed the idea that she and Jeff were lovers. They stood close together, as if they'd known each other a long time, but there wasn't anything between them. The throbbing in his leg picked up a notch, and he shifted his weight to relieve some of the pressure.

"Faith, this is Cort Hollenbeck," Jeff said, placing his hand on the small of her back and urging her forward. "Cort, Faith Newlin."

"Nice to meet you." She extended her hand.

It took him a moment to untangle himself from the crutches. Most people would have been uncomfortable and dropped their arm, mumbling something about it not mattering. She stood there patiently, waiting as if she had all the time in the world.

Her grip surprised him. Not so much the strength of her grasp—given her wardrobe, she wasn't a socialite. No, it was the rough skin he felt on her palm, the calluses. This woman did physical labor on a daily basis.

Their eyes met. Not unattractive, he thought. He studied the straight short nose and full lips that curved up slightly. As he'd decided before—ordinary. Little temptation there. Just as well. He didn't need the complication.

"Ms. Newlin." He nodded.

"Faith." Again her lips curved up slightly, as she withdrew her hand.

"I'm ready, if you are."

"Fine." She glanced at Jeff. "What about medication?"

"Something for pain, some antibiotics in case of infection. I'll get them." He looked at Cort. "You'll want to be armed. A Beretta?"

Cort raised his eyebrows. "Works for me."

"Faith?" Jeff asked.

She shrugged. "I have rifles, but only one handgun. A small revolver." She looked at Cort. "You'd probably be embarrassed to be seen with it."

Interesting. A woman who knew about guns. He hadn't had a chance to think about this new assignment, but so far it wasn't too bad. Close quarters with Faith Newlin. She wasn't a fashion model, but all cats were gray in the dark. Maybe the thought of bullets flying would scare her. Just enough, he thought, trying to remember how long it had been since he'd eased himself between a woman's welcoming thighs.

"I'll get the medication and the gun and meet you at the truck," Jeff said, handing her the duffel bag and leaving.

Faith hung back, but Cort shook his head. "I'll go behind you," he said.

"Suit yourself." Her long hair, pulled back at the front, but otherwise left free, hung over her shoulders. With a quick flick of her wrist, she sent the strands flying out of her way. "I'm parked in the rear lot. Do you want a wheelchair?"

The look he tossed her had often caused armed criminals to flinch. She simply blinked twice and waited patiently for his response.

"No," he said at last.

"It's your neck."

"Actually it's my leg."

She smiled quickly, and he had the thought that it made her look pretty.

"Humor," she said. "A good sign."

As she walked past him, he inhaled the scent of her perfume. French. The name of the brand escaped him. Expensive. Out of place. The information joined the rest of his mental file on her. Shifting his weight, he swung the crutches in front of him and started down the hall.

They'd covered about twenty feet when she started to turn right down another corridor. Suddenly she gasped and jumped back, blocking his path. He couldn't see what had startled her. He heard a loud crash.

Instinctively he dropped the crutches. With one arm, he grabbed Faith around the waist and threw her to the ground. He dropped to the floor, rolled to cushion his fall, biting back a grunt of pain as his weight settled on his injured leg. He came to a stop beside her. With a smooth, practiced motion, he reached for the gun in his waistband.

Nothing. No holster, no weapon. He looked up. Two terrified orderlies stood beside the pile of fallen trays. They started forward to help, took one look at the expression on his face and turned in the opposite direction.

Faith raised herself up on one elbow and studied him. Her blue eyes radiated nothing more than concern. "Did you hurt yourself, Mr. Hollenbeck?"

"Cort," he grunted, between waves of pain. "I'm fine. What about you?"

She pushed herself into a sitting position. "Nothing broken. Do you need help up?"

"No."

She scrambled to her feet. After retrieving the crutches, she stood patiently while he maneuvered himself upright. She handed him the crutches.

"I'm not crazy," he said, knowing exactly how it all looked. Had they told her he'd lost part of his memory?

"That thought never crossed my mind." She turned and continued walking down the hall.

He could feel blood oozing out of the stitches in his leg. Damn. It had finally begun to heal. Maybe he should get somebody to look at it before—

No. It would stop soon enough. Now that he was close to leaving the hospital, he realized how much he'd hated the confinement. He'd been pretty out of it the first week, but the last few days had crawled by. He'd slowly been going crazy trying to force himself to remember.

Faith stopped at the rear entrance and stepped on the automatic door pad. Smiling at the guard on duty, she spoke her name, then Cort's. The older man punched a few keys in his computer keyboard, then nodded.

Freedom. Cort inhaled the dry desert air and held back a sigh. Sweet and clean. Enough to go around.

Suddenly the ground shifted and his vision blurred. Instead of the guard and the woman, he saw the dusky interior of a South American warehouse. Dank smells indicated he was near water. The ocean? Was the scent salty?

Danger! The thought exploded in his mind. Get out. Yet as he turned to run, the picture dissolved. His crutch caught on the lip of the door pad. As the flashback receded, he felt himself slipping. Faith leapt to his side and grabbed the shaky crutch. One strong arm gripped his waist and held him steady.

She had curves under that baggy work shirt, he thought as her right breast flattened against his side. The intellectual information battled with a sudden rush of sexual interest. That, more than the fall, returned him completely to the present.

"You all right?" she asked, looking up at him.

She was wary, but not afraid. She should be. Hadn't Jeff told her what he was capable of? His head began to throb. He'd remembered. Not a lot, but something new. Sweat coated his body. He just wanted to get out of here.

He jerked himself free. "I'm fine. Where's your car?"

She pointed toward a battered four-wheel-drive pickup. He angled himself in that general direction and began to lurch toward it.

Jeff met them at the truck. "This should keep you comfortable." He held a bag of medicine in one hand and a gun in the other.

Cort thought about telling him he'd remembered something, but he held back. He'd know soon enough—when the whole memory returned. Jeff opened the car door and tossed the medication on the dashboard. Cort hopped until the seat pressed against the back of his thighs. After sliding on the cracked vinyl, he lifted his bum leg into the cab and handed Jeff his crutches. Jeff settled them in the back and gave him the pistol.

"Here's a spare magazine and a hundred rounds." He set a small paper bag on the floor of the cab. "Try not to shoot yourself in the foot."

"I'll do my best."

Faith dropped his duffel bag in the back of the truck, then gave Jeff a hug. "Don't forget about my rain check," she said.

"I won't." He held her for a minute.

Cort watched the expressions chase across his boss's face. He knew the flash of pain came from remembering his wife. Cort looked away. Caring turned a man inside out. Exposed him. That's why he would never get involved.

Faith slid in next to him and fastened her seat belt. She stared at him until he did the same. Then she smiled. Again, he thought it made her look pretty.

"You going to hold that in your hand the whole way?" She pointed at the gun.

He stared at the weapon, then thought about how he'd reacted to the crashing sound in the hospital. He was tired, and the surgery two days ago had used up the little reserves he'd had. What he needed was twelve hours of sleep. Until then, he wasn't going to be much good at protecting anyone.

"Here." He handed her the gun. "You keep it until tomorrow."

She studied his face. "Fine with me." She checked the safety, then pressed the button to release the magazine. After pocketing it, she jerked back the slide and looked in the chamber to make sure it didn't contain a round.

He raised his eyebrows. "I'm impressed."

"Then you impress easy." The gun went in the glove box. "And you're exhausted. We've got over a six-hour drive. Why don't you get some sleep? I need to make one stop. I'll wake you there and you can eat something."

"Sounds great." He leaned his head back and closed his eyes. She wasn't the sort of woman he normally picked, he thought as she started the truck and backed out of the parking space. He couldn't remember a single one of his lady friends ever owning a gun, let alone knowing how to handle one. And although she'd been friends with Jeff for years, his boss had never mentioned her.

"Here."

She thrust something soft into his hands. He cracked open one eye. A sweater.

"Use it for a pillow. Lock your door first. I don't want you falling out if I hit a bump."

"Thanks," he muttered as he bunched the sweater and pushed it up against the glass. He pressed down the lock and inhaled deeply. Her scent surrounded him, the elusive essence of that damned French perfume. What was it? He fell asleep still trying to remember the name.

She saw the first evidence of blood after they'd been on the road an hour. Keeping her attention on the sparsely traveled highway, she occasionally glanced at her sleeping passenger. He rested deeply, barely moving except for the rise and fall of his chest. Her gaze swept over him as she noted his size and strength and wondered at the cause of his injuries. At first she'd thought the dark stain on his white bandage was a shadow.

"Damn," she muttered softly. Over the next hour, the stain spread until it was the size of a half dollar. It showed no signs of letting up. He must have torn open his stitches when he'd dropped to the floor in the hospital.

She picked up a cassette and pushed it into the player. The radio was the only thing new in the cab. The vehicle itself had almost a hundred and fifty thousand miles on the odometer, but the engine had been replaced in the last six months and the tires were only two weeks old. She didn't care how the truck looked on the outside; she spent the money necessary to keep it running well. Without her truck available to pick up food, the cats would starve in a matter of days.

Two hours later she saw the sign for her turnoff. She moved to the right of the four-lane freeway then exited onto the two-lane highway that would take her north and home. Her passenger continued to sleep. She turned off at the tiny town of Bowmund and headed for the grain and feed.

At least one thing had gone right today, Faith thought as she signed for the supplies. Everything was ready. As soon as the boxes were loaded, she could head up the mountain. After picking up a quart of orange juice and a plastic wrapped sandwich from the grocery store, she walked back to her truck. Cort slept where she'd left him, resting his head against her sweater and the passenger window.

She eased open her door and slid into the seat. Where was that bag of medicine? She saw the white paper in the far corner of the dashboard. As she grabbed it, she glanced down. The blood on his bandage had widened to a circle the size of a grapefruit.

"If that doesn't stop, we're both in trouble," she said, not bothering to keep her voice down.

He didn't stir. She counted out the antibiotic dosage, confirmed that the instructions said to take the medication with food and touched his arm.

"Cort, wake up. You've got to take a couple of pills."

Nothing.

She pressed harder against his biceps, noting the thickness of the muscle. "Cort, wake up!"

It was like teasing a tiger. Without warning, he jerked upright, then spun and grabbed her. Before she could catch her breath, he'd pulled her head against his shoulder, holding her tight with one arm across her throat and pressing the other arm against her midsection.

"One more move," he growled into her ear, "and I'll kill you."

Chapter 2

Faith didn't move. She didn't even breathe. She held herself still, stifling the overwhelming urge to fight him. She wouldn't win. He had the strength and the skill to snap her neck with one swift jerk.

Her lungs burned for air. Panic threatened. Don't, she commanded herself. She'd been in worse situations. The trick was to keep her head. He would figure out she wasn't the enemy.

The steely arm around her throat loosened slightly. She drew in a deep breath. Her gasp sounded loud in the still cab.

Cort swore and released her completely. She fell forward and supported herself by pressing her hands against the seat. She inhaled deeply and coughed. Thank God. The cab darkened for a second, then came into focus.

After she caught her breath, she gingerly touched her neck, knowing that she would bear bruises for several days. She should have known better than to startle him, she thought, shaking her head in disgust. The same thing would have happened if she'd walked into a cage while a wounded animal was sleeping.

She located the pills she'd dropped when he grabbed her, and she turned slowly to face Cort. He leaned against the door of the cab and stared at her. She couldn't read the expression in his dark eyes. Something flickered there, something black and ugly, but she didn't know what it meant. Was he berating himself, or her? Silence stretched between them, broken only by the sound of their breathing.

"It could have been worse," she said at last, her voice a little raspy from the pressure on her neck.

He raised his eyebrows.

"You could have had the gun."

He didn't answer. Apparently he had no intention of apologizing.

She held out the pills and the container of orange juice. He took them, tossed back the medication and gulped the liquid without taking his eyes from her face. She wanted to look away but sensed he was challenging her. She forced herself to meet his gaze.

"How long since you've been in the field?" she asked.

"Two weeks."

"That explains—"

"Did Jeff tell you I was having flashbacks?" he asked, cutting her off.

"No." She swallowed. *Great.* "Should he have?"

"You tell me."

He held out the empty juice bottle. She took the plastic container and set it between them. Still his gaze locked on hers. He was making her nervous, but she refused to let him see her squirm. She allowed herself to study the straight line of his nose and the stubble darkening the hollows of his cheeks. He was handsome, she thought with some surprise. Perhaps even beautiful, with the wild unholiness of natural predators.

She shifted in her seat and reached for the sandwich she'd placed on the dashboard. "You're probably hungry," she said. "The instructions said to take the medication with food. I have to hook up the trailer and then we'll leave."

He didn't answer. She set the sandwich on his lap and turned toward the door. Before she could touch the handle, he spoke. "I tried to kill you."

"I know. You're also trying to intimidate me."

"What the hell are you still doing in this truck?"

"I don't scare so easy."

"Lady, there's something wrong with you."

She detected a note of grudging respect in his voice. "You're not the first person to notice," she said, looking at him over her shoulder. The early afternoon light caught the gold flecks in his brown eyes. Cat eyes. "How long has your leg been bleeding?"

He glanced down at the stained bandage. "Since I fell on it at the hospital."

"When was the surgery?"

"Two days ago. I think I ripped out some stitches."

"Terrific." She opened the door, then paused. "At the way station, we're over forty minutes from town and an hour and a half from real medical care. Do you need to see a doctor?"

"No."

She pointed to his leg. "If it gets infected, I'll probably just cut it off."

He rewarded her with a slight smile. It didn't make him look any less dangerous. "Deal."

She waited, hoping he would say something more. He didn't. "I've got to see to the supplies," she said. "I'll be right back." She slipped out of the truck and closed the door behind her.

Cort watched as several men finished loading supplies from the feed store into the back of Faith's truck. Carelessly, he picked at the food she'd handed him. His head ached, his leg throbbed and the pain in his gut came from a lot more than medication.

He'd almost killed her. If he'd had a knife or, in that split second when he'd lost track of what was real, his gun, she would be dead. For no good reason. She wasn't the enemy. Just an innocent bystander. He'd never lost control before, and it scared the hell out of him. How was he going to get it back?

He glanced in the side-view mirror and saw Faith talking to a man with a clipboard. She went down the list and pointed at the boxes they were loading into a separate trailer. The man started to argue. Before he'd said more than ten words, Faith planted her hands on her hips and started in on him. In about five seconds, he was nodding and backing up toward the building.

Who the hell was she? He tossed the half-eaten sandwich on the seat and clenched his hands into fists. He'd almost killed her, and she acted like nothing had happened. Jeff had said she needed protection. Cort shook his head. She seemed capable enough to him. He stared at the mirror. Faith stood by the back of the truck, counting the crates being loaded. She moved quickly and easily, as if she'd performed this task a hundred times before. Cool and competent—she turned and he saw the curve of her rear— and very much a woman.

He shifted his leg and felt a spurt of blood, then the warm dampness as it oozed against his skin. He closed his eyes. With a new bandage and a good night's sleep, physically he'd be fine. A couple of days and he would be a hundred percent. But what about the rest of it? What about his memory?

He went over what he'd remembered right before they left the hospital. Salt air. The ocean. He licked his lips as if the taste still lingered. Darkness. He remembered that. And danger. But from what? He strained to see into the gray mist of his mind. Had Dan been there with him? Had he died there?

Nothing. The past refused to focus. He groaned in frustration. What if he never remembered? Had he killed him? Had he killed Dan?

Cort propped his elbow on the door and rubbed his forehead. What was his mission? Dan was a fellow agent. Deep inside his memory, something clicked into place. Had his friend gone bad? Had Cort been sent to kill him? If he'd gotten the job done, he should forget it. Had he, though?

Thoughts circled around and around, until even what he could remember blurred with the fog.

"Stop it," he commanded himself. He would get nowhere like this. Dan was dead. He knew that for sure. The rest of it would come to him. It had to.

He'd gone too far with the last mission, he realized. He'd felt the warning signs of burnout and had ignored them. He should have turned down the assignment and taken a break. He'd been fighting the war for too long. He hadn't wanted to be cautious, and now he was paying the price.

Faith opened the door and slid onto the seat. He ignored her. He heard the click as she buckled her seat belt. He needed a plan. Whatever security he had to provide wouldn't take up too much of his time. He needed to get back in shape physically, and his memory would follow. First— A bump against his shoulder broke into his musings.

"Sorry," Faith said as she rested her arm on the top of the seat and began backing up the truck. "I hate this part."

He glanced out the rear window. "What are you doing?"

"See that big trailer there? It's supposed to be attached to this truck. That's what we haul up the mountain."

The trailer looked to be about as wide as the truck, maybe ten feet long and eight feet high. The painted sides didn't bear a logo.

"What's inside?"

"Food." She adjusted the steering wheel slightly and eased up on the accelerator. "Damn. Why do they have to watch? It makes me crazy."

He followed the direction of her gaze and saw a group of old men standing on the porch in front of the feed store. The building itself looked like it had been built during the forties. "What are they waiting for?"

"Me to mess up. They can't believe that a mere woman can handle a truck, let alone a trailer. They do this every time I come in for supplies."

"You ever mess up?"

A strand of her long hair fell over her shoulder. She flicked it back with a quick jerk of her hand and grinned. "Nope."

He found himself smiling in return. She made a final adjustment of the steering wheel, eased up on the accelerator and waited for the truck to roll to a halt.

"Did it!" she said and faced front. After rotating her shoulders to release the tension, she bounded out of the cab. "I just have to hook us up and then we're out of here. You want something more to eat?"

"No," he said. Then added a belated "Thanks."

As promised, she made quick work of the hitch. In less than ten minutes, the tiny town had been left behind and they began to drive up a steep mountain road.

Cort shifted in his seat, trying to ease the pain in his leg. Faith handled the truck easily, as if she were used to the winding roads. He studied her strong but small hands as they worked the gearshift. Who was she, and why wasn't she frightened of him? He'd almost killed her. She didn't look or act stupid, so what was her story?

He watched the road ahead. Tall trees, a few of them redwoods, came down to the edge of the highway. Recent spring rains left a carpet of lush new grass.

"I'm sorry," he said, staring straight ahead. "For what happened before. I could have hurt you."

"But you didn't. Apology accepted."

"That's it?" He glanced at her. She seemed intent on her driving.

"What more do you want?"

Something. He could have done a whole lot more than hurt her. "I almost killed you."

"I'm as much to blame. I shouldn't have startled you. I know better."

"How? Jeff said you were a civilian."

She gave him a quick smile. "Don't worry. I am. But I'm used to working with dangerous animals."

"It won't happen again," he promised.

"I know."

"How?"

"It won't happen again, because I won't startle you a second time. I'm a quick study."

He shifted in the seat until he faced her. He propped his injured leg on the hump in the floor that divided the cab in half. She rested both her hands on the steering wheel. Short nails, he thought. No polish. Sensible work clothes. He inhaled. But she wore French perfume.

"How do you know Jeff?" he asked.

"We met about six years ago. He was friends with the lady I worked for. When Jeff was hurt in Lebanon—" She glanced at him.

"I know about that," he said.

She nodded. "He came to stay with us for a few months. I helped patch him up. Kept him company. That sort of thing. We became friends."

"So you're a nurse?"

"Not exactly." She flashed him a smile, then sobered. "I guess when you go through what he did, you remember the people who got you through it."

Cort thought about those days. Jeff's injuries had been life-threatening, but it was the loss of his wife and child that had almost killed him. Four years ago. Before Jeff had been promoted. They'd worked together several times. Been gone enough for Jeff's marriage to falter and Jeff to start worrying about it. The worry distracted him and ultimately almost got him killed. He'd made the decision to do whatever it took to save his marriage, then boom. Jeanne and his son were dead.

Cort shook his head. It wasn't worth it. Relationships weighed a man down. Caring about anyone got in the way of getting the job done.

"Tell me about the way station," he said.

"We're about fifteen miles from our nearest neighbors," she said. "I have three college kids coming in part-time to help. We personally own about two hundred acres and have another thousand of leased forest land. There's a fence around most of the compound and a main gate at the entrance. We're pretty isolated."

"What's the way station for?"

She looked at him. Surprise widened her blue eyes. "I keep cats."

"Cats?" He rubbed his pounding temple.

"Jeff didn't explain?"

"No." He cursed under his breath. Cats? What had his boss gotten him into? He glanced at Faith. In her jeans and shirt, with her sensible work boots and unmade-up face, she didn't look like his idea of a person who kept bunches of cats, but then when had he ever met one? "So you keep, what, twenty of them in the house?"

She chuckled. Her smile could only be described as impish. "No cats in the house, I promise. And no more than forty or so at a time. I don't have the room."

"Forty?" He swallowed. Maybe he should have taken his chances with his D.C. apartment and the tourists.

"They aren't a bother."

"I bet."

"Oh, but Sparky does sort of have the run of the place."

"Sparky? Does *he* sleep in the house?"

"No, he sleeps in the office. He's our mascot."

"Great." He pictured some flea-bitten alley cat cowering in the corner.

"He was Edwina's favorite. Edwina is the lady who used to run the way station."

"So there really are forty cats?"

"And Sparky."

Oh, Christ. Cort leaned his head back and closed his eyes. Why was Jeff doing this to him? His boss was normally a pretty fair guy. Had the last assignment been messed up that badly?

He allowed himself to get lost in the pain, controlling his breathing and counting out his heartbeats. It wasn't until the truck slowed that he looked around.

She'd stopped to make a left-hand turn onto a dirt road. A small sign stated that they were entering the Edwina Daniels Feline Way Station.

She stared at the entrance. "The gate's open. I wonder why?" She shrugged. "Maybe the kids knew I'd be coming back."

"What's normal procedure?" he asked.

She pointed to the small black box attached to the sun visor on the passenger's side of the cab. "It's remote controlled."

He picked up the transmitter. "Looks like it's for a garage-door opener."

"It is. We modified it."

Which meant the electronic device on the gate could be defeated by a ten-year-old.

After shifting into neutral, she pulled on the lever that switched the truck from two- to four-wheel drive. "Hold on."

He gripped the window frame with one hand and the back of the seat with the other. His fingers rested inches from her shoulder. The truck turned onto the dirt road and immediately hit a huge bump.

"The gullies got worse with the spring rains," she said.

"I'll bet."

They lurched over a rock as, behind them, the trailer hit the first bump. The combined action loosened his grip and jarred his injured leg.

He swore.

"Sorry." Faith gave him a quick glance. "I'll try to go slower."

"Not on my account," he ground out as fresh blood seeped from the wound. He resumed his hold on the window frame and the back of the seat. This time, a few strands of her hair became trapped under his hand. The soft silkiness distracted him from his pain and he wondered what a woman like her was doing out here, alone except for some college kids and a few dozen cats.

Before he could formulate an answer, they took a sharp turn to the left and rolled onto a paved road.

"What the—" He glanced behind at the dirt torture session, then ahead at what looked like a good mile of asphalt. "You care to explain that?"

"It's to discourage visitors. We keep the bumps and rocks because they'll scare off anyone in a car."

"Probably lose the whole chassis."

"That's the idea."

"And the paved road?"

She shrugged, then moved the lever from four- back to two-wheel drive. "It's convenient. We have another two miles to go."

"You *don't* want anyone near your cats, do you?"

"Only invited guests. The foundation is privately funded. There are about two hundred donors. The bulk of the money comes from Edwina's estate. We have the donors out a couple of times a year for fund-raisers, but we put planks over the ruts so their limos don't lose their transmissions."

"Smart move."

She rolled down her window and inhaled. "Almost home. I can smell it."

He rolled down his window and took a tentative sniff, half expecting to smell eau de Kitty Litter. Instead the scent of leaves and earth filled him. The road was plenty wide enough for the truck. Tall trees and thick underbrush lined both sides of the pavement. Birds and rustling leaves filled the quiet of the warm June afternoon. He inhaled again, noticing the sweet scent of flowers. Peaceful. Exactly what he needed.

Faith chattered about the weather and the house. Cort shifted his position and didn't listen. He craved a good twelve hours of sleep. Then he would regroup.

"We're here," she said, breaking into his thoughts. They rounded the last corner. He was nearly jerked from his seat when she unexpectedly slammed on the brakes.

Less than three hundred feet up the road stood a large open area. Trees had been cleared to create a natural parking lot. The pavement circled around in front of a long, one-story building. High bushes and trees concealed everything behind the structure.

In the middle of the parking area, looking very bright and very out of place, stood a shiny van. The colorful logo of a Los Angeles television station gleamed in the late afternoon sun.

"I told him no." Faith shook her head and looked at Cort. "Reporters. One of them called from an L.A. station and asked for an interview. He'd heard rumors about the kittens. I told him I wouldn't talk to him."

Cort stared at her. Did she say kittens? Before he could ask, she'd pulled the truck up next to the van.

Faith set the brake. Five people glanced up at her. Two looked incredibly guilty, three vaguely surprised.

"This is private property," she told the newspeople as she got out of the truck. "You don't have permission to be here. You're trespassing. I want you out of here, now!"

It wasn't hard for Faith to pick out the reporter. Aside from being indecently handsome, he wore a coat and tie over his jeans. The other two men with him, one holding a camera, the other operating a mike, smiled winningly and began clicking on switches.

"Hey, I'm James Wilson, from Los Angeles. K-NEWS," the reporter said, moving next to her and offering his hand. "We spoke on the phone yesterday. What a great story. I've got all I need from your assistants, but maybe we could talk for a few minutes. It would really add some depth to the piece."

Faith ignored the outstretched hand. "You're right, Mr. Wilson. We did speak on the phone. I told you not to come up here. The kittens aren't to be taped or photographed. This is private property. You are trespassing. Please leave."

His perfect smile faded slightly. "I don't understand."

"It's simple," she said. "You don't have permission to be here, or to write a story. You're trespassing."

"Hey, this was on the wire service. Don't blame me. Besides, the freedom of the press—"

"Does not include trespassing. Leave now."

"Lady, I don't know what your problem is."

She turned away without speaking. She heard the slamming of the truck's passenger door. Cort was about to get an interesting introduction to the way station. It couldn't be helped.

Beth and Rob, two of her college employees, were inching toward the main office building. The low one-story structure stood across the front of the compound.

"Freeze," she ordered.

They froze.

Faith walked into the building, past the offices, to the supply room. She pulled a bunch of keys out of her jeans pocket and opened a metal locker. Choosing a rifle from the assortment of weapons, she picked it up and held it in her left hand. The barrel had been modified to shoot darts instead of bullets. She put a couple of tranquilizers in her pocket and left the building.

"This is private property," she said as she walked back into the sunlight. "I'm only going to say this one more time. You are trespassing. Leave, now." She loaded one of the darts. "Or you'll be sleeping for the next twenty-four hours." The barrel snapped closed with an audible click.

Behind her, Beth and Rob chuckled.

The reporter's handsome face froze. "Listen, lady, there's no reason to get violent. Mac, Vern, tell her."

But his two friends had already abandoned him and were tossing their equipment into the van.

"Wait for me," Wilson called. He spun on his heel and jogged to the van, then ducked into the passenger seat.

Within seconds, the engine roared to life and the newspeople made a tight U-turn, then headed down the drive. Cort stood next to Faith's truck, leaning his weight on the fender and watching the proceedings with interest. She ignored him, popped the dart out of the rifle and lowered the butt to the ground.

"Where's Ken?" she asked, turning back toward the kids.

Beth, a petite brunette with gold-rimmed glasses, stared at her feet. "Putting the kittens back in their cages."

Faith held on to her temper. "Why did you let in the reporters?"

"We left the gate open for you," Rob answered. "They just kind of showed up."

"You didn't ask them to leave?"

Rob shook his head. "Ken said—"

Faith held up her hand. "I'll deal with Ken in a minute. Why didn't *you* ask them to leave? Either of you?"

Guilt was written all over their young faces. Faith hired college students because they had enthusiasm and dedication, plus she preferred part-time help. The only problem was sometimes they weren't as mature as she would have liked.

Beth stared at her shoes. "He was so nice, and it seemed so exciting that I didn't think about how you said you didn't want any publicity about the kittens until it was too late."

"You just thought he was totally cool," Rob said, rolling his eyes in disgust. "Some good-looking older man says a few nice words and you melt like butter."

"That's not true." Beth flushed with anger. She stood a good eight inches shorter than Rob's six feet, but that didn't intimidate her. "I didn't see *you* ordering him off the property. In fact, you were real interested in the sound equipment and asked the guy a lot of questions."

"That's better than swooning. You won't see me on the six o'clock news."

"Stop!" Faith held up one hand. "You know the rules."

Beth nodded. "You're right, Faith. I apologize. I should have thought about what would happen. I know the kittens are important to you and the facility. I wouldn't purposely do something to hurt either."

"Me, too," Rob mumbled, nudging Beth on the arm when she turned and glared at him.

Faith fought back a smile. Eloquent to the last, that boy, she thought. These kids were basically well-meaning. They'd been caught up in the excitement of the moment. She didn't like it, but she understood how it happened.

"I accept your apologies," she said. She heard footsteps behind her, but didn't turn around.

"What's going on? Beth, why are they leaving so soon? I wanted to show them— Oh God, Faith. You're back."

"I'm sure there's an explanation, Ken," she said coldly, still not turning around. "Make it a good one."

"Gee, Faith. I'm sorry. This isn't what it looks like."

Her grip on the rifle tightened. She tapped her booted toe against the asphalt. A couple of deep breaths didn't help, either. "What the hell were you thinking?" she said as she spun to face the young man. Her voice rose in volume. "Reporters? Reporters?"

Rob and Beth slunk away, leaving Ken alone. The young man stood over six feet tall. With broad shoulders, long brown hair and a scraggely beard that hadn't completely filled in, he looked more like a teenager than a college senior. At her words, his bravado faded. He slumped visibly and stuffed his hands in his pockets.

"It wasn't like that," he mumbled.

"It wasn't like that?" she said loudly, then forced herself to lower her voice. "We have a few rules here. They are for your safety and for that of the cats. Rule number one is no reporters without my say-so. Ken, you know where those kittens came from. The last thing we need is word getting around about their whereabouts."

"I'm sorry." Brown eyes pleaded for understanding.

She gripped the unloaded rifle in both hands and tossed it at him. He caught it. "'Sorry' doesn't cut it," she said, pacing in front of him on the asphalt. "I should bust your butt back to the dorm and never let you on this mountain again."

"It was an accident." He shuffled his feet.

"How do you figure? The reporter said the wire service had the story and..." Realization dawned, and she was grateful she wasn't holding the rifle anymore. "It's that girl! You let her take pictures."

For weeks Ken had talked about nothing but Nancy. Nancy the beautiful. Nancy the brave. Nancy the journalism major. He'd asked Faith if she could come and take pictures of the cats for an assignment for one of her classes. Maybe do a story to drum up publicity. Faith had refused.

"Just a few," Ken admitted. He looked up at her. Regret pulled his mouth straight. "She took them to the local paper, and they got picked up by the wire service. That's what brought the reporter out. I'm sorry," he repeated. "Am I fired?" He sounded like a ten-year-old.

She jammed her hands in her pockets. "I don't know," she said at last. "You've worked here two years, and you've done a good job. But in the last few months you've come in late, you've skipped work without calling, now this." She pinned him with her best glare. "You're thinking with the wrong part of your anatomy. All the trouble you're having is because of that girl. Get that under control and you can work here. If not, you're out. Consider this a final warning. One more screwup and you're fired."

"Faith, I'm sorry."

"Put the rifle away, then get out of here. I don't want to see you for the rest of the week."

"I understand."

"Did you at least remember to feed the cats?"

"Yeah. An hour ago."

"Fine." Faith waved her hand in the direction of the supply building. "Get going."

The young man walked off, his body slumped forward, his steps slow and shuffling. He was the picture of misery. Part of her regretted the harshness of their conversation. Still, the lecture had been necessary, and he deserved it.

"Don't you think you were a little hard on him?" Cort straightened from where he'd been leaning against the truck. Using his crutches to support his bad leg, he stepped toward her.

"No." She flushed, realizing she must have sounded like a fishwife. "I have rules—"

"They're just kids."

"They work for me. I expect them to do their job."

He stared down at her, his brown eyes gleaming with amusement. Obviously she'd really impressed *him*, she thought, her temper starting to get the best of her.

"What I don't understand," Cort said, "is what that reporter wanted. All the way up here from L.A. to get pictures of a few kittens." He shook his head. "Slow news day."

If he didn't know about the cats, he sure didn't know about the kittens. Part of her wanted to slap him upside the head until his ears rang. The other part of her wanted him to find out the truth for himself.

"I like the way you handled the reporter, though," he said, looking around the compound. "He won't be back. Still, you have some major security problems. I'll have a look around and see what I can do."

"Good, because we're going to be on the six o'clock news tonight."

He took a step toward the building. "So? What's the worst that will happen? There'll be a cat show here this weekend? At least you've got the parking for it." He jerked his head at the space behind her truck.

His condescending attitude was the final straw. Her hold on her temper snapped. "You think you're so hot, Mr. Spy? I'm just some crazy cat lady, right? A friend of Jeff's, so you're going to humor me? Fine." She pointed to the main building. "Go right through there. Pet any kitty you like."

Cort stared at her. She was so ticked off, he could practically see steam coming out of her ears. She sure was hung up on this cat thing. He'd better give her a chance to cool off.

Awkwardly moving forward, he went through the open door of the building. Once in the dark hallway, he could smell something musty. He inhaled sharply. An animal scent. Not unpleasant. Not Kitty Litter either. He heard odd snuffling noises and a low cough. He walked out the other side of the building onto smooth dirt. The sounds increased. There were a few grunts followed by a muffled roar. A muffled *roar?* He started to get the feeling things weren't as they seemed. His crutches sank slightly into the ground. He adjusted his weight and turned to his left.

And came face-to-face with a tiger!

Chapter 3

The black-and-gold-striped cat stared at him. Cort took a step back. He forgot about the crutches, tried to spin away, and promptly tripped and sat down hard on the ground. The tiger sniffed the air and grunted.

A pair of boots appeared next to him. He looked up past her jeans-clad legs, past her trim waist and worn blue work shirt, to the smile curving the corners of Faith's mouth. It was, he thought with disgust, a very self-satisfied smile.

"Cats?" he said, shifting so the pain in his leg didn't get worse.

She nodded. "Big cats."

"Well, I'll be damned." He held out his hand.

She braced herself and hauled him to his feet. He balanced on one leg while she collected his crutches. When he'd tucked the supports under his arms, he looked around the compound.

Seven large habitats, bigger than he'd seen at any zoo, stretched out from the right of the main building. To the left, a narrow road led into the forest. Past the road, more enclosures formed a curved line. In the center of the open area were a group of telephone poles, a huge wading pool and a stack of bowling balls. The dirt had been freshly raked. All the enclosures were clean. Most had grass and trees, a few had swimming pools. In the far corner, a small cat—smaller than a tiger, he thought, but bigger than a collie—stuck its head under a man-made waterfall and drank.

"You want to explain this?" he said.

Faith tucked her hands into her back pockets. "I told you. I keep cats."

"Uh-huh. You left out one detail."

"No. You assumed." Her eyes sparkled. She rocked forward onto the balls on her feet, then back on her heels.

"I could have been lunch." He used one crutch to point at the tiger's cage.

"Hardly." She pulled her left hand free of her pocket and glanced at her watch. "It's after four. You could have been a snack."

"Nobody gets the better of you, do they?"

She shook her head. "Not without trying hard." She looked at his leg. "How does it feel? You want to relax first and have the tour tomorrow?"

He glanced around again. He'd never been this close to a tiger before. Most of the animals had come to the front of their enclosures to watch him. Gold eyes stared. He stared back. *So this is what it feels like to look into the face of a predator.* The tiger he'd seen first made a coughing noise.

"He's saying hello," Faith told him.

"More likely he's figuring out how many mouthfuls I'd make." His leg hurt, but not badly. Rest could wait. "Give me the nickel tour," he said. "Enough for me to get a feel for the place. I'll see the rest of it tomorrow."

"Okay." Faith pointed to the enclosure in front of them. It was forty feet by sixty. The tiger had stretched out on the grass in front of his pool and rested his massive head on his paws. The afternoon sun caught the colors in his coat, turning the gold a deep orange and making the black stripes seem brown.

"This is Tigger." She shrugged. "I had nothing to do with the name. It came along with him. He's a Bengal tiger. Partially tamed."

"Partially?" Cort raised his eyebrows. "So he'll eat you but feel guilty?"

She laughed. The sound of her amusement, so carefree and open, made him want to hear it again. It had been too long since he'd been around people who laughed. For him, everything was life and death. It was the price he paid for fighting the good fight. Funny, he'd never thought about that particular sacrifice before.

"Most of our cats are partially tamed, which means you can go into their cages, but someone needs to be watching. A few are wild, and they have to be locked in their dens when we come in to clean." She pointed at the compound. "In the back, there. That rock structure."

"What? No carpeting?"

"Hardly. We try to keep the habitats as natural as possible. The water in the swimming pools and ponds is filtered. There's a sprinkler system. Inside the den, the walls are about eight inches thick, to keep the temperature even. We've also got low-light video cameras in there so we can monitor the animals if they seem sick or are giving birth."

He gave a low whistle. "This is some setup." He looked around at the other habitats. "Are they all like this?"

"Yes. The enclosures are different sizes, for different types of cats. Cats that swim out in the wild, like Tigger here, get pools. We don't have habitats for all of them." Her smile faded. "They cost over a hundred thousand dollars each. We're building them one at a time, using both trust money and private donations. In the back are a few cats that live in cages. We're working on getting them their own enclosures." She moved close to the bars. "You can pet Tigger if you'd like. He's really gentle."

Cort shook his head. "No, thanks."

She called the cat's name. Tigger glanced up at her and yawned, showing rows of very large, very sharp teeth, then slowly rose to his feet. Muscles bunched and released with each step. His feet were the size of dinner plates. He padded over to the front of the cage and leaned heavily against it.

"Tigger used to work in the movies, didn't you, honey?"

Faith scratched the cat's forehead and rubbed his ears. The cat made a noise that wasn't a purr, more like a grunting groan, but definitely sounded contented. Cort inched closer, but stayed safely out of paw's reach.

"What happened?" he asked.

"He's a little stubborn and wouldn't take direction."

"Ah, a temperamental artist."

"Something like that." She looked at him over her shoulder. "You sure you don't want to pet him?"

"Positive."

From where he was standing, he had a view of the cat, and of Faith's rear, as she bent to pet the animal. Her jeans pulled tight around her curves. It had been months since he'd spent time with a woman, he thought, then looked around. If he tried anything, she would probably have him treed by a mountain lion.

"Bengal tigers are coming back from extinction. Tigger is doing a lot of breeding with females from zoos around the country, and even with a few in Europe."

Cort stared at the three-hundred-pound male cat. The animal sat leaning against the bars with his eyes half-closed in ecstasy. Faith continued to scratch his ears.

"What a life," Cort said.

"He seems to like it." She straightened. "Over here we have a couple of mountain lions. We're trying to breed them, as well."

"Tigers, mountain lions. What do you need me for?" he asked. "If an intruder shows up, just open one of the cages. You'll solve the problem and cut down on the feeding bill."

"I don't want any of the animals hurt."

"Nice to know I'm expendable."

"It *is* your job."

He looked at the tiger. "Maybe we could work out a swap."

They walked around the right side of the compound. Faith pointed out the various cats. She called each animal by name and explained how they came to be at the way station.

"He was dumped here," she said, pointing at a bobcat. "Someone probably found him as a kitten and raised him, thinking he'd be a fun pet. Then he got big enough to be a problem."

The pointy-eared cat jumped to the front of his enclosure and hunched down like he wanted to play. His short tail quivered.

"Not today, Samson," Faith told the cat. He continued to stare at her hopefully. "As I mentioned, all the cats over here are pretty tame. Samson is declawed. Still, don't go in any cage by yourself."

"I hadn't planned on going in their cages at all," he said, staring at the bobcat. The playful animal made a purring noise, then turned away and slunk to the back of the enclosure.

"On the other side, we have the wilder cats." She turned and pointed across the compound. "We try to have as little contact with them as possible. Sometimes we get an injured animal that we treat, then release back into the wild."

She started across the open area, keeping her stride slow enough that he could keep up. He felt the cats watching him and knew *they* knew he was injured.

"Lunch," he muttered under his breath. They passed the wading pool and stack of bowling balls. "What is all this for?"

"Recreation. When the weather's good, we let the friendly cats out to play."

"They bowl?"

She laughed. Again the sound caught him off guard. Sweet and happy. Innocent of the evil in the world. "The balls are donated by the bowling alley in town. They play with them."

"Play?"

She looked up at him. "They bat them around, jump on them, throw them in the air."

"Bowling balls?"

"The big cats can weigh several hundred pounds."

He shook his head. Who would have thought? He inhaled deeply. The musty smell didn't seem so intense. In another day or so, he wouldn't even be able to notice it. But he could smell Faith's perfume. The sultry French essence teased at him as he still tried to remember the name. He studied the woman walking beside him. Work boots, straight hair, big cats and French perfume. An intriguing combination.

When they reached the other side of the compound, he saw waist-high poles had been set in the ground, about two feet in front of the enclosures. A chain ran from pole to pole.

"This fence is to remind us not to get too close," she said, pointing at the barrier. "These cats will lash out and scratch you."

A powerful spotted cat with huge shoulders and a wide face paced menacingly at the front of the cage. The animal didn't look directly at them, but Cort sensed it knew exactly where they were standing.

"These jaguars," she said, pointing at the two cages on the far end, "are only here for another few weeks. They're a breeding pair."

He stared at the separate cages. "Wouldn't it work better if they were in the same enclosure. I don't know that much about cats, but—"

"I know." She reached up and brushed a loose strand of hair out of her face. "We tried that. They nearly killed each other. You need to know about these cages." She pointed to the corners. There was a gated opening in the front and the back of the steel-enforced cage. "The hinges by the gates are wide. We'd planned to house two Siberian tigers here. They get to be seven hundred pounds. They aren't here yet, and when the mating couple took an instant dislike to each other, we had to separate them. Unfortunately, the jaguars can stick their paws out at the front and back hinges. Just don't try walking between the cages." She smiled up at him. "They'd probably just scratch you up a bit, but if one stood at the front of its cage and the other

stood at the back of the other one, you'd be trapped between them."

He eyed the pacing animal. Rage radiated with each step.
"I'm not planning to walk between any cages, but thanks
for the warning."

He heard footsteps behind them and turned to see one of
Faith's employees approaching. The young woman stared
from him to her boss and back.

"Faith, the food's all unloaded. We're leaving."

"I'll see you tomorrow. Don't forget to lock the gate behind you."

"I won't." The young woman looked Cort up and down,
glanced at Faith questioningly, then blushed suddenly. She
spun on her heel and jogged to the main building.

"Damn," Faith muttered.

He glanced at her and saw matching spots of color
staining her cheeks.

"I should have introduced you," she said. "I forgot to
tell them about the extra security. They don't know who
you are." She sighed. "I'll explain tomorrow."

The same woman who patted live tigers and didn't bat an
eye when a stranger practically strangled her in her own
truck got embarrassed because one of her employees
thought she'd brought a man to spend the night? There had
to be a piece missing. He suddenly realized what it was.

"You married?" he asked.

She looked shocked. "No, why?"

He shrugged, as well as he could, supported by the
crutches. "You seemed upset. I thought maybe you were
afraid your husband or significant other would get the
wrong idea."

"No husband," she said shortly. "I live here alone. We'd
better get your leg bandaged."

"Good idea." The mention of his wound made it ache
more.

He followed her toward the main building. They passed
the narrow road. "What's down there?" he asked.

"The Big House." She reached the glass door and held
it open. "I don't live there anymore. There's an apartment

in this building, at the end of the hall. It's easier to stay here. I use the Big House for fund-raising parties and that sort of thing." She closed the glass door behind them.

He turned and looked at it. "No lock?"

"Just on the side facing the parking lot. The scent of the cats keep four-legged intruders away. I need to be able to get out of here quickly, in case something happens."

He swung the crutches forward and moved to the front door. Cheap lock. He shook the door. It rattled. He shook it again. "Some security. Anyone over a hundred and forty pounds could break through this just by running up and hitting it with his shoulder." He glanced around at the foyer. A couple of chairs and a vinyl sofa stood on either side of the front door. Long hallways stretched out toward both ends of the building. He looked at the low ceiling, then at the wide windows on either side of the front door. "Alarm? Video?"

She shook her head.

"But you have special cameras to watch the cats?"

"They get priority."

"Not anymore. I'm going to call Jeff with a supply list. You need new locks and a decent gate. Some kind of security system. How often you get up in the night?"

"Depends. Why?"

"Motion detectors."

"Wouldn't work. Sparky usually has the run of the place. Come on, that bandage needs changing."

He followed her down the left hall. The linoleum had seen better days, and the walls needed painting, but everything was clean. Prints of big cats hung on both walls. Sparky?

"Who did you say named him?"

"Edwina. He was her favorite."

He should ask exactly what kind of cat—or lion or tiger—Sparky was, but he didn't want to know. Faith led him into an examining room. From the placement of the metal table and the size of the cage in the corner, he knew she treated her cats here.

"Have a seat," she said, patting the metal table.

He set the crutches against the wall and swung himself up. "You know what you're doing?"

She opened a metal cupboard door and rummaged around inside. "Does it matter? I'm the only one here."

"I could change it myself."

She glanced at him over her shoulder. "I know enough not to kill you."

"Great."

He shifted his weight and scooted back on the table until he rested against the wall. The throbbing in his leg increased. "I assume the 'package' Jeff wants me to protect is really a three-hundred-pound feline."

"Nope. Closer to twenty pounds. I'll introduce you to them in the morning."

"Them?"

She looked amused. "Twins."

Twins? Cort fought back a sigh. Jeff was going to owe him big-time for this one, he thought, then turned his attention back to Faith.

She placed scissors beside him, along with clean bandages, antiseptic and a damp cloth. Her long light brown hair fell over her shoulders. She reached in her front jeans pocket and pulled out a rubber band, then drew her hair back and secured it. After washing her hands, she looked at the bandage.

"This may hurt. You want a stick to bite on?"

He looked at her. "A stick?"

"You're a spy. That's what they always do in the movies. I thought it might make you feel better." Her lips remained straight, but humor danced in her eyes.

"You're not digging out a bullet."

"Just thought I'd ask."

She picked up the scissors and cut through the bandage. It fell away revealing his blood-covered leg. Cort told himself it looked worse than it was. Faith didn't even blink. She picked up the damp cloth and began cleaning his skin.

"Here," she said, pointing at but not touching the incision. "You pulled two stitches. I've never sewed up a person before. Would you mind if I used a butterfly bandage instead?''

"Not at all.''

She worked quickly. After wiping away the dried blood, she doused the wound with antiseptic and then taped it closed. She wrapped gauze around his calf and secured it firmly.

"That must hurt a lot,'' she said sympathetically. "There should be pain medication with the other pills Jeff gave me. I'll grab them from the truck. Be right back.''

He was too busy staring at her to answer. Faith Newlin knew about guns and big cats and did a great field dressing. None of this made any sense.

She returned with his duffel bag and the containers of medication.

"Just as I thought,'' she said, tossing him a bottle.

"Great,'' he said, as he caught it. "First thing in the morning, I'll get on the horn to Jeff and get your security under control.''

He slid to the edge of the examining table and stuffed the medicine in his pocket. She handed him his crutches and led the way into the hall. Two doors down she entered a small room. There were rows of file cabinets, a bare wooden desk and a cot against the far wall.

"It's not much,'' she said. "I didn't have a chance to get a bedroom ready for you up at the Big House. Plus, I want to keep an eye on you tonight.''

He lowered himself onto the cot. The blankets were soft, the pillow down-filled. "I'll be fine.''

"There's a bathroom across the hall. It has a shower built in. Do you want to try it or wait?''

He shifted his injured leg, and pain shot up to his thigh. His head still throbbed. "I can wait. Thanks.''

She set his duffel bag on the desk and opened the top side drawer. After clicking on the desk lamp, she pulled out his shaving kit and began putting his clothing in the drawer.

"I can do that,'' he said.

"You're dead on your feet. I don't mind. Are you hungry?''

"No." He leaned back and let the exhaustion flow through him.

When she finished unpacking, she folded the duffel bag on top of the desk and left. She was back almost immediately, carrying a glass of water.

"For your pills," she said.

He raised himself up on one elbow, dug the pills out of his pocket and took one out. As he reached for the glass of water, the light from the lamp caught the side of her face and her neck. Dark bruises stained her honey-tanned skin. He drank from the glass, then set it down on the floor without taking his eyes from those marks. Time and his job had changed him, he knew. But when had he crossed the line and become a brute?

She sat next to him on the cot. "What's wrong?"

"I hurt you." He raised his hand and gently touched the side of her throat. She stiffened slightly, but didn't pull away. Her warmth contrasted with his cool skin as he brushed one finger down the smooth length.

"I told you I understood what happened," she said. "It was my fault. I shouldn't have startled you."

"A high price to pay for a mistake." He dropped his hand back to the cot.

"I'm not afraid. I won't startle you again, so you won't have reason to hurt me."

"A hell of a way to live."

"For you or for me?" she asked.

Blue eyes searched his, looking for something he knew didn't exist. Humanity, the connection, the bonding of two souls. It was beyond him, always had been. He held her gaze, let her search, knowing she would seek in vain.

When he didn't answer the question, she leaned forward. "You don't believe me. That it doesn't matter, I mean."

"No."

She thought for a moment, as if trying to find a way to change his mind. "We had a mountain lion here once. I was pretty new at the time, still idealistic." She sat up straighter on the cot. "He'd been a pet, then abused and abandoned when he got bigger. By the time he was brought to the way station, he was skinny, bleeding and mean. We patched him up and fed him. It wasn't enough. His leg got infected and required surgery. After the operation, he was pretty out of it. I went in the cage to change his bandage and give him water.''

She moved down a little on the cot, so that she was sitting by his thighs instead of by his waist. She began unbuttoning her blouse. He ignored his surprise and forced himself to hold her gaze and not follow the movements of her fingers. But in the periphery of his sight he saw the blouse fall open. She held it together just above her breasts.

"I hadn't bothered to check to see if he was still sleeping. I crouched down to pick up his water bowl.''

She turned away from him and shrugged out of the shirt. He wasn't sure what to expect. Her blouse slipped off her left shoulder. Cort stared. From just below the nape of her neck, across the top of her back, along her shoulder blade and ending on the back of her arm, four scars traced the route taken by the lion's claws. The parallel lines puckered in some places, as if the depth of the slashing hadn't been uniform.

"He was awake and he attacked me.'' She pulled up her blouse and turned to face him. "I was lucky. I got out before he *really* hurt me.''

Though she held the front together, he could see the paleness of her chest and swelling curve of her breasts. Her choice in lingerie matched the rest of her wardrobe. Sensible cotton trimmed in a thin ribbon of lace. A female who dismissed the need to entice a man with satin, though her choice in perfume was anything but pedestrian.

"Do you see why I'm not afraid of you?'' she asked.

No. He and the mountain lion had little in common. The creature of God killed for food or to protect itself. Cort killed because it was asked of him.

She touched his arm briefly. "Sleep now,'' she said. "I'll be right down the hall. If you need anything, call me.'' She rose and walked to the door.

She stood there watching him. Although her hands clutched her blouse together, he could still see the top of one breast. The unexpected view of that female curve hit him low in the gut, spreading need throughout his body. All cats are gray in the dark, he reminded himself, then closed his eyes. Maybe. But something told him Faith Newlin was a special brand of cat . . . and one he should leave alone.

He could hear the tide lapping against the pilings that supported the dock. And he could smell salt air.

The warehouse.

Cort shook his head to clear it. Was he meeting someone, or picking something up? Why couldn't he remember?

Something was wrong. Danger! He heard it, felt it. A voice called to him. Dan? He had to get out, to run. The explosion! There wasn't time. He spun to leave, but something blocked his way. Danger! Run!

"Hush, Cort. You're safe now." Gentle hands pressed against his shoulders.

He forced his eyes open. Instead of a damp South American warehouse, or even the fires of hell, he stared into wide blue eyes and inhaled the scent of French perfume.

"*Je t'aime.*" he murmured.

"A lovely thought," the woman said, then smiled. "But you've just met me."

"Your perfume."

"Ah. Yes. That's it."

He blinked several times to clear his vision and his head. Everything came back to him. The time in the hospital, the cats, the woman. "Faith."

"Good morning. How do you feel?"

He sat up. Sometime in the night, he'd woken up enough to strip off his clothes. The sheet pooled around his waist. He raised his arms above his head and stretched. "Like a new man. What time is it?"

"Almost nine."

He'd been out almost fourteen hours. "Guess I was tired."

"Guess so. You want some breakfast?"

His stomach rumbled.

She chuckled and rose to her feet. She looked fresh and clean. Her long brown hair had been pulled back into a braid. Jeans and boots covered her lower half, but the plaid work shirt had been replaced by a pink T-shirt. She handed him the crutches.

"I put your shaving kit in the bathroom," she said.

He took the crutches and pulled himself to his feet. As he rose, he realized he was wearing nothing but his briefs. A quick glance at Faith told him she didn't even bother to look. Yeah, he'd impressed the hell out of her.

He took an experimental step. The leg felt stronger and his head didn't hurt anymore. He rubbed one hand over his face. Stubble rasped against his palm.

"I need a shave," he said.

"When you're done, I'll have breakfast ready." She ducked ahead of him in the hall and tossed a pair of jeans and a shirt into the bathroom. "The towels are clean. I put a plastic bag out, so you can shower without getting the bandage wet."

Before he could thank her, she was heading down the hall. Her braid swayed with each step, as did her curvy hips. He stared after her until she turned the corner.

By the time he'd made himself presentable, he could smell food cooking. He followed the delicious odors past two more offices, through a door marked Private and into a small living room.

"Faith?" he called.

"In here."

He maneuvered the crutches around the maple coffee table and rocking chair into a cheery yellow kitchen. A Formica table stood in front of a bay window that looked out into the forest. The stove appeared to be older than he was and the refrigerator older still by ten years. But everything gleamed in the morning light. He sniffed, smelling mint along with the cooking.

Faith looked up from the stove. "I hope scrambled is all right." She motioned to the table. "Have a seat."

She'd set a place for him and lined up all his medications in a row. A glass of orange juice sat next to a cup of coffee. He looked at the setting, then at her. "Very nice. Thanks."

He pulled out a chair, sat down and sipped the coffee. She served his breakfast, then poured herself a cup and took the seat opposite him. A stack of papers rested in front of her. As she studied them, she nibbled on the corner of her mouth. Was it worry or simply a habit? Who was this woman who took in stray lions and spies? He buttered the toast she'd made, then sorted through the jars of jelly.

"What are you looking for?" she asked.

"Mint. I can smell it. Can't you?"

She looked down. "Yes." He could have sworn her shoulders were shaking.

"What's so funny?"

She looked up, her face expressionless. The innocence didn't fool him. "Nothing," she said.

"Sure." He cautiously took a bite of the eggs. "This is great. I was half-afraid you'd feed me cat food."

"Eggs are cheaper."

He heard a rumble, like a low-flying plane. The sound continued for several minutes as he ate, then it stopped. He chewed a mouthful of food and swallowed. "What *do* the cats eat?"

"Anything I can get my hands on. Chicken mostly. The bones keep their teeth clean and exercised. Sometimes hunters leave me extra venison."

"Must get expensive."

She nodded. "The biggest cats eat up to fifteen pounds a day."

The rumble started again, broke, became an almost coughing sound, like someone sawing wood, then resumed. "What the hell is that?"

"What?"

"That rumble. Can't you hear it?"

She chuckled. "I'm so used to it, I only notice when it's not there." She glanced at his plate. "Are you done?"

"I guess."

"It's never a good idea to have food around when you meet Sparky," she said.

"Sparky?" He remembered his vision of the mean black alley cat. That was when he'd assumed Faith's cats had been the ten-pound, domestic kind. "Sparky isn't what I think, is he?"

"Probably not." She pursed her lips together and whistled softly, first a high, then a low tone. "Sparky," she called. "Come."

From a room beyond the kitchen, the rumble stopped for a moment. Cort heard the scratchy coughing noise again, then the sound of a thick chain being dragged across the linoleum floor. What he thought was a shadow cast by the overhead lights quickly became a very large, very black, leopard.

"Holy—"

The animal approached slowly. Yellow eyes, more almond-shaped than round, flickered around the room, then settled on him. As the cat walked over to Faith, the smell of mint grew. Cort realized it came from the animal. "Sparky," she said, patting its head. "This is Cort."

The black leopard continued to hold his gaze. The rumbling went on. The cat's massive head rested on Faith's thighs. Powerful muscles rippled as the animal sat down. A faint pattern of spots was barely visible in the dark coat. Its long tail moved back and forth in a slow but menacing rhythm.

"Is this your idea of a pet?" Cort asked, wondering what Jeff had been thinking of when he'd sent him here.

"No. Edwina is the one who took him in. He was less than four weeks old when his mother died. He was hand-raised after that. Edwina couldn't bear to put him in a cage, so here he is." She rubbed the animal's forehead, then scratched behind its ears.

Like a huge house cat, the leopard arched toward the stroking and butted his head against her leg, asking for more. This gentle butt, however, nearly knocked her out of her chair.

"Easy," she admonished, giving the animal a slight slap on its shoulder.

Sparky was properly cowed and broke his gaze with Cort to glance up at Faith and yawn.

A perfect domestic scene, if he ignored the glistening teeth designed to rip and tear flesh and bite through bone.

"Why does he smell of mint?" he asked.

"Leopards conceal their own scent. In the wild he'd use certain herbs or animal dung."

"I can see why you'd want to discourage the latter."

"You bet. There's a mint patch for him out back."

"Where does he sleep?"

"In the office." Faith continued to stroke the leopard. "Or with me. Give me your hand."

He offered his left.

Faith grinned as she took it. "You're right-handed, aren't you?"

"I don't take chances."

"Sparky won't hurt you without provocation. He's just a friendly little kitty, aren't you, boy?" She found a particularly sensitive spot behind its jaw, rubbed vigorously, and the purring deepened.

Faith laced their fingers together. "Sparky," she said. "This is Cort. He's going to be staying here awhile." Her soft voice, slightly higher pitched than her normal speaking tone, soothed both him and the cat.

The leopard remained indifferent to the stranger's hand being drawn closer and closer to his head. Faith continued to stroke the cat. She moved her free hand lower onto the animal's shoulder and placed their joined hands on its head.

Cort resisted the impulse to pull back. The short black fur felt coarse under his fingers. Thick, not at all like a domestic cat. But everything else seemed familiar, just on a larger scale. Ears moved back and forth as if following the conversation. The rumbling purr continued, unbroken, except when Sparky shifted to lean more heavily on Faith.

Power, Cort thought, looking at the long legs and thick ropes of muscle visible under the fur. A perfect killing machine. Elegant. Beautiful. A creature without a conscience. Is that what Jeff saw when he looked at him?

"He likes most people," she said, patting Sparky with his hand, then slipping her fingers away.

He hesitated. Their eyes met, and he continued stroking the cat. "Most? When do I find out if I'm one of the lucky ones?"

"He wouldn't have come in here if he didn't like your scent."

Sparky straightened, as if he'd just realized Faith wasn't the one touching him. He rose to his feet and walked the two steps over to Cort. Even though the kitchen chair was relatively high off the ground, Sparky practically stared him in the eye. The cat sniffed at his hand, then his arm. Cort wanted to get the hell away, but he held his position. He knew that much.

Predator to predator. He recognized Sparky's need to understand the intruder. If this was her chaperon, it was no wonder Faith wasn't married.

Sparky made the coughing sound again, then turned away and walked next to the refrigerator. The one-inch-thick chain trailed behind him. The rumbling purr became a humph as he laid down, then resumed.

Faith began to clear the table. When she went to put the butter away, she nudged Sparky out of the way so that she could open the door. Cort wasn't sure if he should respect Faith or have her committed.

"Do you want to drive around the compound?" she asked. "I've cleared my morning so that I could show you anything you would like to see."

Before he could respond, a loud shriek pierced the morning. Even Sparky stopped purring.

"Damn," Faith muttered, apparently more annoyed than concerned as she walked out of the room. "What are you two up to now?"

Cort grabbed his crutches and followed her. The shrieks came again, this time followed by plaintive mewing.

"You can't be hungry," Faith said, moving down the hall toward a dim light in a room on the right. "I just fed you."

The mewing got louder. Cort continued to hobble behind her. When they entered the room, he saw a big cage that filled most of the floor space. Inside, blankets formed a soft nest. Newspapers lined a far corner of the cage. The striped bundle in the middle of the blankets moved as they walked closer. Two white tiger cubs looked up and mewed piteously.

"Here they are," Faith said as she crouched down beside the babies. "Jeff sent them along to me last week."

"This is what the reporter was after?"

"Yes. They were confiscated at the border. Something about being added to the collection of some big-time crook." She looked up and smiled. "Think you can keep them safe?"

William Thomas paced the small motel room. He needed a drink, but he couldn't afford to miss his phone call. What would happen to him now? he wondered for the hundredth time. What would they do to him? Second chances didn't exist in his organization. But it hadn't been his fault. They had set the rules. No killing, they'd insisted. If he'd iced the border control officer none of this mess would have happened.

He swallowed thickly and again wished for that drink. Maybe he could run to the liquor store across the street. It wouldn't take long and—

The ringing of the telephone cut into his thoughts. He picked it up immediately.

"Yes?" he said curtly.

"I'm very disappointed, Mr. Thomas."

"I know. It was an accident. The rules I had to work under were too restrictive."

"I don't care about accidents. I want the job done."

"Of course." William forced himself to speak calmly. The fact that they hadn't killed him yet meant he might be given the chance to redeem himself.

"Our mutual employer is still out of the country," his caller said, the voice low and cold. "You have exactly twenty-one days until his return. If the cubs are recovered by then, he would be very forgiving of your little accident."

"I can get them back. As soon as I find out where they are—"

The man on the phone cut him off again. "They were on the news last evening."

"What? The cubs?"

"Yes. A reporter, a James Wilson, filed a story. Locate him and you'll locate the cubs."

"Consider it done."

"Mr. Thomas, I shouldn't have to remind you that you can't afford to make another mistake."

William wished he could ignore the implied threat, but doing so would cost him his life. "I need to be able to do whatever is necessary," he said. "You can't tie my hands and then complain that the job isn't done."

"Recover them. *At any cost.*"

William nodded. He'd just been given permission to get rid of anyone who stood in his way. Better. Now he could finish the job. "You can count on me."

"Twenty-one days, Mr. Thomas. Our mutual employer spent a lot of money on the cubs. They are the centerpiece of his collection. If you don't succeed, we will be forced to discontinue our association. Do you understand?"

Who wouldn't understand a .45 slug between the eyes? "I understand."

There was a click, and the line went dead.

Chapter 4

"Hush, babies," Faith said as she crouched down and opened the cage. "Come on. We're here." The larger of the two tiger cubs tumbled toward her, mewing loudly. "You're lonely, aren't you?" When the kitten reached her, she picked it up and cradled it in her arms. "All this fuss over twenty pounds of trouble."

Cort looked stunned. He reached out to pat the cub. The white-striped cat made a garbled sound that was supposed to be a growling hiss and hunched back against her.

"Hold your hand out," she instructed. "Let it sniff you."

"It?" His gold-flecked eyes met hers. He shifted his weight and leaned on the crutches, offering his fingers to the cub.

"One's a boy, the other's a girl, but I still have trouble telling them apart."

"How old are they?" he asked.

"Around three months. We can't be sure. They can see what's going on around them, and that doesn't happen until about two months. You want to hold it?"

She looked at Cort. The scar on his chin looked less raw this morning, and the shadows under his eyes had faded. Except for the crutches and the gaunt hollows in his cheeks, she wouldn't know he'd ever been injured.

"Sure," he said, shifting his weight so he leaned against the wall. He set the crutches next to him, securing them near the cage.

"Here, baby," Faith said, moving close to him and petting the cub. "They thrive on attention. In the wild, they're totally dependent on their mother. They won't even stray from her side until they're more than a year old. They want to be cuddled, don't you?" She softened her voice and nuzzled the kitten's soft ears. "You're a sweet baby. Hold your arms out, Cort, and cradle it while I'm still holding on."

She moved until she was inches from him, then felt his hands slip between her and the cub. His knuckles brushed against her belly. A shiver raced through her, and she had to fight not to jump. What on earth . . . ?

"You got it?" she asked.

"I think so. God, he's so soft. Come here, monster," Cort said, keeping his tone low and calm. "Get a load of those feet."

She gave the cub one last pat and stepped back. "They'll both grow to be several hundred pounds."

"That's a lot of kitty." Cort held the kitten in his arms. The animal looked from her to Cort, then mewed and snuggled close to his chest.

"It likes you." Something sharp nibbled on her ankle. "You want attention, too, don't you?" She leaned down and picked up the smaller cub. Icy blue eyes stared back at her. The small triangular nose quivered as it inhaled her scent. "The changes have been hard on them. I don't know how many people have handled and fed them, but it's pretty obvious they haven't had a stable life."

"So now you're doing cat therapy?"

"Cort!"

He grinned. "How rare are white tigers?"

"It depends," she said. "Some people are breeding white tigers, but they aren't true mutants. You can tell by the eye color. A true white tiger has blue eyes. Just like yours, huh?" She scratched the cub's head. The baby arched back against her hand and wiggled to get closer. "They have brown stripes on white fur, and the nose and lips are pinkish gray."

"I never thought of tigers as having lips."

He held the cub securely, but without too much pressure. The lonely cat sniffed at his neck and face, making throaty noises and generally looking pleased.

"Not quite the same as fighting warlords and terrorists, is it?" she asked.

Their eyes met. She felt that same shiver again, but this time he wasn't even touching her. Her heartbeat clicked up a notch, pounding harder and faster in her chest. Her palms suddenly felt damp, and she fought the urge to moisten her lips. What was happening to her?

"So who takes care of them?" he asked. "You?"

"I've been sharing the duties with the kids, when they're here, but it would be better to have just one person. After all the cubs have been through, they need some stability."

Cort shifted suddenly and disentangled the cub's claws from his shoulders. "I'm not a scratching post," he told the animal. "They're feisty little buggers, aren't they?"

"Yeah, and hungry. They get fed every few hours. They have to be rubbed down and massaged to keep their circulation and bowels going. They need attention and affection and a lot of other things I don't have time for."

"You want a volunteer?" he asked.

"I wasn't hinting."

"Yes, you were."

"Okay, maybe I was. But it's a lot of work and time."

He glanced around the small room. "Once I get the security system installed, maintenance shouldn't take much of my day. If they don't object to a gimpy role model, I'll give it a try."

She told herself the sensation of nerves in her stomach came from relief and nothing else. Certainly not from being near Cort. He was here to protect her and the cubs. She knew better than to risk being attracted to any man.

"Are you sure?" she asked. "I really didn't mean to make you think you had to help. Keeping the cubs safe is my main priority."

"Mine, too." He gave her a slow smile. It caused lines to crinkle by the corners of his eyes. She felt her own lips tug in response. "I'm here because of them, Faith. If I help you with feeding and whatever else you do, I'm also looking out for them."

It seemed easiest to accept gracefully. After all, she really didn't have time to take care of the cubs along with all her other duties. "Thanks." She placed the baby she was holding back in the cage and reached for the other one. "Let me show you the feeding schedule. Then we can tour the compound. By the time we're done, it'll be time to feed them and you can get your lesson in Tiger Mothering 101."

She secured the cage. Cort collected his crutches. The cubs stared up at him and began to mew. He looked at her. "How do you resist them?"

She shrugged. "Practice, and the knowledge that if they had their way, someone would be with them twenty-four hours a day." She shook her head. "That's the worst of it. People smuggle in rare animals because they want to own something unique, but they don't bother to consider the animal itself. They don't think about the special diet and attention, the needs of babies this tiny." She crouched down and patted the smaller of the two through the wire cage. "Poor sweeties. We need to find you a good home, and fast." She rose and started out of the room.

"How long will that take?" Cort asked, hobbling behind her.

"It depends. It's not that easy to hand them over to a zoo or a breeding center. Tigers are expensive to keep and cubs are demanding. Most facilities don't have the room, the personnel or the funds. Jeff wants to make sure he gets it right the first time. That's why they're with me. I can hold them longer than most places."

They entered her office. Photos of big cats lined the walls. Her scarred, thrift-store desk took up a good portion of the space. File cabinets and a couple of chairs filled the rest. Faith waved him into the seat in front of her desk. Cort settled into the chair and placed the crutches on the floor.

"How's the leg?" she asked as she pulled open a file cabinet drawer and withdrew several forms.

"Not bad. I should be walking without help in a day or so."

"Good." She turned around and looked at him.

In his jeans and long-sleeved cotton shirt, he looked like any local. Most of the men living on the mountain did physical work for a living, so his broad shoulders and defined muscles wouldn't set him apart. It had to be something else that made her heart flutter foolishly. Maybe it was the shape of him—lean and graceful with a concealed power. Even with the bandaged leg and crutches, he reminded her of her cats, moving carefully, deliberately, the wary instincts of a predator never far below the surface.

"These are the forms I use to keep track of the cubs' care." She handed him several papers. "I don't think you'll have any trouble with them."

He glanced at the sheets and nodded. "Looks simple enough."

"When we feed them, I'll go over the amounts of formula each needs." She closed the file cabinet and sat in the old rickety wooden chair behind her desk. "They usually just scarf down whatever we give them. These are not picky eaters."

"Good." He read on. "Playtime?"

She nodded. "They need a certain amount of social interaction. You'll probably want to wear gloves."

The flecks in his eyes seemed to glint with amusement. He smiled. "Gloves?"

"You've seen their claws."

"Felt them, too." He rubbed his shoulder. "Could be worse, I suppose. You could be asking me to wrestle Sparky."

She smiled. "Not until you're feeling better."

"Great." He leaned forward and placed the papers on her desk. He bumped several other sheets, and they fluttered to the ground. "Got 'em," he said, reaching down and grabbing them.

"Thanks." She took the offered forms and grimaced. "Government paperwork."

"Aren't you used to it?"

"No. We're privately funded. I'm helping Jeff with the cubs as a favor, but for the most part, I don't work with government agencies." She stared at the papers stacked on her desk. "Most of these files are for a new project I'm thinking of starting. I counted. There are one hundred and eighty-seven forms there. Who knows how many agencies and bureaucrats for me to deal with."

"What for?"

She tossed the sheets on the desk and leaned forward, lacing her hands together. "I want to breed snow leopards."

She half expected him to laugh. She'd mentioned the project to one of the way station's contributors, and he'd patted her on the head and told her not to bite off more than she could chew.

"Why?" Cort asked.

"They're almost extinct. I bought some land a few years ago in North Dakota. It's away from everything. The climate is good for the leopards. If I could get a few breeding pairs and mate them in captivity, in a couple of generations there would be enough to release several back into the wild. They would help not only with the numbers, but by increasing the gene pool. That's the problem when a species becomes endangered. There aren't enough genes to create a healthy population." She stopped suddenly, aware of how she was going on.

But Cort seemed interested. He adjusted his injured leg, then rested his hands on the arms of the chair. "What's all the paperwork for?"

"I have to get permission from federal, state and local governments. I have to have the approval of all the neighbors. There are zoning permits, financial qualifications. I've seen an attorney, and she gave me some direction, but I'm a little overwhelmed by the whole issue.''

"Why? You run *this* place."

"It's not the same. The way station was already established when I arrived. Edwina was a little eccentric, but she had a head for business as well as cats. My changes around here have been minor." Faith fiddled with a pencil, fighting the familiar feelings of inadequacy. "I have a two-year degree in animal husbandry, but no formal business training, which presented a problem. Before her death, Edwina had asked me to take charge, but several of the board members tried to get it away from me."

One gold-blond eyebrow raised slightly. "Why? You're damn good at your job."

"How would you know?"

He pointed at his leg. "You did a terrific field dressing."

"Why, thank you. I'll explain that to the IRS and my attorney when I set up the nonprofit foundation."

She was smiling, but Cort saw the faint worry lines puckering between her brows. He was intrigued by what Faith was telling him, yet knew better than to get involved. Until the cubs had been moved somewhere else, she and this facility were his responsibility. When the danger was over, he would be long gone. It was one of the advantages of his job.

"You ready for the real tour?" she asked, obviously trying to change the subject.

"Sure." He collected his crutches and stood. "But first I'd like my gun back."

She studied him for a second, then pulled open her desk drawer and drew out the Beretta and its magazine. He took them from her, loaded the gun, chambered a round and checked to make sure the safety was on. Then he slipped the gun into the waistband at the small of his back and turned toward the door.

"So if we're invaded by a small third-world country, you're prepared," she said.

"Always."

"Good to know." She led the way into the hall.

As they walked past the room containing the cubs, the kittens cried out. They were so small, he thought, remembering holding one of them. Hard to believe something like that would grow into a five-hundred-pound killer.

They walked to the foyer and out the front door to the parking lot where Faith had scared off the newspeople. This morning the circular area stood empty. She waited while he maneuvered his way down the single step.

"Beth will be here in a couple of hours," Faith said, leading him to the left. "She has morning classes. The two guys have different schedules on different days, but someone comes here every day. Most days there are two of them."

"I'll need to look at their personnel files," he said. "Run a few things through the computer."

She paused and looked at him. In the bright morning light, her skin glowed. The faint color on her cheeks owed its presence to her temper rather than makeup. Clear blue eyes framed by dark lashes bored into his.

"I trust my kids."

"This is routine," he said, leaning on the crutches. "Maybe something happened to one of them in the last month or so. I'm not accusing anyone, but it's better to know."

She folded her arms over her chest. "What does your spy computer say about me?"

"Jeff didn't tell me."

"But I've been investigated." She wasn't asking a question.

"You wouldn't have been allowed in the hospital yesterday if you hadn't been cleared."

She stared at him for several seconds. "I don't envy you your world, Cort," she said, dropping her arms to her sides. "Come on. The Jeep is this way."

A three-car garage jutted out on one side of the main building. She lifted the single door and stepped into the shadows. Ten seconds later he heard an engine start up. She backed an open, black-and-white-striped Jeep out in front of him. He stared at the vehicle. It looked like something from an animal park—a zebra on wheels.

She stepped out and lowered the garage door. "Don't ask," she muttered. "I had nothing to do with it. The vehicle was a donation. We were all humiliated when it was delivered."

He tossed his crutches in the back and climbed in. His bum leg bumped the side once and he fought back a curse. When the pain eased, he turned to her. "Why zebra stripes?"

"I have no idea." She slid in beside him. "I guess they thought the cats would think they were back on the Serengeti." She rested her hands on the steering wheel. "What do you want to see first?"

He thought for a minute. "How much of the perimeter is fenced?"

She smiled. "Perimeter? Should we be wearing fatigues and a little beret?"

Her humor surprised him. He knew Faith wasn't happy about him investigating her employees. He understood her reluctance and admired her loyalty, however misplaced. He thought about the casual way she'd handled the Beretta yesterday and reminded himself she wasn't like any of the women he'd known. He would do well to remember that.

"We'll save the camouflage for night maneuvers," he said. "How much of the compound is fenced?"

She shifted into gear and started down the driveway toward the main road. "Not enough of it. We count on the forest to keep most people away. There are a few places where it would be pretty easy to hike into the facility. Most people just want to get a look at the cats, so the gate and the road discourage them."

As they drove down the paved driveway, she pointed to where the fencing started and ended. When the asphalt gave way to dirt ruts, she slowed down and eased forward in second gear. About twenty yards from the gate, she pulled a remote-control device from her jeans pocket and pushed the button. The gate swung open.

"Let's start here," he said. He climbed out and hobbled over to the gate. "Worn hinges. You could cut through this with a nail file." He leaned on the frame. It groaned and gave slightly. "Item one, a new gate."

Two hours later, they stopped at the top of a sloping rise. Most of the trees had been logged in the last twenty years, and the new growth didn't yet block out the terrain or the sun. Cort squinted and peered down in the direction of the way station.

"Can't do much about fencing up here," he said. "It's a roundabout route, but fairly impassable, especially at night."

"Good." Faith leaned against the Jeep. "You're really taking this seriously, aren't you?"

He glanced at her. A couple of strands of hair had escaped from her braid. They floated around her ears and temples. He thought about smoothing them back in place, then dismissed the idea as foolish. He didn't want to start something he had no intention of finishing.

"It's my job."

"I know. I guess I didn't want to think the cubs were really in danger."

"Would that have affected your willingness to take them in?"

She thought for a moment, then shook her head. "No. They had nowhere else to go. I would have spent the last couple of days being nervous, though."

He scanned the quiet hilltop. A faint earthy smell mingled with the sweetness of spring flowers and Faith's French perfume. Birds chirped from nearby branches and small creatures rustled in the underbrush.

"Nothing's going to happen," he said.

"I have every confidence in you."

"Thanks."

"You want to talk about it?" she asked softly.

"What?"

"The dream."

He swung around to face her. She leaned against the vehicle. With her elbows propped up on the closed driver's door, her chest thrust forward, enticing him with her feminine shape. He ignored the faint stirrings inside and concentrated on her statement.

"What dream?" he asked, even though he knew.

"From this morning. I heard you calling out." Her face was as open and readable as a child's. She wasn't judging.

"No." He spoke sharply. The word cut through the late morning like a gunshot. She tried to control her reaction, but his skilled eyes saw the slight stiffening of her muscles and the way she forced herself to relax.

"Just asking," she said. "You ready to head back?"

He hobbled over to the Jeep without speaking. She didn't look up at him. Nothing in her manner indicated anything had happened, but he felt like a jerk. He was here to do a job. Whatever personal problems he brought with him had no business spilling out into the assignment, or involving Faith.

"How much did Jeff tell you?" he asked, settling his crutches in the back of the vehicle.

She opened her door and got inside. "Only that you'd been injured on your last assignment, and that you were having trouble remembering everything that happened."

"That about sums it up," he said curtly, sliding in beside her. Faith started the engine and made a tight turn in the small clearing.

Cort's feeling of helplessness returned. He couldn't force himself to remember. He couldn't do a damn thing except wait for his past to catch up with him. In the meantime, he could wonder if he'd killed his friend.

That was the problem. In his line of work, he wasn't supposed to have friends. If he'd remembered his own rule, none of this would matter. Dan's death would simply be another casualty of war. Nothing personal about that. It was the price paid for fighting the good fight. But it *was* personal, and it was too late to change that fact.

"I've been thinking about painting the hallway of the main building," Faith said as she drove down the narrow path. "It really looks shabby. Maybe a light cream or even white."

He stared at her. What the hell was she talking about? She spoke about remodeling, moving from paint to flooring, then about replacing the vinyl couch. A shaft of sunlight filtered through the trees overhead and highlighted her right side. He stared at the snug-fitting jeans hugging her slender thighs and the way her breasts bounced with each bump in the road. Inside, heat coiled, the awakening desire defusing his temper. He moved his gaze to the muscles in her arms and up to the wisp of brown hair floating beside her ear.

His stomach clenched. There. Where the pink T-shirt met her neck. The faint shadowing in the shape of a man's hand, his hand, wouldn't let him forget what he'd done. He started to curse himself, but her quiet voice kept getting in the way. She soothed him, and he realized she spoke to call him away from his demons.

"Is this what mother tigers do?" he asked.

She stopped speaking in midsentence and glanced at him. "Excuse me?"

"You're talking to relax me. Is that what cat mothers do? Is this human purring?"

She smiled and returned her attention to the road. "And here I thought I was being subtle."

"You were. I'm very observant."

"I guess you'd have to be. Tigers don't purr. None of the big cats do."

"Wasn't Sparky purring? He looked like a big cat to me."

"Leopards are big cats. And yes, he makes a purring-like noise. Only leopards bred in captivity and hand-raised purr."

She drove around the compound and turned east on a narrow road. He stared at the greenery around him. The crisp smells and budding trees were so different from what he'd left in South America. There he'd seen . . .

He shook his head. Damn. He didn't know what he'd seen there, only that it had been different. He forced himself to concentrate, but his mind refused to open and the mist only got thicker. He balled his hands into fists and tensed his muscles. He *had* to remember. He had to. If he didn't—

"Cort?" Faith spoke his name. He looked at her. She'd stopped the vehicle and put her hand out, as if she'd considered touching him but had thought better of the idea. "Are you all right?"

"I'm fine."

She held his gaze, then slowly, deliberately, placed her hand on his curled fingers. She worked against his fist, forcing him to relax. Her skin, rough calluses at the base of her fingers, smooth everywhere else, felt warm and alive.

"You'll remember," she said. "Give yourself a break."

In her casual clothes, with her hair pulled back in a sensible braid and her face devoid of makeup, she wasn't anyone he would look at twice. But there was a gentle set to her mouth and a fearless compassion in her eyes. He knew why the cats trusted her and allowed her to help them heal. He knew why Sparky purred for her. He wanted to lean close and taste her generous mouth. Sex had always been his way of getting lost. He smiled. She would be shocked at his actions. Not because she was inexperienced—she moved with the easy grace of a woman who knows and appreciates her body—but because she didn't see him as a man.

He hadn't realized it until now, but the clues had been there all along. The way she calmly excused his attack on her by comparing it with that of a wounded panther. Her impersonal dressing of his wounds, the instinctive way she stroked him now, soothing him with the healing touch of her hand.

He thought about pulling her close and showing her he was very much a man, with a man's needs, but he dismissed the idea as soon as it appeared. Sleeping with Faith would simply complicate their situation.

He pulled his hand away from hers and reached up to gently touch her cheek. She started at the slight contact. Her eyes widened with surprise, as if one of her cats had spoken her name. Then he opened the door and stepped out.

"What's this?" he asked, pointing at the tall, two-story house in front of them. The Victorian-style manor looked completely out of place in the middle of the forest.

Faith joined him. He leaned on the front of the Jeep, testing his bad leg. It didn't hurt too much, and so far hadn't started to bleed.

"Edwina used to live here. She loved the cats but didn't want to be too close to the compound. We call it the Big House."

"Who owns it now?"

For the first time, Faith looked uncomfortable. She stuffed her hands in her pockets. "She left it to me in her will. The foundation owns the way station and all the land except for one acre and this house."

He glanced from the building to Faith and back. "You mean you've stuck me on a cot in some back office and I could be sleeping here?"

She smiled. "Yeah. It has big bathrooms and everything. You're welcome to move in. Most of the rooms are empty, but a couple of the bedrooms are furnished."

He shook his head. "It's tempting, but I've got to stay near the cubs. Why aren't you living here?"

"I never really fit in." She stared at the Big House. "It will always be Edwina's place, not mine. I did live there with her, but when she passed away, I moved into the apartment behind the office. Much more my style."

"So what's this old place for?"

"Parties."

"You don't strike me as the party type."

"I'm not." Her shoulders slumped. "It's for fundraising. We have gala events about three or four times a year. We bring out the tamer cats, serve fancy food and collect big checks."

"Don't sound so enthused."

"It's awful." She looked up at him. Her mouth pulled into a straight line. "Black tie, caterers. It takes tons of time, but it's necessary. We need the funding. I even have to give Sparky a bath."

"He must hate that."

"It's not fun for either of us." Her eyes widened. "You're making fun of me."

"How bad could it be, Faith? You make it sound worse than getting a tooth pulled."

"Fine. See how much you like it. I hope you brought a tux."

"What?" He glared at her.

"Oh, didn't I mention it? There's a fund-raiser next week."

He thought about the faulty gate and the fence that didn't run all the way around the property and the hundreds of ways a really determined individual could break into the compound. "No, you *didn't* mention it. You can forget about it."

"Sorry," she said blithely as she climbed back into the Jeep. "The invitations have already been mailed. It's too late to call the event off."

Cort glanced at the empty bottle and scribbled the amount of formula the cubs had eaten. From inside the cage the larger of the two, the male, tumbled with a knotted towel and growled as he wrestled his imaginary prey. Every few minutes he looked up to make sure Cort was still within sight. The female cub sat near the gate and mewed piteously every few seconds.

"I'm not going to hold you," Cort said, trying to ignore her. "I've spent the entire morning with you."

She was unimpressed. Her vivid blue eyes locked onto his. With big ears and clumsy puppy feet, the cubs were growing on him. In less than four days they'd figured out he was a soft touch and spent most of their time trying to manipulate him. She meowed again. When he didn't respond, she hung her head dejectedly and trembled.

Cort swore, opened the cage door and hauled her onto his lap. Instantly the cub cuddled next to his chest and began chewing on the rolled cuff of his shirt.

"You are the worst," he told her. She just gazed up at him. Cort rubbed her fur, scratching the spot that she loved best behind her ears. He glanced at his watch. "You're making me miss lunch."

She yawned, showing small white teeth that would grow large and deadly. Before she could trick him again, he placed her back in the cage next to her brother, latched the door closed and walked into the hall. She mewed once, then snuffled a few times and settled down to sleep.

Faith wasn't in her office, so he limped toward the compound. His wound was healing and he'd stopped using the crutches the day before. As he stepped out into the bright spring sunshine, a black shadow crossed his path.

Cort stared at the leopard. Although he'd grown comfortable with the tiger cubs, the sight of Sparky roaming free through the offices and outside always brought him up short.

The big cat made a coughing noise low in his chest and moved close enough to butt his head against Cort's thigh. Cort reached down and patted the animal. Sparky looked up. Wide, almond-shaped yellow eyes held his own. Behind the facade of domestication lurked the cold determination of a killer. As he stared down at the leopard, recognition flashed. He was like this predator: a creature who killed in the night, a creature without a soul.

The cat broke away suddenly, raced across the compound to the central play area and leapt onto the telephone poles planted in the raked earth. Except for the red collar around his neck, he looked like an escaped wild animal. The first jump put him almost halfway up the pole. Using his claws, he climbed to the top of the first pole, crouched and jumped to the cross beam six feet below. He landed perfectly in the center of the beam, then ran across it and up the pole on the opposite side. Black fur gleamed in the bright light. The pattern of his spots was barely visible. Cort walked haltingly around the perimeter of the play area, watching the beautiful cat. He leaned against the safety chain, taking the weight off his healing leg.

"Cort!"

He looked at Ken jogging toward him. "Did Faith warn you about the jaguars?" the young man asked as he approached.

Cort looked over his shoulder at the two flat-faced cats pacing and snarling in their cages. "She said not to get too near them."

"Good." Ken stopped in front of him. "They can fit their paws through the sides of the gate. You could get a nasty scratch."

"Or worse," Cort muttered, not liking how they were eyeing him. "When are they going back to the zoo?"

"Another couple of weeks. Then we'll be getting the tigers."

Cort studied Ken. The college student had been suspended from work until today. Cort remembered how he'd thought Faith had overreacted to the newspeople taking pictures of the cubs. Of course, four days ago he'd thought the "kittens" were the domesticated kind.

"Faith says you're in charge of security," Ken said.

"That's right."

"I saw the new gate and the fencing. So you work for the government? The CIA?"

"Not exactly." He started back toward the office building.

Ken fell into step beside him, matching his gait to Cort's slower limp. "You think there's going to be trouble?"

"You planning to cause any more?"

The kid flushed. With his big frame, beard and long hair he should have looked tough. Instead, he looked like a boy being reprimanded for stealing candy from a local store.

"I didn't mean for that to happen," he said glumly. "I'm really sorry. I would never deliberately put the cubs in danger."

"Then follow the rules and keep me informed of anything unusual you see. Strangers coming by, people asking questions, anything out of the ordinary."

"Okay. Anything happens, you'll be the first to know."
Ken stopped and looked at him. "Thanks for letting me
help." He offered Cort a quick smile. "I've got to finish
cleaning the cages." He trotted off.

Cort watched him leave, then turned back toward the
building. Had he ever been that young and enthusiastic? It
had been so long, he couldn't remember. Ken was impressed by the new gate and a little fencing. Hell of a lot of
good that would do against someone determined. They
were all sitting ducks out here. In the past he wouldn't have
doubted his ability to keep Faith and the cubs safe, but
now— He shook his head. He wasn't so sure. In four days
he hadn't remembered a damn thing about his last mission. What if he never remembered?

He walked a little faster, putting more weight on his
healing leg. He tried lengthening his stride, but his calf
muscle cramped and he almost went down. He stopped to
rest for a second, then continued moving.

From the corner of his eye, he caught a flash of black
flying through the air. Before he could prepare himself,
something plowed into him, and he hit the ground. Instantly he was transported back in time.

The explosion nearly deafened him. Below him, the
wooden floor of the warehouse shook with the impact.
Dust billowed around, filling his lungs. He tried to cough,
but he couldn't seem to draw in air. A burst of light split the
night, illuminating the stacks of boxes. Where there should
have been a wall, he could see through a gaping hole to the
sea beyond.

He inhaled again and tasted the salty air. And something else—smoke. He tried to raise his head, but couldn't.
Still he could feel the heat of the flames, hear the snapping
as the fire began to consume the wood building. In the distance, men screamed out in agony. His head. He reached up
to touch the bump on his forehead and felt instead a warm,
wet tongue.

As quickly as it had begun, the flashback receded. Cort
dug his fingers into the dirt of the compound as if he could

hold on to the past, but it slipped through his fingers like sand. He gritted his teeth. He *had* been in an explosion. He'd been unable to move. Someone must have pulled him to safety. But who? And what the hell had happened to Dan?

Chapter 5

Faith was standing by Samson's cage when she saw Sparky leap up and Cort hit the ground face first. She dropped the buckets she'd been carrying and took off at a run. By the time she reached Cort's side, Sparky was licking his face and grunting nervously. She pushed the leopard out of the way.

"Cort?" she said, dropping down beside him. "Are you okay? Can you hear me?"

He groaned and shook his head. "What the hell...?"

"Sparky jumped you. I think it's because you're still limping. He probably thought you were playing."

"Great." He pushed as if to sit up.

"Don't move," she said, touching his arms and then his back. "Anything hurt?"

"I just got tackled by a three-hundred-pound leopard. Everything hurts."

"Don't try to get up."

"I'm not going to lay here and eat dirt."

She sat back on her heels. "You must be feeling all right if you can complain."

He rolled onto his back. Dust coated the front of his shirt and jeans. His hair hung over his forehead. "Thanks for the expert medical assessment."

She bit back a smile.

He raised himself up on one elbow and glared at her. "That cat is a menace."

"He's very sweet and he likes you."

Cort rubbed his head and shifted until he was sitting up, then brushed the grit from his hands. "I'd hate to see what he could do if he didn't like me."

She leaned forward and stared at his face. The cut on his chin had stayed closed and his eyes seemed clear. She bent over and ran her hands along his legs. She could feel his warmth through his thick jeans. As she touched him, his muscles rippled in response. She ignored the answering tightness in her stomach and concentrated on locating sudden swelling or lumps. Nothing out of the ordinary. Just long, lean legs.

"Everything seems in place," she said, not quite able to meet his gaze. "Does anything feel broken?"

He stretched out his legs and rotated his ankles. "Nope."

She glanced over her shoulder at Sparky. The leopard sat a short distance away. He looked like he expected to be punished. "You're going to have to tell him you're still friends," she said.

Cort rolled his shoulders. "Friends? Are you kidding? That cat could play pro football. As a defensive tackle. I bet a lot of teams would be interested. You could go for the big bucks."

He grinned at her. The midday sun caught the gold in his short hair. His flecked eyes glinted with amusement. Despite the dirt on his work shirt and jeans, he'd never looked more handsome. Her hands still tingled from their contact with his body. She didn't like knowing he affected her. It was easier when she thought of him as one of her patients, or simply as the guy Jeff had sent along to keep the cubs safe.

She got to her feet and held out her hand. When Cort took it in his, she braced herself and he pulled himself to his feet. She hated that she liked the feel of his fingers against hers. She hated it more that she didn't want him to let go. For a second they stood there, staring at each other. She wondered if he would pull her close and . . . The erotic visions that filled her head frightened her. Deliberately, she pulled free of the casual contact and stepped back.

Sparky approached her and butted her thigh. "I'm not the one you need to apologize to," she told the animal.

Cort glared down. "She's got that right, buddy."

Sparky looked at him and coughed.

Cort shook his head. "All right, Sparky. Come." He patted his leg. The black leopard stepped over to him and sniffed his arm. "I forgive you." He grabbed the collar and tugged on it until the leopard looked at him. "Just don't do it again."

Sparky twisted his head so Cort scratched his ears. Faith grinned. Cort looked up at her. She tried to smother her smile, but he saw it.

"What's so funny?" he asked, obviously annoyed at being observed making up with the cat.

"Nothing."

"I know Sparky's a wild animal. He was just reacting. I'm not a complete jerk. I wouldn't hold it against him."

"That's why I'm smiling."

Cort pushed the leopard away and started toward the main building. She walked beside him.

"I really understand," she said. "That's why I wasn't upset with you."

He stopped suddenly and stared at her. The emotion left his face as he once again became a cool professional. "What are you talking about?"

"The drive up here. In the truck. When you—"

"When I tried to kill you," he said bluntly, cutting her off.

She ducked her head, sorry that she'd brought it up. "Yes." She tossed her long hair over her shoulder and stared up at him. "It was just like this. That's why I didn't mind. You simply reacted."

If anything, her explanation made him grow more still and distant. His mouth tightened into a straight line and all the light faded from his eyes.

"There is a difference," he said slowly. "I am not one of your cats. I am a man. I wasn't reacting; I tried to kill you."

"Now you're trying to scare me." Unable to stare at the emptiness in his eyes, she lowered her gaze. The right sleeve of his shirt was torn and blood trickled down his arm. "You're bleeding."

"I hit a rock on my way down."

She pulled open the tear. Dirt and tiny pebbles clung to the gash. "Why didn't you say something? We've got to get this clean and bandaged."

She hurried in front of him and held open the door to the office building. He hesitated as if he wasn't going to accept the change in subject or her offer of aid, then he followed her into the examining room and sat on the metal table.

"You'll have to take off your shirt," she said as she washed her hands. She dried them, then reached for the antiseptic. After pulling a gauze bandage and tape from the drawer under the counter, she turned toward the table.

He'd done as she asked and removed his shirt. She stared at his broad, bare back. Despite his lean build, muscles rippled with each movement. The tanned skin looked warm and inviting and she curled her fingers around her supplies to keep from reaching out to him. Her throat tightened.

It had been a long time since she'd been with a man. Even longer since she'd allowed herself to care about one. She let herself get lost in the day-to-day cycle of dealing with the cats and never thought about her owns needs. It was easier that way. She couldn't get hurt. But sometimes the loneliness overwhelmed her and she ached for all she'd given up.

Faith drew in a deep breath and walked over to the metal table. The hair on Cort's chest was slightly darker than that on his head. She forced herself to look no higher than his throat. She didn't want him to figure out what she was thinking. A man like him would never be interested in a woman like her. He was wild and untamed, like her cats.

Forgetting that would be as dangerous as walking into a wounded panther's cage.

"This shouldn't sting," she said, sliding a towel under the wound and flushing it with the cleaner. "Even Sparky doesn't flinch and, at heart, he's a baby." The liquid washed away the dirt and pebbles. When the wound was clean, she reached for the antiseptic.

As she uncapped the bottle, the smell of alcohol filled her nostrils. But it wasn't enough to erase the musky scent of the man. Even without trying she could see the bare, broad expanse of his chest. As she worked, she almost brushed against him. She wanted to. Desperately. Between her thighs a hot ache came painfully to life.

"This one *will* hurt," she said, damping a wad of cotton with the antiseptic. "But it's the best I have." She held his arm in one hand and ignored the warm feel of his skin and hard muscles just below the surface. Ignored how touching him made her want to be touched. "Deep breath. Now." She pressed the treated cotton against him. He tensed once, then relaxed.

She set the cotton down and picked up the bandage. As she began to peel back the covering, Cort reached out and gripped her wrists. He pulled her until she stood between his spread knees.

"Look at me," he growled.

She licked her lower lip, then slowly did as he asked. Past the waistband of his jeans, past his flat stomach, the hair of his chest. Past his broad shoulders to the cut on his chin and the faint shadow of stubble darkening his jaw. Past his straight nose to his oddly flecked brown eyes.

Something hot flared to life there. She wanted to respond, but she was afraid. He held her forearms tightly and shook her.

"I am not one of your cats," he said.

"I know."

"I don't think you do."

"Why does it matter?" she asked desperately.

"What are you hiding from?"

Part of her noted he hadn't answered her question, so she wouldn't answer his. She knew exactly what she was hiding from. Him. Pretending he was just like one of the cats made him safe. It was dangerous to think of him as a man, because he tempted her. He made her think of family and forever, and she'd learned long ago she didn't have what it took to inspire a man to want either.

His grip on her loosened, and she jerked away. She thrust the bandage at him. "Here. Finish it yourself." Then she fled the room.

William Thomas paused outside the news reporter's dressing room. On the drive over to the TV station, he'd planned several different ways to approach the man and get the information he needed, but he had dismissed them all. It would have been easiest to simply pull out his gun and demand he tell him everything. But if he didn't waste the reporter afterward, the jerk was likely to blab the entire incident to someone, and then Thomas's advantage of surprise would be lost. No, he would have to come up with a plausible story. He adjusted his jacket to make sure his gun was concealed then knocked once on the door.

"Come in," the reporter called from inside.

Thomas took a deep breath and forced himself to smile. "James, my man. How's it going?" he said as he pushed open the door. "It's been a long time." He walked forward confidently and held out his hand.

The handsome reporter stared at him. Instinctively James Wilson took the offered hand and shook it, then frowned. "I'm sorry, I don't remember meeting you."

Of course not, you little twit, Thomas thought. We've never met.

"Harry Williams," William Thomas lied. "Work for the *Times*. We covered that big scandal downtown together."

Keep it vague enough and they'll believe, Thomas reminded himself. People are basically stupid and trusting. If you say you know them, they'll do their best to remember you. Thomas was banking on the fact that in Los Angeles "downtown" could mean anywhere from the West Side to

East L.A., and that a scandal could have occurred in city politics, at one of the big universities, or in the movie business. Surely James had covered at least one story like that.

"Of course," James said suddenly, his brow clearing. "The bribery case."

"Bingo," Thomas said jovially. "Been meaning to look you up. We were supposed to grab a drink some night, but hey, you know how that is."

"Sure," James said, eyeing Thomas's cheap sports coat. "I'm afraid I'm working the four o'clock news so I can't—"

Thomas gave a hearty laugh. "That's not why I stopped by." The laughter turned genuine when he saw James's look of relief. He knew the newsman's type. The big dressing room with a long vanity and a closet full of suits didn't hide the truth. James might like expensive clothes, whiskey and women, but underneath, he was a wimp. Wouldn't last a day on the streets. "I saw that piece you did on the tiger cubs."

"What a disaster that day was." James shuddered and turned back to the mirror. "The woman in charge is crazy."

Thomas pulled a notepad out of his pocket and pretended to consult it, even though he'd had the information memorized for three days. He'd wanted to come to Los Angeles and confront the reporter as soon as he'd heard about the newscast, but James had been in Sacramento covering some hearing.

"Faith Newlin," he said.

"That's her." James looked at him in the mirror. "Are you doing a story on the way station?"

"Kicking it around. Probably for the Sunday magazine."

James shook his head. "Don't bother talking to that woman. Do you know she threatened to shoot me?"

Thomas clucked with artificial concern. To be perfectly honest, he didn't blame the woman one bit. He wouldn't mind shooting the yuppie reporter himself.

"I checked with the station's attorney." James picked up a brush and smoothed his perfect hair. "I wanted to sue her for distress, but they said that since there hadn't been any actual damage, it might not look good for the network.''

"But you got a great story."

James grinned. "Pets and kids get 'em every time. I don't usually like either, but those tiger cubs were something else. Still . . . that woman." He shook his head. "I won't be going back there again."

"She's up north, isn't she?" he asked casually, as if he really knew but couldn't remember. He'd checked up on the foundation that supported the way station to get an address, but all they listed were a post-office box and some attorney's office in L.A.

"Outside of Bowmund." James grimaced. "Are you sure you want to do this, Harry? She's dangerous."

"I'm sure." It was find the cubs or die. Not much of a choice.

James looked through the clutter of papers on the vanity. "I've got the address here, somewhere. They're having their annual fund-raiser at the end of the week. The station was going to send me back, but I told them that woman doesn't deserve the free publicity." He pawed through a stack of invitations until he found what he was looking for. "Here it is." He read off the address, then tossed the invitation into the trash.

Thomas thanked him. James glanced at his watch. "Look, it's almost time for the broadcast. I'd love to talk some more, but—"

"No problem," Thomas said, pocketing his small notebook. "Thanks for the information. I appreciate it. I'll give you a call in a couple of weeks and we'll get that drink."

"Sure." James stood up and the two men shook hands.

Thomas left and quickly walked down the hallway. He ducked into a supply closet and closed the door behind him. The news sound stage was on the other side of the wall. He could hear the crew getting ready for the live broadcast, then the call for silence. The broadcast began. Several minutes later, he heard James's voice droning on about some bill up for passage in Sacramento. He cracked the door to make sure the hallway was empty, then walked purposefully toward James's dressing room.

The invitation lay where the reporter had tossed it, right in the white plastic trash container. Thomas pulled it out and pocketed it. Five minutes later he pulled onto Prospect Avenue and into the rush-hour traffic. He'd been worried about having to sneak in and steal the cubs in the dead of night. Luck was on his side. With a big party at the way station, he could walk in with the other guests and take the cubs without anyone being the wiser.

After feeding the cubs and settling them down for their afternoon nap, Cort wandered toward Faith's office. She'd pleaded too much work as a reason for avoiding him at lunch, but he knew it was something more than that. He flexed his arm and felt the bandage move with his skin. Something had happened when she'd tended his cut. In a flash of temper, he'd forced her to acknowledge he wasn't just one of her cats. He paused at the entrance to her office and shook his head. It came from thinking with the wrong part of his anatomy, and from living in close quarters with a woman who turned him on.

She sat at her desk, with her head bent. She wrote furiously on the papers in front of her. Afternoon sunlight filtered through the window. The overhead fluorescent glared harshly on her. Often she wore her hair in a braid, but today a headband held it away from her face. A single, shiny strand slipped over her shoulder and onto the page. She brushed it away impatiently.

The scent of Sparky's mint, the smell of furniture oil and the whispered fragrance of French perfume mingled together. In the compound, cats paced restlessly and called to one another, but here there was only quiet. Faith was a woman, he was a man, and they were alone. It was tempting to think about touching her and tasting her. Tempting to wonder what she would feel like next to him, under him.

But would she be tempted? And why did he care? He was here to get a job done. She would be a complication he didn't need, a temptation he had no time for. He was reacting to circumstances, not the woman, and he sure better not forget that.

This arrangement of theirs got to him. Their domesticity was as foreign to him as the jungles of South America would be to her. It was different from his normal life. He allowed himself a small smile. Who was he kidding? He had no normal life.

"How's it going?" he asked.

She jumped in the chair. Her pencil went flying, and she looked up at him. "How do you *do* that?" she asked. She leaned forward and stared down. "You're wearing boots. I can't believe you snuck up on me."

"I wasn't sneaking." He moved into the room and took the chair in front of her desk.

She shuffled her papers together and tried not to look at him. He knew she was trying hard, because she kept glancing at him out of the corner of her eye and then looking disgusted with herself. He liked that he got to her.

"Are the cubs fed?" she asked.

"Both Big and Little tiger are sleeping soundly."

"Big and Little? Is that what you're calling them?"

"Yeah. What do you think?"

She grinned. "It's kind of basic, but it works. Having any trouble with the forms?"

"Nope." He motioned to the papers scattered on her desk. "What about you?"

She bent down and retrieved her pencil from the floor. "Don't even ask. It's a nightmare. Every government agency has its own rules. You have to document the documentation." She leaned back in her wooden chair and stretched her arms above her head. Her back arched and her shirt drew taut across her body.

The unobstructed view of her generous curves reminded him of his original premise that rooming with Faith Newlin wasn't going to be tough duty. The unconscious grace in her movements made him wonder what else she did gracefully and well. To distract himself, he looked around the office. Like the rest of the building, it needed a coat of paint.

"You don't spend a lot of money on decorating, do you?" he asked.

"The cats are my first priority."

"I guess." Pictures of the animals hung on all the walls. He glanced at a pair of photographs in dark wood frames. "Are those the snow leopards?"

She swiveled around until she could see them. "Yes. They're a breeding pair."

He got up and stepped over to the wall. "Looks like the pictures were taken from a long way off."

"A plane." Faith rose and stood next to him. Her arm brushed his. He pretended not to notice. "These two were illegally brought into the country. I don't know if it was for a private collection or what, but they escaped and were captured by animal-control people." She picked up the smaller of the two frames. "They brought the cats here and I looked after them." She glanced up and smiled. "They were so beautiful and wild."

He stared down at her blue eyes, at her faint dusting of freckles and the generous curve of her mouth. Not beautiful, he thought, but intelligent and warm and attractive enough that conventional beauty didn't matter. It occurred to him that he could get to like her. He didn't have many friends in his life; it was too dangerous. The weight of relationships slowed him down. But in another time and place, he wouldn't have minded getting to know her.

"How long were they here?" he asked.

"About four months. We healed them, fattened them back up. The hardest part was making sure not to domesticate them." She placed the photo back on the wall. "They were flown back to Asia and released in the wild. These pictures were taken about a year ago. They're both still alive."

He placed his hand on her shoulder. Her blue eyes widened slightly, but she didn't step away. If anything, she seemed to sway toward him. He told himself he was fourteen different kinds of fool, but he didn't care. "You must be very proud of yourself."

"I am. I'm glad they survived."

Her bones felt delicate. He knew she was strong and re-silient, yet there was a fragility about her that intrigued him. He also knew she'd probably drop-kick him if he ever said that thought aloud. He gave her a brief squeeze and stepped back.

"Is that why you want to start a snow-leopard breeding program?" he asked.

She nodded slowly, as if trying to remember what they were talking about. "There are so few of them left. With-out adding to the wild population, they're going to disap-pear altogether. Just three or four breeding pairs would greatly increase the gene pool. When I found out these two made it, I bought some land to start my own breeding cen-ter. Now I just have to worry about all the paperwork, get-ting the foundation up and running, finding donors."

He perched on the corner of her desk and took the weight off his healing leg. "What will happen here if you leave to start your snow-leopard program?"

"Several zoos have approached me about buying the place. They would use it for an isolation facility, either for quarantined animals, or for breeding the more endangered species."

"Sounds like you've got it all figured out."

"Maybe." She leaned over and picked up the forms. "I'm just not sure I can pull this off. I would have to run the new foundation and I don't have a lot of business ex-perience. I'm not sure I could get funding. I have this pic-ture of slowly starving to death our first winter."

"At least the snow leopards would keep you warm."

"Yeah, they are furry little creatures, aren't they? Oh well, I'll deal with that problem later. Right now I have a benefit to plan."

He folded his arms over his chest. "I'm not happy about this."

She wrinkled her nose. "Fortunately, your being happy isn't a priority."

"Gee, thanks." With him sitting on the desk, they were almost at eye level. She was one tough lady. "Did you put a call in to Jeff?"

"Earlier today. I'm expecting him to return it shortly." She glanced at her watch. "In another hour or so."

"We're going to need extra security for the party," he said. "I want to talk to him about that. I've already sent the guest list through the computer. Everyone is clean. You do realize that reporter you scared off is invited."

"I know," she said. "I don't think he'll show up. Do you?"

"Highly unlikely. Are there any changes?"

"A couple. I'm expecting more." She bent over and pulled open a desk drawer. She drew out a folder and handed it to him. "Some of the invitations say 'and guest,' so we don't have all the names. They're supposed to call and let us know how many are coming, but they don't always. Also, here are the names of the caterer's employees, and the guys who'll be parking cars. But these haven't been finalized, either."

He opened the folder and scanned the typed sheets. "Are you trying to make my job harder, or is this a natural trait?"

"I guess you're just lucky." She leaned over and looked at the bandage partially visible under the T-shirt he'd changed into. "How do you feel?"

"Sore. I haven't checked in the mirror, but I think I have paw-shaped bruises on my back."

She chuckled. "I'll bet. I'm heading up to the Big House. The bathrooms there have tubs. I'm going to take a bath. You're welcome to join me." As soon as the words came out of her mouth, she blushed scarlet and stared at the ground. "That's not exactly what I meant," she stammered.

"Too bad." Her invitation conjured up a vivid picture of a delightfully naked Faith Newlin soaking in a tub of water.

She risked a quick glance, then busied herself with straightening the papers on her desk blotter. "The guest room has a Jacuzzi tub. It might help with any stiffness."

"Thanks."

"If you want to go get a change of clothing, I'll meet you by the garage in a couple of minutes." She fled the room without waiting for his agreement.

Cort rose and trailed after her. He could use a good soak to ease the tightness from his muscles. More than that, he wanted to talk to his boss. The missing pieces from his memory were gradually being filled in. Jeff might be persuaded to give him a couple more. He had to learn the truth. If he didn't, he couldn't go back. And he had to go back. Fighting in the trenches was all he knew.

Chapter 6

Faith shifted her tote bag over one shoulder and bent down to pull the roast out of the refrigerator. After collecting a few potatoes and some vegetables, she put them all in a plastic bag and dropped them in the tote.

No doubt Cort was waiting for her by the Jeep. She should go face him and get it over with. But just thinking about what she'd said was enough to send heat flaring on her cheeks.

You're welcome to join me. Oh! She wanted to scream. How could she have blurted that out? She hadn't been thinking anything remotely sexual. She sighed and made her way down the hall. She'd never been a good liar, especially to herself. She *had* been thinking about how handsome Cort was, and how he seemed to fill her office, but she certainly hadn't been thinking about having a bath with him. Still, it was an intriguing thought. She wasn't a virgin; she knew what went on between a woman and a man.

As she entered the foyer, she instinctively glanced out at the compound. Ken and Sparky were playing tug-of-war with Sparky's favorite blanket. Sparky was winning. She pushed open the door.

"Ken?" she called.

He looked up. Sparky took advantage of the distraction, jerking his powerful head once and pulling the blanket free. Ken promptly sat down on his butt.

"That's cheating," he yelled at the victorious cat. He stood up and brushed off his pants. "Yes?"

"Cort and I are going up to the Big House. Please feed the cubs before you leave and make sure everything is locked up."

"No problem." He tossed her a grin, then started after the cat. "Come back here. I demand a rematch." Sparky sprinted up one of the telephone poles and looked down at him.

Faith closed the door and stepped out the front. Cort was leaning against the Jeep. His black T-shirt emphasized his blond good looks and her heart started making a funny thumping against her ribs.

"Thought you'd changed your mind," he said, stepping forward to take her bag.

"Just giving Ken instructions. He'll take care of the cubs' next feeding."

Cort lifted the tote from her shoulder and looked surprised when he felt the weight of the bag. "What do you have in here?"

"Dinner." She climbed into the vehicle. "I have to count glasses and plates, see what we have before I call the caterer. I thought I'd cook a roast while I was there. The oven at the Big House is better, and I can keep an eye on it while I work."

He settled in beside her and peered in the bag. "How do I know you're not feeding me tiger or leopard food?"

"You'll just have to trust me."

"Not something I do easily."

She believed him. Jeff never talked much about his work, but the few times he'd opened up to her, she'd been appalled by the horrors he'd seen. Cort would have shared those experiences. She didn't understand these warriors who risked their lives and fought ever-changing enemies.

"Lucky for you the meat is still in the store wrapper. You can read the label yourself."

"I'll risk it," he said.

When they reached the Big House, Faith parked in front. She pulled the keys from her jeans pocket and unlocked the front door.

"It's always a little musty," she said. "The cleaners come two days before the party and air the whole thing out. The caterers arrive the next day and then the guests."

He stepped into the house and gave a low whistle. "This is some place."

She glanced around at the familiar high ceilings and papered walls. "Let me get the roast going, and I'll show you around."

In the kitchen, she turned on the oven and prepared the meat. After she slid the pan in the oven, she turned to Cort. "We can cook for about a hundred with this kitchen."

He stared at the two large stoves, the extrawide triple sink and the subzero refrigerator. A butcher-block island stood in the center.

"All the party dishes are stored in there," she said, pointing to the pantry on the right. "Through here is the dining room." She led the way.

The rooms were large. Hardwood floors gleamed despite a layer of dust. The wallpaper was subdued and elegant, with a cream-and-rose print. Small couches had been pushed up against the walls and covered with sheets. Chairs stood in tall stacks in all the corners. Round tables had been pushed together in front of the big stone fireplace. Velvet drapes covered the tall windows, rich brocade trimmed the valances.

"We use the downstairs for our fund-raisers. We have conversational areas in these two parlors, then set up a buffet here in the dining room. There's a study over there." She pointed to closed double doors. "That's where we hold the petting zoo."

Cort glanced at her and raised his eyebrows. "Something tells me you don't bring in lambs and baby goats."

She shook her head. "The friendliest of the cats. Samson, that bobcat in the last habitat. He loves the attention. His being declawed is a real plus. There are a couple of panthers that like people, and of course, Sparky."

"Sparky ever take one of your guests down?" he asked.

"No. I told you, it means he likes you."

He rubbed the cut on his arms. "If anyone gets out of hand, we'll just tell him to go long and let Sparky tackle him."

Faith grinned. "I'll keep that in mind." She shifted the tote bag to her other shoulder and started up the stairs. "The house was built in the early part of the century. Edwina's grandfather made his fortune in lumber and construction."

"It's a beautiful place. I'm surprised you don't want to live here."

"It's expensive to keep the house heated. With the weather mild, it's fine, but in the winter, this place is drafty and cold." At the top of the stairs, she paused. "Edwina's suite of rooms is over there." She pointed at the closed door. "It's empty now. After she was gone it seemed easier to move to the way station and live in the apartment. We save a lot of money on utilities, and I'm closer to the cats."

He moved past her to the glass case lining part of the long dark hallway. "What's this?" he asked, pointing at the many ribbons and trophies.

She switched on the overhead light and stepped next to him. "My secret life."

He opened the cabinet and pulled out one of the statues. "You're a sharpshooter?"

"One of my many talents." She smiled.

His brown eyes flickered over her face. "Jeff didn't tell me."

"I'm not sure he knows."

He put the trophy back. "You ever shoot at anything other than targets?"

"If I have to."

He didn't return her smile. "If someone shows up to take the cubs, are you prepared to defend them?"

She bit her lower lip. He was asking if she could kill a man. She thought about the white tiger cubs, sleeping peacefully in their cage. And the snow leopards that had been illegally smuggled into the country, then mistreated.

She nodded slowly. "I would do my best."

He held her gaze. "Can't ask for more than that."

They were standing close together. She wasn't sure why she hadn't noticed before, but suddenly she was aware of his arm only inches from her breasts and the way his scent drifted to her. The empty house was a welcome sanctuary from her pressures at the compound. She knew she would never enter here again without remembering how Cort looked standing next to her.

She stepped back to break the spell. "The guest room is through here," she said, walking around him and pushing open a door. A king-size bed stood against one wall. A rich mahogany dresser and armoire matched the headboard. She pulled a towel out of her tote bag and tossed it to him. "The tub is in the bathroom, over there." She pointed to a half-open door. "I think it's big enough to swim in."

He looked around. "There's no phone."

"I know. I have one in my room, and there's another downstairs. They're extensions of the main number at the way station, so we won't miss Jeff's call."

He dropped the towel on the bed and looked around. "It's a great old place."

"You're welcome to sleep here, if you want."

"No, Faith." He placed his hands on his hips and stared at her. "I take my responsibilities just as seriously as you do."

Faith leaned back in the tub and sighed. Hot water lapped around her shoulders. The scented bubbles teased her nose. Soft music from her portable radio filled the bathroom. This was her idea of heaven. The tension in her back eased, and she closed her eyes. She had a thousand details to worry about with the upcoming fund-raiser. She should be planning the menu or worrying about decorations, but she didn't care. Right now she didn't want to think about anything.

Her eyes drifted shut. The music swept over and through her, carrying her along on the sweet melody. She moved lower in the tub, until the water crept up the back of her neck. Warm, she thought. It reminded her of Cort's hand on her shoulder, and the feel of his body so close to hers. The brief contact had shaken her to her toes. She'd tried not to let him know how he affected her.

It was just because she lived out in the sticks and had limited her contact with men, she told herself. It wasn't anything to do with that man specifically. He wasn't interested in her, and she wasn't interested in him.

She hummed with the song on the radio and thought about how his bare chest had looked that morning when she'd dressed his cut. Broad and strong and tanned. She'd wanted to touch him, had thought about running her fingers along his ribs and—

She sat up suddenly, ignoring the water sloshing over the side of the tub. Cold air stung her wet torso. She had it bad for Cort. Faith drew her knees up and hugged them. There wasn't anything she could do about it, either, except pretend this—this attraction or whatever she wanted to call it— didn't exist.

She stepped out of the tub and grabbed a towel. As she dried off, she forced herself to think about the upcoming party and the tiger cubs. She walked naked into the bedroom, ignoring her reflection in the mirror over the dresser.

The entire room made her uncomfortable. From the pale cream carpeting to the lacy bedspread and frilly drapes, this was a feminine room. Edwina had decorated it for her when she'd first come to live with the older woman. It had been her welcoming present. Faith had never had the heart to tell her friend that ruffles and lace made her feel awkward and out of place.

She picked up the clean undergarments she'd brought with her and slipped into the panties. Sensible cotton. She fingered the plain white bra. No silk for her. As she fastened the front closure, she sighed. What was the point?

The cats hardly cared what she wore. It didn't make sense to spend extra money on lingerie no one but her was going to see.

She glanced at the fresh clothes she'd brought, then walked over to the closet and pulled open the door. A dozen outfits hung on the rack. There was room for four times that many. On the floor sat three shoe boxes. The top shelf contained a bag of stockings.

These were her fancy clothes. The things she wore to the fund-raisers. They were part of a life that wasn't real to her. She fingered the midnight-blue velvet of a long dress. She became someone else when she wore these clothes. Rich men spoke to her, but their eyes dipped to her breasts. Wealthy matrons assumed she was one of them and whispered confidentially about the best caterers and florists. Wives squealed at the beauty of the cats and conveniently forgot about the fur coats they had waiting in the cloakroom. Husbands cornered her to find out if she was adverse to having a brief but torrid affair.

Faith shook her head and closed the door. They weren't all like that, she reminded herself. Many of the people came because they genuinely cared about the cats. But the foundation required money to keep it going, and that meant she had to play her role.

She picked up the clean jeans and knit top she'd brought with her. Sometimes she wanted to be more than she was. Not the woman in the velvet dress, not the competent genderless caretaker, but someone in between. A woman who wore pretty things from time to time. She slipped into her jeans. That wasn't true, she admitted. It wasn't about wearing pretty dresses and shoes; it was about fitting in. Just once, she wanted to be like other people who seemed so naturally to join up, two by two. She wasn't like that. She could give her love away, but it was never returned. She'd never been enough. She'd learned it was safer to give it all to the cats. At least they needed her.

She slipped the white knit top over her head, then pulled out a brush. After taking the pins out of her hair, she let it fall down her back and began brushing out the tangles.

She'd just finished securing her French braid when the phone on the nightstand rang.

She picked it up. "Hello."

"Tell me there's no crisis," Jeff said.

She laughed. "Why do you always assume the worst?"

"It's my job, Faith. How are you?"

He sounded weary, she thought, wishing he were here for her to talk to. Although what would she say? There were some things even Jeff wouldn't understand. She had a feeling that her attraction to one of his operatives fell in that category.

She quickly brought him up-to-date on the cubs and the security measures Cort had already installed.

"He wants to talk to you," she said.

"About what?"

"I'm not privy to that information," she said, then chuckled. "But he did want me to mention that the foundation is having a fund-raiser at the end of the week. We're expecting about a hundred and twenty guests. I think he wants some extra people for that."

She held the receiver away from her ear and listened to him squawk. At regular intervals she brought the mouthpiece closer and said his name. About the fourth time she did it, he got quiet.

"I absolutely forbid it," he growled.

"I didn't ask permission."

"Faith, those cubs are important. I don't want anything happening to them."

"I understand that, but you dumped them on me with no warning. I'm happy to keep them for you. However, this party has been planned for months. Unless you're prepared to offer me a half-million dollars, which is about what we'll be raising, I can't stop it now."

He didn't say anything.

"I'll go get Cort," she said.

Jeff sighed. "Fine."

She set the phone on the bed and crossed the hall to the guest room. After knocking on the door, she waited. He didn't answer, so she knocked again.

"Cort, Jeff is on the phone."

Could he have fallen asleep in the bath? She knocked a third time, then pushed the door open. As she entered the room, the bathroom door opened and Cort stepped into the bedroom.

He stood before her, naked. More beautiful than any of the wild cats in the compound. The soft lamplight made his tanned skin glow. Long, lean muscles covered his strong frame. Despite the bandage on his calf, he was the perfect specimen of a man.

He held a towel over one shoulder. A single drop of moisture dripped from his neck onto his chest and got lost in the matting of hair. Her fingers curled into her palms. She looked at his tapered waist and narrow hips, then at the wide thatch of blond hair surrounding the partially erect proof of his gender. Below that, long legs stretched down endlessly.

She thought of how incredible he would look moving through sunlight, each muscle bunching and releasing with powerful male energy. She could see the coiled strength just below his skin. Her gaze trailed up his body. So stunning. He took her breath away.

He pulled the towel down and let it hang from his hand. The movement startled her. She looked at his face. In a single heartbeat, everything changed. As she met his gaze, she knew he wasn't like the wild cats she so loved. He was a man, and she wanted him.

Sexual need snapped between them like the crack of a whip. She swallowed against the tightening of her throat. Her breasts swelled as her nipples poked against her bra. Between her legs, moisture dampened her sensible cotton panties. She watched an answering interest stir Cort's body, lengthening his maleness. She took a single step toward him.

He smiled. A very knowing, very satisfied male smile. Reality crashed in around her. She had been staring at him, practically begging him to touch and take her. Embarrassment flooded her, and with it horror that she had completely lost control.

"Jeff is on the phone," she blurted out, then turned and ran out of the room.

Cort started after her. He'd seen the humiliation in her eyes. "Faith, wait."

But she was already halfway down the stairs. He paused, torn between duty and desire, then cursed and made his way across the hall to her room and the phone.

"What?" he barked into the receiver.

"Took you long enough," Jeff drawled. "What the hell have you been doing?"

Cort sat on the edge of the bed and ran his hand through his damp hair. It was all bad timing. But the look on her face...how was he supposed to resist that? Had any woman ever looked at him with such appreciation and raw desire?

"Cort, are you listening?"

"No. What did you say?"

"Tell me about this party."

Cort explained about the fund-raiser. He forced himself to ignore what had happened with Faith and concentrate on the business at hand. "I want you to send me a team. I've already faxed the guest list to your office. To date, everyone has been cleared."

"I'll take care of it." Cort heard the scratching of Jeff's pen, then his boss said, "How's everything else going?"

"I've got most of the security measures already installed. It's been quiet. No one's made any kind of move."

"They might use the party as a cover."

"I've already thought of that. I'm going to make sure the cubs are well guarded." He ran through the list of other precautions he'd taken. "Could you rent me a tux? This affair of Faith's is formal."

Jeff laughed. "Don't want the hired help standing out. We're about the same size. I'll send up mine."

"You own a tux?"

"Comes with the job, buddy."

Cort grimaced. "You should never have gone inside, Jeff. You gave up all the action."

His boss was silent for a minute. "I couldn't do it any-more. Not after what happened to Jeanne and my son, J.J."

"I know." Cort felt like a heel. He'd spoken without thinking.

"You could do worse," Jeff said. "The field gets old."

"Sit behind a desk?" Cort switched the receiver to his other hand. "I'd rather be shot at dawn. I want to be out there, face-to-face with the bad guys."

"Let me know when you change your mind. You're up for a promotion."

It was a familiar argument. Jeff offered him a promo-tion and a raise. The only problem was, Cort had to come in from the field to get it. Not him. He wanted to be where he could see the action. Great battles were never fought behind desks.

"Anything else?" Jeff asked.

Cort drew in a deep breath. He had to know and Jeff was the only one he trusted to speak the truth. "Did Dan die in the explosion?"

Silence.

"I know about the warehouse going up in flames. I re-member being there, but that's all." Cort waited, but Jeff didn't answer. "Tell me, dammit. I know I went down there to be with Dan. He was my friend. I have the right to know what happened to him." He realized he was squeezing the receiver tight enough to crack the plastic, and he forced himself to relax his grip. "Did I kill him?"

"It really matters to you, doesn't it?" Jeff asked.

"Yes."

"You didn't kill him."

Cort slumped forward and rested his elbows on his knees. "Thanks."

Before he could ask anything else, he heard Jeff shuf-fling papers. "I'm glad you're getting better," he said. "How's Faith?"

Cort thought about the look on her face when she'd stared at his naked body. The desire there had him responding instantly. Then she'd become aware of herself, of the situation, and she'd run off.

"She's fine," he said.

"The way your memory is returning, you should be ready to come back to work as soon as the problem with the tiger cubs is taken care of."

"Looks that way," Cort answered, hoping he was right.

"Think about the promotion," Jeff said. "You would be surprised what a difference you can make from the inside."

"It's not for me."

"The offer stands. Take care of yourself and Faith, buddy. I'll be in touch." He hung up the phone.

Cort replaced the receiver. Relief overwhelmed him. He hadn't killed Dan. Thank God. He leaned back on the bed and stared up at the ceiling. How would he have handled that? He'd killed before. In his line of work, that couldn't be helped. But it had always been a simple decision. The bad guys had been the ones shooting at him. But Dan? Cort sat up and rubbed his jaw. This is why he didn't like relationships. Entanglements complicated everything.

Would he have done it? If Jeff had told him to kill Dan because he'd gone over to the other side, could Cort have iced his friend? He thought for a moment, then nodded. He was a damn good operative. He followed orders. So what the hell kind of human being did that make him?

He didn't like the question, so he rose to his feet and walked back to the guest room. No answers awaited him there. He wanted— He paced restlessly. He wanted to talk about it.

The need startled him. He'd never been the kind to share his troubles. But everything blurred together. Dan. The parts of the mission he could remember. What he couldn't remember. What the death of his friend meant. Why, given the order, he would have been able to pull the trigger.

He suddenly remembered Jeff hadn't answered the question about whether or not Dan died in the explosion.

"Tricky devil," Cort muttered. And wondered what Faith would make of the whole thing. She—

He cursed. He'd completely forgotten how she'd run out on him. He started out of the room. Realizing he was still wrapped in a towel, he pulled the ends tight around his waist and hurried down the stairs.

He found her in the pantry off the kitchen, surrounded by the caterer's menu and cupboards full of dishes and glassware. She sat on a high stool, a clipboard rested on her knees. The setting sun shone through a window, back-lighting her delicate profile.

She didn't notice him. He leaned against the doorframe and studied the way her nose tilted up slightly at the end, how she moved her lips when she counted. A pulse fluttered at the base of her throat. She wore a clinging white top, tucked into the waistband of stone-washed jeans. With her hair pulled back in one of her fancy braids, there was nothing to obstruct his view of her torso. As she raised her arm to push some wineglasses aside, he saw the curve of her breast. The size and shape looked to be a perfect fit for his palm.

"Faith."

She jumped at the sound of his voice and spun on the stool to face him. Color flooded her face. She raised the clipboard in front of her chest, like a barrier. Her gaze avoided his.

"Dinner will be another hour," she said softly. "I just put the potatoes in to bake. I have to count the dishes, but you're welcome to use the TV in the study, or whatever you want."

"Faith," he said again.

She still didn't look at him. He walked forward and placed one finger beneath her chin. Slowly, he pressed until she was looking up. Embarrassment clouded her blue eyes.

He hated seeing her like this. It was fine to make her squirm when *he* teased her. He liked the flush of color that stained her cheeks when he winked, or she accidentally said something suggestive like her invitation to join him in her bath. But not this bone-numbing humiliation. Not for her.

She was strong and capable. That's how he wanted—no, needed—her to be.

"I would have looked," he said.

Instead of smiling, she jerked her chin free and turned her head away.

"You're an attractive woman. Why wouldn't I have looked?"

"Just leave me alone. I'm fine."

He didn't believe her. She would retreat inside herself, and he would miss the—he tightened his jaw, but dammit, he couldn't hide from the truth—the friend she'd become. He didn't have many friends. Only Dan and Jeff. Dan was dead and Cort didn't know why or how. He grabbed her shoulders. The clipboard clattered to the floor. She stared up at him.

"You are a stubborn woman," he said.

Her lips quivered slightly. It was almost a smile. "I know."

"Don't be embarrassed. I liked you looking at me."

Fresh color crept into her cheeks. She tried to twist away, but he held her shoulders tightly and she couldn't slip off the stool.

"Don't," he said, and bent down to kiss her.

He'd only meant to reassure her. But at the contact of her mouth against his, he realized he'd made a tactical error. She was soft, too soft, and the feel of it made him hard.

Hunger swept through him. He wanted to tell himself it was all about the amount of time that had passed since he'd last made love to a woman. Any woman would scratch the itch. But he wasn't thinking about any woman. He was thinking about Faith. He squeezed her shoulders and she sighed.

He brushed her lips once, then twice, and raised his head. Wide blue eyes stared into his. She looked as shocked and stunned as he felt. If he had a lick of sense he would back off now and make a strategic retreat. A cold shower would go a long way to stopping this before it started.

"Cort?" she whispered, and he was lost.

He moved close to her, pushing her legs apart so that he could step between them. He brought his arms around her and hauled her against his bare chest. Her breasts flattened against him. Her hands touched his back. Her tentative stroking on his skin contrasted with her normal competence at everything else, and he groaned.

Before she could withdraw or protest or change her mind, he bent down and claimed her mouth again. He told himself to go slow, to move casually and not frighten her away. But when he touched her lips, rational thought fled.

Faith caught her breath at the sweet contact. Cort angled his head so their mouths pressed more firmly together. She'd spent the last twenty minutes berating herself for standing there gawking while he was naked. Now, with that vision fresh in her mind, it was easy to give herself up to his kiss.

He smelled of soap and male skin. Her hands brushed up and down his back, then held on to his shoulders. The tip of his tongue delicately touched her bottom lip. The damp caress made her lips part instantly. She liked the feel of him, the way he held her close. She liked—

His tongue touched hers. Her mind exploded in a conflagration of sensation, as if someone had set a match to dry tinder. Fire raced along her arms and legs. Need followed, making her ache and hunger with a power that frightened her. His tongue swept inside her mouth. She responded to each stroke, surging against him, trying to pull him closer. Her fingers clutched at him, touching his damp hair, then moving rapidly up and down his spine. Her chest grew tight and her breasts throbbed with each heartbeat.

He moved to kiss her jaw, then down her neck to the top of her shirt. He nibbled at her sensitive skin and bit her earlobe. She gasped and arched her head back, needing more.

Both his hands moved to her waist, then reached up toward her aching breasts. She tried to lean back to give him room to move, but he bent down and claimed her lips again. This time she was the aggressor, pushing her tongue into his mouth. As she tasted his heat, his hands cupped her breasts.

She froze, unable to believe the glorious tingling that swept through her. Her hips surged toward his, and she felt the length of his desire press against her jeans-clad core. She rhythmically moved her hips. His matched the thrusting as his fingers swept over and around her breasts. Her nipples puckered in anticipation. Her hands gripped his waist. He shifted, and she felt his towel fall away.

As she reached down to slide her hands across his bare buttocks, his fingers brushed her hard nipples. She moaned her pleasure. He gently squeezed the sensitive points, then pressed slightly. Her head lolled back. He kissed her neck, leaving a wet trail from her jaw to her shirt collar.

It had never been like this, she thought hazily, as his hands pulled her shirt from her jeans. She'd never been so ready, so hungry for a man. There was an honesty to their mating. No words or empty promises, no false pretense. Just a man and a woman with a need too large to be ignored.

He pulled up her shirt and deftly unhooked her bra with one hand. She stroked and squeezed his firm buttocks. He surged against her. As he cupped her bare breasts and his thumbs teased her nipples, she shifted on the stool, bringing her center more firmly against him.

He breathed her name. Supporting her hips, he drew her legs around him. Fire burned in his brown eyes. The lines of his face tightened as he reached for the waistband of her jeans. She'd only had two lovers in her life. Each of the physical relationships had begun slowly, awkwardly, with fumblings and bumped noses. Neither had been as right as this primal mating.

He unfastened the first button. Faith leaned forward and kissed his bare chest, tasting his warm skin. She licked his nipples, making him squirm. Inside, the wanting grew until she knew she would perish from the need. She wiggled her hips impatiently. He grabbed the zipper and tugged it down. As he reached his hand inside her jeans, he lurched suddenly.

Faith straightened and wrapped her arms around his waist to support him. He grabbed for the counter. Their eyes met.

"Guess the leg isn't a hundred percent," he said hoarsely, glancing at his bandaged calf.

She nodded slowly. Self-awareness returned, pushing away the passion.

"We can continue this upstairs," he said.

She bit her lower lip. Could she? Mate like one of the cats, without thought or concern for anything save pleasure? She'd never known how people did that. Both her lovers had claimed possession of her heart before she'd given her body. Unfortunately, after taking the latter, they were no longer interested in the former. She looked at Cort, at his nakedness, the proof of his need thrusting toward her. She wanted him. But was that enough? He was like the snow leopards. Beautiful, wild. Something to admire from afar, but never claim.

"I can't," she whispered.

He swallowed hard, then touched her chin, forcing her to look at him. "I understand. No hard feelings."

"Thank you. Maybe we can just forget it."

One corner of his mouth lifted up in a smile. "You go ahead, Faith. I don't want to forget."

Chapter 7

"This is really great," Cort said, slicing off another bite of beef.

Faith toyed with her food, but didn't bother looking up or answering. It was the third compliment in ten minutes. So much for forgetting about the kiss.

It was all her fault. She shouldn't have kissed him back. She shouldn't have let him know how he affected her. She shouldn't have let him kiss her in the first place. She sighed. She shouldn't have stared at him when she'd seen him standing there naked.

The round oak table sat in an alcove of the kitchen. Behind her were the two professional stoves, the triple sink and expensive refrigerator. She'd wanted to run back to the compound and hide out in her office. With dinner already cooking and work she couldn't put off any longer, she'd had to stay. An hour had passed and she was still shaken.

She glanced at him. Cort was looking at *her*. The fact that he was dressed and sitting there as calmly as if nothing had happened didn't help. She wanted to turn away and hide. She wanted to stop the blush she could feel heating her cheeks. Instead she put down her fork and drew in a deep breath. They had to work together. He seemed to be handling what had happened exactly as she'd requested. Despite his claim to the contrary, he seemed to have put the entire event out of his mind.

"You must think I'm completely inept," she said at last.

He shook his head. "I don't think you're inept. I think you're very honest and you make a great pot roast."

She smiled slightly. "It's a tri-tip."

"Whatever. Do you want me to apologize?"

"Do *you* want to?"

"No. I'm not sorry." He leaned forward across the table and took her hand. "We're working in close quarters. We're both without significant relationships in our lives. I find you very attractive. It's perfectly natural."

She wasn't especially petite, but his wide palm and long fingers dwarfed hers. He said it was perfectly natural. She wished she could believe it was nothing more than hormones and circumstances.

"You're right," she said, withdrawing her hand from his and picking up her plate. She rose and walked over to the sink. "I know it didn't mean anything. Is Jeff going to get you the necessary security people?"

He set his plate next to hers on the counter. "All taken care of. He'll also run a last-minute check on any changes in the guest list, along with substitutions in the catering staff."

She ran water and rinsed the dishes. After pouring them each coffee, she returned to the table. He picked up a pad of paper and sat in the chair next to her.

Working quickly, he drew a rough floor plan of the house. "Tell me what happens at one of these parties. How are the rooms set up?"

She leaned over the drawing and pointed. "We put chairs and sofas in conversation groups."

He sketched them in. "Like this?"

"Yes. The buffet is in the dining room. The big table runs lengthwise. We have a wet bar in both parlors. The cats are brought into the study through the French doors.

That's why we use that room. They don't have to walk through the crowd.''

He asked her questions about the party. As they worked together, she felt some of her embarrassment ease. Every now and then their arms would brush, or his breath would stir a loose hair or two at her temple, and then her body would quiver with awareness. She watched him speak, the way his mouth moved, the flash of white teeth. She remembered the feel of that mouth on hers. Had it only been an hour or two before? It seemed longer.

"What about the guests themselves? Everybody I checked out was rich, right?" he asked.

"We invite a few members of the press. A couple of old friends of Edwina's. Otherwise, yes."

He leaned back in the kitchen chair and placed his hands behind his head. He raised one ankle to the opposite knee. "You could find yourself a wealthy husband, and all your worries about the snow leopards would be solved."

She smiled. "We don't get a lot of single men at these functions. All of them are married, most of them are elderly. Feisty executive types don't have much time for wildlife."

"You've never been tempted?"

"By one of them?" She shook her head. "Not really."

"And you've never been married?"

"No. What about you?"

He folded his arms over his chest. "Never. I travel fastest when I travel alone."

"Where exactly are you going?"

She'd meant the question to be humorous, but he took it seriously. "Wherever they send me. It's not right to have a wife and kids in this business. Look at what happened to Jeff. Losing Jeanne almost killed him."

"But while she was alive, they had something very special."

He raised his eyebrows. "Such as?"

"A relationship. A close bond between a man and a woman. You've never been tempted?" she asked, repeating the question he'd asked her.

"Not my style. When I go out on assignment, that's all I can afford to think about."

She leaned forward and rested her arms on the table. "Why do you do it?"

"It's my job. All I've ever wanted to do. Fight the good fight."

"But it's not a war. Don't you get lonely?"

He waved his arm to take in the large kitchen and the big house behind that. "You want to compare life-styles?"

That jab hit home. She stared at her hands.

"Faith, I'm sorry." He leaned forward and deliberately bumped her elbow with his.

She looked up at him. The cut on his chin had almost healed. He would carry a scar as a reminder of that mission. Gold-blond hair tumbled across his forehead. She wanted to brush it back, but she didn't. It wasn't her place.

He bumped her again. "I have a hard time answering personal questions."

"I understand. People ask me strange things, too. They don't understand my commitment to the cats. I guess it's similar to how you feel about what you do."

"Friends?" he asked.

She nodded. "Friends."

Cort resisted the need to tease her until she smiled. It was the easy way out, and for once, he didn't want that with a woman. There was something fundamentally honest about Faith. She didn't play games. When she made a decision to do something, she did it without reservation.

Which made her reaction to their kiss all the more interesting. He'd expected to be turned on by touching her. He hadn't expected to be consumed by white heat. Even thinking about his tongue in her mouth and her breasts in his hands was enough to get him hard again. If his bum leg hadn't given out on him, who knows what would have happened. He wasn't sure if he was grateful for the interruption, or mad as hell.

He looked around at the drinking glasses Faith had stacked on the counters. She'd already gone over the menus and approved the liquor list. Setting up the fund-raiser was an incredible amount of work. She never even batted an eye.

"I told Jeff we'd be keeping the cubs under guard during the party," he said.

"That's a good idea. Too many people would upset them. Even though most of our guests are aware of the dangers with the cats, even the domesticated ones, most can't resist wanting to pat a 'kitty.'"

He rotated his arm and looked at a healing bite. "Those tiger cubs aren't *close* to domesticated."

"They're sweet."

"They have very sharp teeth."

She smiled. He'd seen her smile dozens of times, but the way it changed her whole face—brightening her eyes and making her look pretty—never failed to surprise him.

"They're supposed to have sharp teeth. They're carnivores."

"Will they be released into the wild?"

She sipped from her coffee mug, then set it down. "They can't be. Aside from the fact they won't have the skills to feed themselves, we have taken away their very necessary fear of humans. Besides, their white coloring would put them at a disadvantage. They'll be safe in captivity."

"You don't sound very happy about it."

"Are you?"

He thought about the cubs, the way they were starting to follow him around. They recognized his voice and were always willing to play. He had to admit they didn't look right behind the bars of a cage.

"I guess not." He rose from his chair. "Come on. I'll help you count plates."

Once in the pantry, he climbed up on the stool and began handing down dishes. He told himself he was crazy, but he could swear he smelled the lingering scent of their desire in the small room. If he closed his eyes, he would be able to taste Faith's sweetness and feel her responsive body trembling next to his. He banished the memories. If he closed his eyes he would fall off the stool and break his fool neck. Then he'd be useless to Faith and Jeff.

But for once the thought of his job and what he couldn't remember didn't tie him up in knots. It was coming back to him. Slowly. And now he knew he hadn't killed Dan.

Faith took the salad plates and carried them into the kitchen. "That's a hundred," she said. "We need another fifty."

He passed her a stack of ten. She took them and set them on the counter. Her arm muscles flexed with the movement. She wasn't anyone's idea of an ornament. She'd been wild in his arms. What would she be like in bed?

"How come you never married?" he asked.

She looked up, obviously surprised by the question. "I've never been asked."

"Was there anyone serious?"

"A boy in college. I'd thought—" She took another stack of plates and set them on the counter, then counted. "Ten more, please. I'd thought we might, you know. But after graduation, he sort of disappeared."

"What do you mean 'disappeared'?"

"Left without saying goodbye. Packed up and moved away. We had a date and he never showed. I went to call him and the phone was disconnected." She picked up the salad plates and walked into the kitchen.

"I'm sorry," he said.

His initial flash of outrage made him want to find the man and punch him out. He stepped off the stool and picked up a stack of dishes. Who was he to cast stones at the guy? He thought about his own past. Had he done any better?

He was about to ask another question, but when she came back she wouldn't meet his eyes. There was something sad about the set of her mouth, as if remembering the past was painful for her. Clumsy bastard, he told himself.

She cleared their mugs off the small table in the alcove and set them in the sink. "What about you?" she asked. "You can't always have traveled alone."

He should have expected the question. Normally he didn't talk about himself, but he owed her. "There was someone once," he said, hoping it would be enough.

Faith leaned against the counter and looked expectant.

"We broke up," he said, and went back for more plates.

Faith followed. "You must have loved her very much."

Cort started pulling down dinner plates and slamming them on the counter without worrying about their breaking. Why did it always come down to loving someone? For once, he wanted to blurt out the truth. No, he hadn't loved her. She'd been convenient. He'd been young and horny and she thought the world of him. In the end, he couldn't wait to leave her. He hadn't loved her, because he hadn't loved anyone. Even then he'd known it was faster and safer to travel alone.

He opened his mouth to finally speak the truth. "I—"

Faith's blue eyes widened. In the muted light from the kitchen, her skin looked smooth and soft as satin. He already knew how it tasted. She could control a three-hundred-pound leopard and face down wild jaguars without batting an eye. But he saw the wistful expression on her face, and he knew that under the tough facade she was a romantic dreamer who still believed in love and happily-ever-afters. Her commitment to the cats proved it. He could kill if it were required, but he couldn't destroy her dreams.

"Yes," he said. "I loved her very much." The lie tasted heavy and bitter. He wanted to call it back and speak the truth, but the moment passed as she nodded.

"You've never forgotten her. I know what that's like. Not for me. If someone had loved me like that, well, he would be here with me." She sounded sad. "My father loves a woman like that. Not my mother. His second wife. When I was growing up, my father traveled on business. He was gone a lot, and we had to move with his job. My mother and I begged him to find another line of work. Something that would keep us all together." She leaned against the pantry counter and traced a circle in the center of the top dinner plate. "But he wouldn't."

She looked up at him and smiled. "He was a little like you. He wanted to go his own way. When my mother died, he put me in boarding school for a couple of years. I didn't want him to leave me there. He told me it was the only way."

Cort perched on the stool. "Then what happened?"

"He met another woman. She's different from my mother, but nice." Faith smiled faintly. "I like her. She told my father if they were going to get married, he would have to change his ways. He did. They live in Vegas. He works for a casino. They have three little girls and he's there for them every night. He goes to soccer games and school plays." She drew in a deep breath and tucked a loose strand of hair behind her ear. "All the things he didn't have time for with me."

"Faith, I—"

"Don't apologize," she said. "I'm not angry. I guess I envy them. What my father has with my stepmother. What Jeff had with Jeanne. It must be wonderful to be so special to someone. To have that bond. I wanted to but I've never been able to find anyone who could love me back. I understand why you can't forget her, Cort. She must have been an incredible woman."

If he'd felt awkward before, now he just felt as low as a snake's belly. He wanted to ease the hurt in Faith by telling her most relationships weren't as wonderful as she made them out to be. Love wasn't real. It was an excuse for sex. He'd never loved a woman in his life. But if he told her the truth, he would make her feel worse. He stood up and grabbed the stack of plates. Better for her to believe what she wanted. Easier for both of them.

As he passed her on his way to the kitchen, she reached up and touched his arm. "Cort?"

"Don't, Faith. Don't say a damn word."

She nodded once, then drew her hand away.

He could feel the hurt radiating from her. It burned in his gut and there wasn't anything he could do about it. This was why he preferred to travel single, he reminded himself. Relationships always got in the way.

"Oh, sit still," Faith told Sparky.

The black leopard glared at her, his yellow eyes little more than slits.

"You can bring down a good-sized deer. Why are you afraid of a little water?" She raised the bucket up to rinse off the suds.

Sparky made a choking sound low in his throat, then flattened his ears as the water cascaded off his back.

"He doesn't look happy," Cort said as he strolled across the compound and stopped next to her.

"He isn't. He hates getting a bath. It's not being wet, but the fact that he doesn't smell of mint and dirt anymore."

Cort crouched down and patted the cat's face. "Could be worse, pal. I have to wear a tux tonight."

Sparky looked unimpressed.

Faith unhooked his chain from the telephone pole at the center of the compound. "Hold this," she said, handing the end to Cort. When he took it, she stepped back about fifteen feet.

He looked puzzled. "Why do you want me to—" Sparky rose to his feet and braced himself. Cort glared at her. "Why, you little—"

Faith started to laugh. "Too late." She yelped and turned away as Sparky started to shake. Water flew everywhere. When she looked back, Cort was drenched and Sparky was licking his front paws.

She walked over and took back the chain. "Thanks."

Water dripped from Cort's face. The front of his blue shirt clung to him. Drops formed a pattern on his jeans. The devilish light in his eyes promised retribution.

"You could have warned me," he said, wiping his face.

"And spoil the surprise?" She tugged on the chain. "Come on, Sparky. I don't want you rolling in the dirt and getting muddy." The big cat slowly followed her.

"What about me?" Cort asked, holding his arms out to his sides.

"I don't want you rolling in the dirt, either."

He jogged after her, his limp barely noticeable. When he reached her side, he placed an arm around her neck and squeezed gently, before releasing her. "I should have done you in when I had the chance."

"Try it. I'll sic my watch cat on you."

Their eyes met and they both smiled. She was glad they could still be friends. The first day A.K.—After Kiss, as she thought of it—had been awkward, but she'd forced herself to behave normally around Cort, however funny she felt inside. She still had trouble looking at him without remembering how incredible he'd been standing naked, or the feel of his mouth on hers, but if she concentrated, she could push the memories aside. The upcoming fund-raiser had really helped. With a thousand details to take care of, it was easy to get lost in her work. In the last couple of days, she and Cort had slipped into a kind of teasing relationship that made her wonder if she was going to feel lonely when he was gone.

"When do the rest of the security people get here?" she asked. A team of four had arrived yesterday.

He checked his watch. "Within the hour. The cubs will be in the office and under guard at all times. Only you or I will be allowed in that part of the building."

"Be sure to tell the guards not to try to play with them. The cubs will be upset enough by the noise from all the cars pulling in."

Cort grinned. "I'll do better than that. I'll show them my bites. That'll keep them in line. What about you? Are you ready for tonight?"

They reached the main building. He held the door open for Faith, then stepped in after her. She walked into her office and led Sparky over to the blanket she'd stretched out on the floor. "As much as I can be. The caterers finished setting up this morning. The flowers are in place and most of the food is prepared." She grabbed a towel from the stack on the chair and knelt in front of the leopard. "Your favorite part, Sparky."

The leopard crouched down and closed his eyes in anticipation.

"Want some help?" Cort asked.

"Sure. Grab a towel. I rub him dry. It adds a nice shine to his coat and keeps him from going to roll in the mint."

Cort settled on Sparky's other side, picked up a towel and began rubbing the big cat. "You seem a little nervous," he said, glancing up at her.

"It's the party. They always make me crazy."

"Why?"

She leaned forward and took one massive paw on her lap. Wrapping the towel around his foreleg, she pressed out the moisture. "Anything can go wrong. I worry about a guest getting drunk enough to want to provoke the cats. I don't like playing hostess. I'm not great at small talk with people I don't know. It was easier when Edwina was alive." She patted Sparky's head and looked into his bright yellow eyes. "We miss her, don't we fella?" The leopard nudged her hand and made a purring noise low in his throat. She moved to Sparky's side and rubbed his shoulder. "Our donors are seriously rich." She smiled. "We don't have a lot in common."

"The cats," Cort said, brushing the towel across Sparky's flank.

"That's true. So I smile until my cheeks hurt, and answer questions about panthers and leopards. And I remind everyone how big cats are losing more and more natural habitat every day, and they write me checks." She wrinkled her nose. "The worst part of it is that I'm going to have to do even more fund-raising if I start the snow-leopard project."

He raised his eyebrows. "If?"

"The jury is still out on that one."

"You can do it."

"Thanks for the vote of confidence."

Sparky stiffened suddenly and Faith looked up. One of the security guards, a tall bald man in his late forties, stood in the doorway.

Faith wrapped the towel around Sparky's neck like a collar. His neck wasn't dry enough to put his leather one on yet. "Sparky, you remember Andy," she said, keeping her voice low and pleasant. "Andy, crouch down and hold out your arm." She didn't bother looking at the man, but kept her eyes on the leopard.

Nothing happened. Before she could repeat her request, Cort walked over to the man. "Do it," he growled. "Unless you want to be lunch."

Andy obeyed. Sparky sniffed the offered hand, then turned away in disinterest. The man rose. Faith released the leopard and Sparky began grooming.

"What do you have to report?" Cort asked.

The older man looked a little shaken. "Jesus, I don't know if I'll ever get used to that thing roaming around here loose." He grinned at Faith. "Great watchdog. You think when this is over I can get a picture of me and him to show my kids?"

"Sure thing," she said.

The man was as tall as Cort, but heavier. He pulled a walkie-talkie out of his utility belt. "This is for you, Boss. Frequency is all set. Every unit has been tested." He turned to Faith. "The planking is all in place over the dirt part of the driveway. Two guards are posted there. They've been logging in the catering people. All the extra lights are strung and working." He looked back at Cort. "So far, no surprises."

Cort took the walkie-talkie and stuck it in his pocket. "Let's keep it that way. When do your kids arrive?" he asked Faith.

The three part-time employees were working the party. They were responsible for bringing the cats up to the main house and showing them to the guests. "Any time now."

"And the guests start arriving when?"

"About seven."

"Then I guess we're all set," he said.

She followed the two men from the office and closed the door behind her. "I'm going to go up to the Big House," she said. "I have to check on the food and then get ready."

"I'll see you at the party."

She left the men and drove up to the house. People swarmed over the main floor, taking care of the last-minute touches. The house glowed from its recent cleaning. The crystal chandeliers glittered. Bright flowers lined the mantel. She spoke to the woman in charge, made sure everything was going well, then escaped upstairs to her room.

She stared at the contents of her closet, at the dressy clothes hanging there. These nights were the only ones when she became like other women. When she wore makeup and curled her hair. The expensive gowns and jumpsuits made her fit in with her guests. In the past she hadn't cared what she looked like, as long as she was presentable. But this night was different. She wanted to be special. A foolish dream, she told herself. Cort wasn't for her. He wouldn't care what she dressed in, because he saw her as little more than a co-worker. But there was nothing wrong with pretending, even for a night.

Cort adjusted the gun at the small of his back, then shifted the walkie-talkie to his left jacket pocket. The house was quiet. The catering staff had returned to the back rooms to change into their uniforms. None of the guests had arrived. As it always did at the start of any mission, a calm came over him.

A whisper of sound caught his attention. He turned and looked toward the staircase. Faith stood poised at the top. If he wore a tux, it made sense that she would be formally dressed, as well. But he wasn't prepared for the transformation.

The cream jumpsuit clung to her curves, outlined her generous breasts, narrow waist and slender hips. Sequins sparkled from the padded shoulders and angled down toward her midsection. The sleeves puffed out at her upper arms, then fitted snugly from her elbows to her wrists. Cream suede boots hugged her calves.

As she walked down the stairs, his gaze reached her face. Makeup accentuated her blue eyes and highlighted the shape of her mouth. Sparkling earrings dangled almost to her shoulders. She wore her hair swept up and away from her face. Curls tumbled down her back. She was beautiful.

When she stood on the last step, he moved close to her. She tried to smile, but trembled too much.

"I'll take your silence as a compliment," she said, twisting her hands together. "If you hate the way I look, please don't tell me. I'm nervous enough."

"You look terrific," he said, not quite believing the transformation.

"Really?" She flushed. "Thanks. I'm so nervous."

He took her hands in his. "Don't be. You'll do great."

She looked down at herself. "I think this color might be a mistake. What if I spill something? And I'm going to get cat hair all—"

He cut her off. "Faith?"

"What?" She looked worried. "What's wrong? Is it my hair? You hate—"

"Do you have more of that lipstick?"

She frowned. "Of course. But why do you—"

"Because I'm about to smear it."

He leaned forward and touched his lips to hers. Her eyes fluttered closed, and he felt the familiar heat throbbing in his body. He was about to draw her close to him when he heard the faint scuffing of shoes on the front porch. He stepped back.

Faith looked dazed. She touched her fingers to her lips. He wiped the back of his hand across his mouth, then grinned at the lipstick he'd brushed off. Ken opened the front door and stuck his head in the door.

"They're here," he said. "Show time."

Chapter 8

William Thomas tapped his fingers impatiently on the steering wheel of his dark sedan. He was next in line. The limo in front was waved through. He eased his foot off the brake and the big car rolled up to the guard posted at the open gate.

"Good evening, sir," the armed guard said, and took his invitation. He scanned the thick, creamy paper. "And you are...?"

"Johnson," Thomas said. "Mark Johnson. From K-NEWS."

The reporter and his producer, Mark Johnson, had been invited to the event. A quick call to the station had confirmed Johnson was out of town. It was unlikely any of the guards would know who the man was. Safer to impersonate him than a well-known newscaster.

"May I see your driver's license?" the guard asked.

Thomas pulled out the forged ID. He loved Los Angeles. You could buy anything you wanted if you knew where to go. The driver's license was genuine, if stolen. The picture had been taken that morning.

The guard looked from the photo to his face, then smiled and handed back the ID. "Just follow the driveway up to the main house, sir. Enjoy your evening." He checked Mark Johnson's name off the list.

Thomas waved and pressed on the gas. The sedan with its tinted rear windows rolled along the planking, then onto smooth asphalt. As he moved up toward the main house, he glanced over his shoulder. The big collapsible cage he'd purchased was completely covered by a dark blanket. He patted the gun concealed under his jacket and allowed himself a small smile. It was almost over.

Faith greeted her guests as she circulated through the room. She resisted glancing at her watch. Last time she'd checked, only fifteen minutes had passed. The evening was crawling by. Her forced smile became genuine. Why was she surprised? These evenings were always long and awkward.

She stopped by the bar and ordered another glass of club soda. As the bartender poured, she leaned against the brass railing and glanced around the room. Quiet conversation filled the huge parlor, competing with the tinkle of glasses and cutlery. The excited buzz was already starting as it grew closer to the time when they brought in the cats. Jewelry sparkled, expensive fabrics gleamed. All in all, a beautiful scene.

The bartender handed her the drink, and she nodded her thanks. Across the room, a pair of broad shoulders caught her eye. Cort. Before tonight, she'd only seen him in casual clothing. Or nothing at all. She'd liked him best in the latter, but the tux he wore came in a close second. The black wool emphasized his strength and lean grace. He moved through the room, watching, nodding when noticed, but mostly staying in the background. She tried to catch his eye, but he was intent on his work and hadn't once looked her way. Gone was the passionate man who had kissed her until she trembled. In his place was a handsome stranger intent on doing his job. There was an air of danger about him that made women look twice and men step back to let him through. She felt safe knowing he was around.

"Faith, darling, you look fabulous." An older woman swept across the room and stopped in front of her, kissing the air next to her cheek. Her husband trailed behind.

"Margaret, Milton. How good of you to come."

Margaret was a carefully preserved woman of sixty who still looked to be in her late forties. Her purple silk dress showed off a figure that had defied gravity. Milton didn't resist aging as strongly. His white hair hung down to the collar of his expensively tailored formal wear. They could be difficult at times, but Faith had always liked the couple. They were two of Edwina's oldest friends and had always looked out for her.

"Where are those lovely cubs we've been hearing about?" Margaret asked, then sipped from her champagne.

"I'm afraid they're not on display."

Margaret made a moue of disappointment. "Oh, I did so long to see them."

"We have them under guard. They would be upset by all the people. They're still babies."

Milton nodded sagely. "Sensible. Don't want any trouble. You bringing out Sparky?" The old man had a soft heart for the leopard.

She smiled. "Of course. He should be ready. Why don't I take you in the study now, so you can spend a minute with him?"

The older couple glanced at each other. "We'd love to," Margaret said. She leaned forward and whispered. "Milton has done very well in the foreign market. There's a little extra in your check tonight, dear."

Faith squeezed her hand. "Thank you."

She led them to the study and ushered them inside. Sparky sat on a blanket, trying to chew the red bow around his neck. Samson, the bobcat, quivered with excitement. An older panther lay on a sturdy metal table in the corner.

Margaret rushed over to Samson, who greeted her like a long-lost friend. Milton let Sparky smell his arm before patting the leopard he'd known since the cat was a cub. Faith backed out of the room and closed the door behind her. She looked at her watch and decided she'd slip away and check on the cubs.

The road from the way station wound around for almost a mile, but there was a narrow path that cut through the woods. It was about a ten-minute walk. Lights had been strung from the trees and all the overhanging brush had been cut back. Later, she would lead the group over to the compound to unveil the two new habitats paid for by some of the guests.

"Where are you off to in such a hurry?" Cort asked from behind her.

Startled, she spun to face him. "Where did you come from?"

"I saw you leave."

"But I didn't ever see you looking at me," she blurted out, then wished she could call back the words.

Cort didn't seem upset. "I'm good at my job. You're not supposed to see me watching you. Where are you going?"

"To check on the cubs. I want to tell the guards that we'll be bringing people over in about a half hour. A few will wander into the main building. I wanted to warn them to be firm but polite."

Cort took her arm and turned her around until she was facing the Big House. "I'll do that. You go back to your guests."

"But I—"

He squeezed her arm briefly. "You're doing fine. Everyone is having a great time and no one knows you're nervous."

"*You* know."

"It's my job to know. Go on." He waved her along the path. "I'll see you by the habitats in a half hour."

Thomas hovered at the back of the crowd. The woman in charge, Faith Newlin, was making a speech about the generosity of the family that had donated the big cage structure in front of them. He took a couple of steps to one side and slipped into the shadows. This was his chance. While everyone was busy, he would find the cubs.

A few casual questions had told him the tigers weren't part of the show. That would make his job easier. They were, according to a plump but talkative matron, under guard at the main building. He spun on his heel and stared at the low, one-story structure in front of him. Lights shone from several windows. That had to be it.

He walked along the back of the building, counting windows and trying to figure out where the cubs would be. The dense undergrowth didn't allow him to easily go around the structure, so he headed for the glass doors and pulled them open.

The shabby foyer was empty. In front of him stood another set of doors. They were sturdy and looked new. He pushed on one. It swung open to reveal the parking lot filled with expensive cars and limousines. Excitement flickered in his belly. He could move his car close to the building. That would make his job a lot easier. He would have to carry the cubs out one by one. No way he could wrestle the cage inside, take them, then carry it out without being noticed. He eased the door shut and looked down the long halls.

On his right, overhead lights shone on signs for the men's and ladies' restrooms. To his left, the hallway stretched down with closed doors on both sides. He stepped to his left.

Thomas slipped his hand into his jacket and rested his palm on the handle of his pistol. He slipped inside the first door. A metal table attached to one wall and open shelves containing bandages and medicine told him this was a medical office. He continued down, opening the doors, one after the other. On the fifth one, he walked into a small area dominated by a cage. He allowed himself a small smile. In the center of the cage, the cubs lay curled up together sleeping. Perfect, he thought. They'd be easier to handle and—

"Excuse me, sir. This room is off limits to our guests."

He turned toward the voice. Thankfully, he had the sense to drop his hand to his side. The khaki-uniformed security guard looked a little startled at seeing him, but not unduly alarmed. Thomas thought about taking out the man. The guard wasn't much over six feet. Before he could decide, another guard joined him.

"What's the problem?"

"I was explaining to the gentleman that this room is private."

"My mistake," Thomas said, figuring he couldn't take both of them without a commotion that would alert the other guards in the area. "I was looking for the restroom."

The first guard smiled and stepped back. "At the other end of the hall, sir. It's marked."

"Thank you." Thomas adjusted the jacket of his rented tuxedo and stepped past the guard and into the hall. As he walked down the corridor, he counted doors so he'd be able to find his way in from the outside.

He went through the front doors and into the parking area. Several limo drivers clustered together talking. He circled around the cars, found his rental and slowly maneuvered it as close to the main building as he could. He climbed into the back seat and pulled the blanket off the cage.

He'd rented this car specifically because, although it was a sedan, it was the executive model with an extrawide back seat. He worked quickly and in about ten minutes had the cage up and secured. He tossed the blanket over the gleaming metal so someone walking by couldn't see it, then left the car and headed back to the building.

The cubs were in the second room from the end. He closed his eyes and thought about the layout of the room. There hadn't been any chairs. The guards weren't stationed with the cubs. Apparently they were patrolling the halls. He would have to be prepared to take one or both men out quickly, if he had to. He would come around the building, through the bushes, and break the window. The cluster of trees would hide his activity from the parking lot. That would make his job easier.

As he entered the main building, he glanced at the screens covering the windows, then patted his pockets. The tools he'd brought with him would be enough. He adjusted his tuxedo jacket and stepped through to the compound. It was just a matter of time.

Cort circled around the crowd of people by the new habitats. He kept an eye out for stragglers and anyone who looked too curious for their own good. He wished there was a way to keep people out of the main building, but Faith had pointed out her guests would need access to a restroom. He walked over to Andy.

"Send two more guards to patrol the outside of the main building," Cort said.

The older man pulled out his walkie-talkie and spoke into it. "Done," he said a moment later. "Seems to be going well, boss."

"So far," Cort answered.

He moved away, scanning the area. One guard had been posted by the two jaguar cages to make sure no guest came to any harm. Three couples strolled by Tigger's habitat and spoke to the big cat. The situation wasn't as controllable as he would like, but it felt damn good to be working again. Every sense was on full alert. His leg felt a hundred percent. He'd been at the way station long enough to become familiar with the noises and smells. It all seemed right. He glanced at his watch. Another couple of hours and it would all be over.

He turned his back on the crowd and studied the main building. Nothing moving there. He walked toward the jaguar cages to make sure the guard was alert. As he moved through the darkness, something flashed in his mind. He froze. Not a memory. More of a picture. Of walking somewhere else. Where? The dock? He closed his eyes and tried to remember. Nothing.

Cort swore. When was it going to come back to him? Why couldn't he remember? He had to. He shook his head and continued toward the guard.

"Anything?" he asked the man.

"Nope. A couple of old guys came by, but I told 'em to move on, and they did."

"Good. I—" Cort paused. A sixth sense made him turn toward the narrow road leading from the compounds to the Big House. He thought he saw something—or someone—moving there. "I'll be back later," he said, walking toward the main building.

He broke into a jog, trying to remember the people who had been around a moment before. They weren't there now. Some had gone inside, others had joined the main group. Had one of them tried to slip around the building?

He saw a man silhouetted against the dense brush and broke into a run.

"You there," he called. "Stop."

The man froze for a second, then dove into the bushes. Cort raced after him, pulling his radio from his jacket pocket. He was about to call Andy when he stepped from the path into the underbrush. Instantly time tilted. He felt the sturdy floor of the dockside warehouse. The smell of the sea invaded him. He could taste the salt. Up ahead. There. Dan! Cort crouched low behind a stack of crates. His fellow agent opened a briefcase filled with documents. Cort strained to see what they were. The other men—there were six of them—stood with their backs to him. But he knew them. Terrorists, arms dealers, working for no country, instead selling to the highest bidder. He remembered his mission. To get proof that Dan was selling out his country. He stared in disbelief as he watched his friend take the money. Dan's betrayal tasted bitter on his tongue.

The scene shifted, grew foggy, then cleared, but it was later. The meeting was over. Cort approached the open area cautiously. He heard a noise behind him and spun. Dan!

"What the hell are you doing here?" Cort demanded.

Dan flushed, then grabbed his arm and jerked him close. "We've got to get out of here. They're going to come back."

Cort started to resist, then a cold feeling slid down his spine. He pulled free and started to run for the exit.

He was too late. The explosion caught him up in its power and tossed him aside like a doll. He struggled to get to his feet, to breathe, but he couldn't. Then strong hands tugged on him, pulling him to safety. Where there had been smoke, now he could breathe fresh, salty air. He coughed.

"Why?" he asked groggily, barely able to focus. His head. What had hit him?

A branch snapped.

The sharp noise jerked him back into the present. Cort blinked in the darkness of the forest and reached for his gun. As he pushed aside the flashback, he scanned the trees and bushes. The lights strung along the walking path didn't reach far into the gloom.

He circled to the front of the building, but couldn't find any trace of the intruder. He collected two of the guards and had them go around the building twice. They found some footprints made by dress shoes. All the guards wore boots. Cort stared at the tracks. They led from the main compound into the bushes, then disappeared into a pile of leaves. Maybe someone had gotten drunk and wandered off the main path. Perhaps a guest was simply trying to get a look at the cubs, but that didn't mean he was going to kidnap them.

The two guards posted with the cubs had mentioned that a half-dozen people had been near the restricted room. A couple had been lost, but the others were obviously hoping for a peek at the prized kittens. None of them, according to the guards, had looked dangerous.

By the time the last of the guests left, Cort knew that whoever had been stalking around the compound was long gone. If the extra guards hadn't scared him off, the big lights he had set up in the front of the main building would have. While Faith said her goodbyes, he had Rob and Ken help him move the cubs' cage to an interior room. Then he locked the door, pocketing the key as he left.

He walked into Faith's office and sat behind the desk. He didn't bother flipping on the overhead lights. Tiredness settled on him like a thick blanket, but he knew he wouldn't sleep much tonight. The cameras in the hallway had recorded twenty guests entering the main building. Fifteen of them had obviously been searching for the cubs. Aside from that, he'd seen nothing out of the ordinary. He didn't know who had been in the bushes or who he'd been chasing.

But he had remembered. Not all of it, but enough. He still didn't know how Dan had died, but he'd recalled most of the mission. Dan had been involved with dangerous characters. What had possessed his friend to cross the line? Had there been money troubles at home? He rubbed his forehead and tried to remember if Dan had a family. He didn't think so. They'd shared a common belief that traveling alone was always safest. Which made their friendship unusual for both of them.

Cort leaned back in his chair. The explosion and fire in the South American warehouse had been deliberately set. Someone had tried to get rid of Dan. *Or him.*

The thought made him sit upright. Was that it? All this time he'd assumed the bomb in the warehouse had been because of Dan's activities. Cort frowned. Had he been fingered, as well? Was someone after him? How much of the mission did Jeff really know?

He didn't bother glancing at his watch. He drew the phone close and punched out the familiar numbers.

"Markum."

"Could someone be after me?" Cort asked without bothering to introduce himself.

"Something happen with the cubs?"

"A guy was creeping around in the dark. Was it about me or the cubs?"

Jeff exhaled loudly. "As far as I know, you're clean. I wouldn't have sent you up to stay with Faith if I'd thought there would be any danger to her or the cubs."

"They killed him, didn't they? The arms dealers turned on Dan."

"So you remember."

"Not all of it." Cort leaned forward and rested his elbows on the desk. "Enough. Did the deal go bad?"

Silence.

"You can't be sure they aren't after me."

"Not a hundred percent, but—"

"Then replace me."

"You want to come out?" Jeff asked.

Cort felt something bump his leg. He looked down. Sparky sat next to him and butted his thigh. Automatically he reached down and scratched the big cat's ears.

"If there's even a possibility that I'm endangering them, then yes."

"I don't think you are. No one but me knows where you are. Your requests for assistance are being handled outside the agency."

Cort stared at the leopard. He glanced around the small office, at the photos on the wall, barely visible from the light in the hallway. He thought about Faith and the way he'd kissed her. He was starting to care about her and this place. He couldn't afford the distraction.

"I want out, anyway," he said abruptly.

"Why?"

"I'm a hundred percent, Jeff. Put me back in the field."

"You're still on medical leave and those cubs need protecting."

"There has to be someone else you can send."

"Sure." He heard Jeff flipping through papers. "Smith is available at the end of the week. Can you wait that long?"

Cort grimaced. "Smith? He's a jerk. Who else?"

"That's the best I can do."

"It's not good enough. I won't leave until I'm sure Faith and the cubs are safe."

"Then stay where you are," Jeff snapped. "You're supposed to be my best operative. Who can I send in who's better? Or is there something you're not telling me? Another reason you want to come out?''

Cort thought about how Faith had looked that night, a beautiful woman in expensive clothes and makeup. He thought about how he preferred her in jeans and boots, with her hair hanging straight down her back. He remembered how he'd lied to her about his past relationships and the pain in her eyes when she talked about her father deserting her. He thought about how easy it would be to go to her bed and share the passion lurking so close to the surface. The fire between them would probably burn hot enough to scar, but it would be worth it. He thought about how, when this was over, he would return to his world, because fighting was all he knew and believed in. Then he thought about Jeff's questions. There were a dozen reasons why he wanted to come out. He couldn't tell his boss even one of them.

"No," he said. "There's no other reason to come out."

"Then stay put and do your job." He hung up the phone.

Cort sat in the dark listening to Sparky's breathing as the black leopard slept at his feet. He knew he would pay a big price for letting himself like Faith. Caring could be deadly. Look at what had happened to Jeff's family.

But his boss had been right about one thing. Cort was the best. It was up to him to protect Faith and the cubs. No matter what, he couldn't let his feelings get in the way.

Chapter 9

Faith filled Cort's coffee cup. "You want to talk about why you didn't sleep much last night?"

Cort took a sip. "Is it that obvious?"

Only to me, she wanted to say, but didn't. "The dark circles under your eyes give you away."

"I had a lot on my mind."

It was past noon. The day after a fund-raiser was usually slow. Beth and Rob had arrived a half hour before to clean cages. Cort had already been out patrolling the compound when she'd gotten up shortly after eight.

Sparky came into the kitchen of her apartment, dragging his blanket behind him. He walked over to Cort and dropped it at his feet.

"I think he wants to play," Faith said as Sparky stared hopefully.

"Beast," Cort said, then jerked his head toward the door. "Come on, Faith. Let's make it two against one."

She followed him outside. The bright sunshine promised a warm afternoon. After all the planning and hard work, it felt good to be out from under the party. She took hold of the blanket at the middle. Cort stepped up behind her and held on. Sparky grabbed the dangling end. He shook his head playfully and almost ripped the cloth from her fingers.

"You got it?" she asked, not turning away from the leopard.

"I'm ready," Cort said.

She could hear the smile in his voice and feel him so close behind her. The nearness made her insides feel funny, as if a jolt of electricity had passed through them.

"Go!" she called.

Sparky immediately hunched down with his rear end pointing skyward, and started to pull. She could hear his grunts as he strained against them. Faith tightened her grip, but the blanket was slowly being pulled through her hands.

"He's strong," Cort said from behind her, his voice tense with strain. "No you don't, cat. You're not going to get the best of me."

Sparky's yellow eyes glittered with excitement. He made low growling noises deep in his throat. The powerful muscles in his shoulders bunched with the effort. Faith held on tight. She felt herself starting to slide forward.

"He's pulling us," she said.

"That's not possible. Between us, we weigh more than he does."

"I don't care what you think. It's happening. Look." Sparky backed up toward the play area in the center of the compound. Faith's boots slipped in the dirt. From a habitat, one of the cats howled encouragement. She started to giggle.

"Don't you dare laugh," Cort ordered, bumping against her. "You'll lose your strength."

"I can't help it. They're rooting for him." The laughter became louder, and she felt her fingers slip. She let go of the blanket and immediately sat down hard on her behind. Cort jumped to avoid running into her. Sparky took advantage of his momentary loss of balance, jerked the cloth free and sprang victoriously onto the telephone poles. He held the blanket between his forelegs, as if it were his prey, and gnawed on one end.

Cort placed his hands on his hips. "We almost had him."

She shaded her eyes and stared up at Cort. He looked tall and strong and very handsome. He'd rolled his long-sleeved blue shirt up to his elbows. Jeans clung to his narrow hips and powerful thighs. She tried to ignore the quivering in her chest and the heat blossoming in her breasts. "We didn't almost have him, Cort. He never loses in tug-of-war. Even when he was a cub, he was strong."

Cort held out his hand. She grabbed it, and he pulled her to her feet. As she brushed off her backside, he looked around the compound. "How did you find this place? Were you always interested in big cats?"

"No." She started back to the office. He moved into step beside her. "I never had pets when I was growing up. We moved too much. Then, after my mother died, I was sent away to school. Besides, my father always hated cats."

"Is that why you work with them?"

She grinned. "I never thought of it like that, but maybe. I got a summer job here the year before I went to college. I didn't know what I wanted for a career, but after that first week, I knew this was where I belonged."

He held open the door and she ducked inside. Cort hovered in the foyer. He looked tired and out of sorts.

"Is it about last night?" she asked.

He raised his eyebrows. "Is what about last night?"

"I heard we had a possible intruder. Is that why you're so jumpy?"

He shook his head. "Whoever the guy is, he's long gone."

"Then I know just the thing to make you feel better."

She'd expected him to be curious about her announcement. Instead he took a step closer and she saw passion flare to life in his brown eyes. The cut on his chin had healed. Suddenly she wanted to touch the scar, tracing it up from his chin to the corner of his mouth. She wanted to be close to him, to inhale the scent of his body. To feel him on her, and in her, tasting her, touching her, until nothing existed except the moment of their joining.

Need swept through her. She started to sway toward him. He moved close, as if to catch her. She wanted to say yes. But she couldn't. Her self-respect had been hard won, and she wasn't about to throw it all away by giving her body without her heart. Cheap affairs had never been her style. She didn't know how not to care. And Cort had made it very clear he wasn't interested in any kind of a relationship. He preferred to travel light. At first she hadn't understood his reluctance to commit to someone, but now that she knew about the heartbreak in his past, it all made sense. Oh, but he tempted her.

She cleared her throat. "I was thinking of going shooting up in one of the canyons. Want to come along?"

The passion receded. "Shooting?" He raised his eyebrows.

"I haven't been in a while. I mostly use my rifle. Come on, it'll be fun."

He seemed to consider his options. She half hoped he would pick sex and simply pull her into his arms. Once he held her, she wasn't sure she would have the will to resist. Instead he smiled. "Okay, let me get the Beretta and I'll meet you by the truck."

She collected her weapons and ammunition and carried them outside. Cort helped her load everything. She went into the kitchen, grabbed a six-pack of sodas, then stuck her head out the back and told Beth they would return in a couple of hours.

They drove up the mountain in silence. Cort saw Faith glancing at him every couple of minutes. He wanted to tell her that he was fine, but he knew she wouldn't believe the lie.

He hadn't known how much Faith was getting to him until he'd asked Jeff to take him off the case. Since then he hadn't been able to think about anything else. It wasn't hard to figure out his concern. Jeff had said he hadn't killed Dan, but Jeff hadn't been in South America. Cort didn't have to have been the one who pulled the trigger to be responsible for what happened to Dan. Was he putting Faith in the same kind of danger?

He leaned his head back and watched the passing scenery. Lush growth spilled onto the narrow two-lane road. It was too late in spring for many of the wildflowers to still bloom, but wild berry bushes were already budding fruit. Squirrels jumped from tree to tree, and a rabbit crossed the road a hundred yards ahead of them.

Faith slowed the truck, shifted into four-wheel drive, then turned off onto a dirt path. Branches slapped against the cab as the vehicle slowly moved up the mountain. Ten minutes later, they rolled into a small clearing. A locked shed stood on one side.

She stopped the truck and smiled at him. "We're here."

He stepped out into the warm afternoon. Taking a deep breath, he smelled wild roses and the soft grass under his feet. "This is exactly what I needed."

"Good." Faith unlatched the gate on the bed of the truck and lowered it. "Let's see how you do shooting a rifle." She picked one up and tossed it to him.

He caught it easily, then collected three more. Faith lifted the heavy case of ammunition. She wore jeans and a T-shirt. As she picked up the case and set it on the ground, the muscles in her arms bunched and released. She was strong. She bent over and reached for the zippered case containing her handgun. Her jeans molded to the firm curves of her rear. She was also very much a woman. In the past he'd always been attracted to ultrafeminine types who would collapse at the first sign of trouble or physical activity that wasn't directly related to sex or their aerobic workout. Faith was different. She didn't need to pretend. Hell, she didn't have time. Working with the cats required total commitment.

She unlocked the shed and pulled out paper targets. "It's just through here," she said, pointing to a break in the trees. She handed him the targets, then picked up the box of ammunition and led the way.

The path ended in a narrow canyon. Brush had been cleared back to the trees, creating a narrow corridor perfect for shooting. Frames for targets had been set up in front of a muddy hillside. Most were stationary, but a couple were on jointed sections that moved with every breath of the wind.

For the first half hour, they shot using handguns. Faith couldn't match him on speed or accuracy, but she was better than most people he knew. The sound of the gunshots gave him a sense of something familiar, and something about his last assignment, but when the memory didn't focus, he tried to ignore the sensation. He'd finally learned the best way to remember the past was to let it come to him. Trying hard to recall things only made the fog thicker. At the end of each clip, they compared targets. He tried not to gloat, but couldn't help grinning when they took down the last one.

"You completely missed the bull's-eye," he said, slipping off his ear protection and pointing from the neat collection of bullet holes that punctured the center of his target to the scattered spray on hers.

Faith shook her head disgustedly. "I never was much good with a handgun."

He took her target and held it up in front of him. The bullet holes formed a pattern in the center of his chest. "I don't think you have to worry about an intruder."

Her blue eyes widened. She stared at her gun and then at him. "You asked me once before if I thought I could kill someone." She flipped on the safety and popped out the magazine. "I'm still not sure. I hope I never have to find out."

Cort remembered his own questions about Dan's death and understood her feelings. He admired her ability to admit she wasn't sure. So many rookie agents talked about wanting their first kill, as if it were a badge of honor to be won. There was nothing noble in taking another person's life.

"I'll do my best to keep you safe," he said.

"Just what every woman needs. Her own warrior prince." She grinned up at him.

The makeup from last night was long gone. Her hair hung straight again, pulled back in a ponytail. He could see the freckles on her nose, the faint lines by the corners of her eyes, and he could smell her French perfume. Her shirt was faded, and her jeans had seen better days. None of that mattered. A powerful need swept through him, stirring his blood and making him want to take her here on the spring grass, surrounded by the trees.

She picked up a rifle and handed it to him. "Prepare to have your butt whipped."

He took the weapon and loaded it. The desire was as controllable as any bodily function. He could feel it, but he didn't have to do anything about it.

"You sound pretty confident," he said.

"I am." She smiled smugly. "But doubt me all you want."

She set up the targets. Two of them went on the swinging frames. A light breeze stirred the paper, rocking it from side to side. Cort stepped up to go first. He was used to following a moving target with a pistol, but not with a rifle. Every time he got it lined up in his sights, it moved.

"You have to anticipate which way it's going to go," she offered.

"Thanks," he said dryly, as he took a breath, held it and squeezed the trigger.

The target fluttered as the bullet went through it, but he could see he wasn't even close to center. He took several more shots, but didn't get any better.

Faith stepped next to him and gently pushed him out of the way. "Let me show you how the pros do it, honey," she purred. Her self-satisfied grin told him he was about to be had.

She didn't disappoint him. She put a dozen bullets into a space the size of a half-dollar. By the time she was done shooting, there wasn't anything left of the paper at the center of the target. She put a second sheet in place and kicked the frame so it wiggled wildly. Even with the additional movement, her shots all went in dead center.

Cort took the rifle from her. "I've been hustled."

She nodded modestly. "You should have looked more closely at those trophies. I told you I was a sharpshooter."

"Is this something you learned to do in your spare time?"

"No. Actually, I was forced into it." She reached for a can of soda and tossed him one. Then she popped the top of her own and sat down under a tree. She dropped her ear protection on the ground. "I learned to shoot a rifle because we use them to tranquilize the wild cats."

Cort settled next to her. They both leaned against the rough bark of the maple tree. He stretched his legs out in front of him. "Why you?"

She shrugged. "When I first came to work for Edwina, I worked part-time, like the kids I have now. She saw I was interested and committed to the animals. When she mentioned a full-time job after I had my associate degree, I was more than willing to switch and study animal husbandry. It's difficult for people to get jobs working with animals. There aren't a lot of openings at zoos, and private places like this don't have the money to hire people. Edwina already had an older man working full-time, but he wanted to retire and go live with his daughter. I could do everything he could, except shoot."

She took a swallow of her soda. "I remember the first time he brought me up here." She smiled. "I couldn't even keep my eyes open enough to aim at the target. I was terrified. I'd never handled a gun before in my life. Plus, tranquilizing a cat is complex. You have to know the body weight so you get the correct dosage. The dart has to land in a big muscle group. If it hits bone, you'll break it. If the dart passes through soft tissue into the animal's internal organs, you can kill the cat." She pulled her knees up to her chest. "That's why I aim for the rear flank. If I miss, the dart usually hits the ground."

"That's a big responsibility."

"It's the one part of the job I don't like."

"But you do it." He shifted toward her and studied her face. A few strands of hair drifted around her cheeks. He reached over and tucked them behind her ear. "You always find a way to surprise me."

She glanced down. "What do you mean? I'm just—"

"You're not 'just,'" he said, cutting her off. "I admire the way you don't let being scared get in the way. That's a rare strength."

"You're flattering me. I wish it were true. If you knew how many times I've been afraid."

He touched his finger to her chin and urged her to look up at him. "Everyone is afraid. Most people let the fear win. You don't."

He smelled her perfume. It mingled with the warmth of her body, creating an essence that drew him closer. He wanted to kiss her full lips and feel the passion that had flared between them before. Instead, he traced the line of her jaw, then dropped his hand.

"Believe me, Faith. You're a hell of a woman."

She dismissed him with a shrug. "If I'm so damn strong, why am I scared of opening a snow-leopard breeding center? I think about it every day. I know it's the right thing to do. I have all the forms. I have the land. I can apply for permission to import two breeding pairs. If I packed up and moved today, I could be in business in less than six months."

"So what's stopping you?"

"Me." She set her soda on the ground. "I've never done anything like that. Edwina left me the foundation intact. I just have to keep it running. It's very different to start over from scratch."

He snapped off a blade of grass and toyed with it. "Once you were terrified of shooting a rifle. Now you're a marksman."

"I'm still scared. Every time I shoot a cat, I feel like I'm going to throw up."

"But you do it, anyway."

"I have to. They're depending on me."

"You'll move when you're ready," he said.

"I hope you're right." She wrapped her arms around her knees and stared into the distance.

Cort drained the last of his soda. It was peaceful out here. Faith didn't fill the quiet with chatter. She was easy to be with. He could talk to her or be silent with her. She wasn't afraid of hard work. She was a good leader. She'd given him instructions as to the care and feeding of the cubs, then left him to do the job. He knew she checked on him occasionally, but otherwise she trusted him to get it all done.

Cort used the same management style when he had people under him. Out in the field, there wasn't much chance for close supervision. He'd been alone when he'd been sent to South America. Why had he agreed to go? He grimaced. He knew the answer to that: Because it was his job.

"What's wrong?" Faith asked suddenly. "You look—" she leaned close to him and her mouth drew straight with concern "—as if you'd lost your best friend."

He jerked his head back and started to stand. She placed her hand on his arm. "Cort, don't turn away from me. I wasn't prying."

He hesitated, then settled back down. He hated to admit it, but he wanted to talk. To her, specifically. "I did just lose my best friend. Except for Jeff, my only friend." He looked at her. "Does that shock you? That I only had two friends in my life?"

"No," she said simply. "Not with what you do. Jeff's the same way. It's the job. You learn not to trust people."

"I guess you would understand. You live out here alone. You know what it's like to be on your own."

She turned until she was facing him, then sat cross-legged. "That's all I've ever been." She paused, as if considering her words.

He found it hard to volunteer information, but he wanted her to ask questions. He trusted her. It was risky to trust anyone, but Faith— It wasn't just because Jeff trusted her. It was because she was honest and dependable and strong.

"Have you remembered more of your last mission?" she asked.

"Some. I know where I was. I can't tell you the location."

"I understand." She smiled. "Classified. Can we narrow it down to a continent?"

"No." He laughed, then sobered. "I was supposed to check out an agent who might have gone bad."

"Had he?"

Cort stared past her into the trees. "Yes."

"I'm sorry."

He shrugged. "It happens."

"Is he dead?"

He looked at her. "Why do you ask?"

"I don't know. I just wondered." She spread her hands, palms up. "But he is, isn't he?"

Cort didn't answer.

She caught her breath. "Did you kill—"

"No."

"Then I don't understand why you're so troubled."

"I could have," he said sharply. He rose to his feet and started to pace in the clearing. "I could have been the one to kill him. I still don't remember enough."

"Did they tell you to kill him? Was that the mission?"

He hadn't wanted to admit it to himself, but he'd figured out the truth. "Yes."

"I've already told you I don't envy you your job," she said, standing up and leaning against the tree. "I wouldn't want to make choices about life and death, right and wrong. I know you've talked about fighting the good fight, but I don't understand the rules of your war. How do you know the enemy?"

He shoved his hands in his pockets. "You don't always. But I can't give up. That would mean they would have won."

"Who are *they?* That's what I don't understand. I guess I'm naive, but I like things to be black and white, or even in color. I couldn't live in your world of gray."

He stood in front of her and looked down at her open face. There were no secrets in her blue eyes, nothing artificial about her life. She lived in a world of defined choices.

Maybe that's what was wrong with him. Maybe it was the lack of color. Gray was cold and empty. It left him very much alone. He reached out to her, then dropped his hand. She saw the appeal and stepped close to him, wrapping her arms around his waist, burying her head in his chest. He hugged her tightly.

"I'm sorry I don't know how to help," she murmured.

"You've done more than you know."

He absorbed her warmth as if the heat itself would heal him. How long had it been since he'd allowed himself to hold another person? Not for sex, but because he liked the feel of her body next to his. He'd closed himself off because he couldn't let himself trust.

For what? He didn't know the who's and why's anymore. He didn't know anything. All he'd ever had was the good fight. Even that had been lost. He'd been sent to kill his friend. Circumstance had rescued him, but he knew he could have pulled the trigger. He had become the job.

He closed his eyes against the past and wondered if once, anywhere, he'd ever made a damn bit of difference.

William Thomas sat in a booth near the rear of the fifties-style diner. He'd barely had time to order coffee when a battered pickup pulled into the parking lot and a tall, bearlike young man stepped from the cab. Thomas allowed himself a small smile. Right on time.

Ken walked into the diner, looked around, spotted William Thomas and approached the booth. "Good to see you again," he said, holding out his hand.

"Young man." Thomas shook his hand, then indicated the empty seat opposite. "Please. Would you like anything?" he asked as the waitress returned with his coffee.

Ken slid in and smiled at her. "A cola, please." When she'd left, he turned to Thomas. "I've been really excited about what you told me. Is the job still open?"

"Of course. That's why I wanted to meet with you." Thomas smiled at the young man. "You're exactly what I'm looking for."

He wanted to reach across and grab the kid by the lapels of his ill-fitting sports coat and shake the information out of him, but he forced himself to go slow. Security had been tight at the party three nights ago. Too tight. He hadn't been able to get back into the building. Between the men patrolling and those bright lights they'd set up, he hadn't had a chance. But his life was on the line, so he'd come up with a new plan. And it all revolved around this college kid.

"You've worked at the way station how long?" he asked.

"Two years." Ken handed him a folder containing several typed pages. "Here's my résumé. As you can see, I have a lot of responsibility there. I know about the care and feeding of all the cats. Faith, uh, Faith Newlin—she's the lady who runs the way station—depends on me when she goes away. I'm sure I'll be right for you. Where did you say you were setting up your facility?"

"Texas," Thomas said, mentioning the first state that came to mind. He flipped through the pages without really seeing them. Before he'd left the party, he'd circled the compound one last time. He'd seen Ken putting a small, mean-looking cat into a cage and had struck up a conversation with the boy. The alternative to failing to get the cubs back was a .45 in the back of his head, so it wasn't too difficult to come up with a story to draw the kid out. He'd told Ken he was opening a way station of his own and was looking for someone to run it. The college student had taken the bait.

"I graduate in another month," Ken said, trying to hide his eagerness. "I was going to stay and work for the summer, but I'm sure Faith wouldn't mind if I—"

"What about security?" Thomas interrupted. "I noticed a lot at the party. Is all that necessary? It was an expense I hadn't considered."

"Don't worry about it." Ken leaned back in the booth. "The extra security was for the party. Usually there's no one there but staff."

"Usually?"

Ken straightened his jacket. "Yeah, well, there's a guy there now, but that's because we have—" He stopped suddenly and looked uncomfortable.

Thomas was silent. He learned long ago that most people couldn't stand silence. They would blurt out the first thing that came to mind just to fill the empty air.

"There's some rare tiger cubs staying for a couple months," Ken said. He paused. "I'm helping another guy with security."

Thomas didn't even have to look at him to know he was lying. One man. He smiled. Easy enough to take care of. He would simply drive in tonight and take the cubs.

He turned his attention back to Ken. He would continue with this mock interview. He didn't want to make the boy suspicious. A casual glance at his watch told him that he had plenty of time until nightfall. He would play out the game, then make his move.

Chapter 10

The absence of sound woke him. Cort sat up on his cot and listened. Normally the cats were active at night, playing, calling out to each other, roaring into the blackness. Nothing stirred outside his window, not even the wind.

He reached for his jeans and pulled them on, then slipped on boots and grabbed his pistol. The hallway was dark. First he checked on the cubs. They were sleeping in a bundle in the middle of their cage. Since the party three days ago, he'd kept them in the windowless room. He felt better knowing someone couldn't break in through a window. He backed out of the room, then secured the lock. He moved quietly to Faith's room and pushed open the door. She slept in her bed, her brown hair spread out on her pillow. He allowed himself a heartbeat of appreciation, then eased the door shut and went to her office.

Sparky stirred restlessly at his entrance and padded over to greet him. His chain stretched taut from its hook in the wall. Cort bent down and released the animal. Instantly Sparky raced into the hallway and toward the door leading to the compound.

Cort followed him. He wished he could ask the animal what he heard or smelled. He checked through the glass in the door, but couldn't see anything. In the faint moonlight, Tigger paced in his habitat. The other cats seemed equally restless, but silent. Sparky butted him, then scratched at the door. Cort opened the lock and let the cat slip into the night. Before following, he chambered a round of ammunition, leaving the safety on. He cracked the door and went outside. As soon as he stood in the compound, he could feel the presence of someone. He crouched down and moved swiftly to the cover of the trees. Sparky had disappeared, and he didn't dare call out to the animal.

Cort closed his eyes and forced himself to concentrate. Could it be a four-legged predator, rather than a man? No, Faith had told him the scent of the cats kept any other animals away. Someone was after the cubs. He crouched low in the brush. He could circle around the building, but that wasn't where he sensed his enemy. Why would anyone hide out around the compound? He thought about the clearing they'd found a half mile up the mountain. Were they trying to come in that way, rather than through the front? Damn. Since his last mission, he didn't trust his instincts. He paused, torn by indecision, then moved slowly toward the habitats.

It took him thirty minutes to circle through the facility. He moved silently around the cages, trying to stay downwind of the more vocal cats. Twice Sparky appeared at his side. The leopard seemed to be hunting, as well, and having as little luck. Neither found any signs of an intruder, and Cort never heard a car or a truck. When he reached the main building again, all feeling of someone being there had disappeared. He put Sparky inside, but didn't chain him, then got the Jeep and drove it down to the main entrance.

He stared at the closed gate. A light mist of dew covered the ground. He bent down and touched the dirt by the road. It clung to his finger. No one had driven this way tonight. They would have left tire marks. He stood up and brushed his hand on his jeans. Was he crazy? Jeff had told him to stay and do his job because he was the best Jeff had. Was that still true? How much of his edge had he lost in South America?

He got back in the Jeep and jerked the steering wheel around. When he'd parked the vehicle, he took one last look around the compound. The cats were stirring now, behaving normally. A couple played with the bowling balls in their cages. The familiar *thunk* of the heavy balls hitting steel bars should have made him relax, but it didn't.

He opened the door to the foyer, then blinked at the lights in the hallway. Faith appeared at the doorway to her office. The sight of her caught him like a fist to the belly. She stood in a pool of light, naked beneath her cotton gown. The thin fabric hung to her ankles but concealed little. He could see the shape of her breasts, the darker color of her nipples and the small triangle of shadow at the apex of her thighs.

Long hair tumbled over her shoulders. Her feet were bare. She wore no jewelry, no ornamentation save her faint smile. Sparky sat at her side. The black leopard contrasted with her white nightgown. Cort understood why ancient men had worshiped women. Primal female power called to him, and every part of his body longed to respond. Between her thighs he could forget all that troubled him.

"What happened?" she asked.

"I though I heard someone. I didn't find anything. Neither did Sparky."

She nodded. "He would have treed a stranger. He's done it before. He won't, as a rule, attack." She rested her hand on the cat's head. "What else is wrong, Cort?"

He forced himself to look away from her. "What if no one was there? What if I've lost it?"

"If you've lost it, we'll find it for you. I believe you're right. Someone was there, but now they're gone. Come on." She held out her hand. "I've warmed some milk."

He ignored the outstretched hand. "I'm not some child you can coddle after a bad dream." The sharp tone of his voice had often made green agents tremble with fear. Faith simply looked at him. Sparky yawned. Cort stuck his gun in the small of his back and wondered when he'd stopped being intimidating.

"I'd planned to put rum in it," she said, turning away. "You look like you need a drink."

She hadn't shown her feelings, but he knew he'd hurt her. "Dammit, Faith." He hurried after her, stepping over the leopard who had settled in the hall. "I didn't mean—" He grabbed her arm and forced her to stop. "I didn't mean it like that."

He held her firmly, yet without bruising. Faith stared at his hand, at the scratches from playing with the tiger cubs, then looked at his bare chest. There was a scar from a bullet on his right arm, and the scratch she'd treated over a week ago. Had he been here that short a period of time? It felt as if he'd always been in her life.

Taking a deep breath, she raised her eyes to his. "I know what you meant," she said. She pulled her arm free. "Come into the kitchen. You could use a drink."

When he'd settled into one of the straight-back chairs, she poured warm milk into two mugs and added a healthy dose of rum. After sprinkling nutmeg on top, she handed him one.

"Cheers."

He touched his mug to hers. "I shouldn't drink on the job. It clouds judgment." He laughed without humor. "Hell, I don't have any judgment left." He sipped. "It's good."

"Thank you." She flipped off the overhead lamp and took the seat opposite him. Light filtered in from the hall and glowed from above the ancient stove. "What happened tonight?"

He shrugged. The movement caused muscles to ripple across his bare chest and down his arms. She clutched her cup to keep from reaching out to touch him.

"Something woke me up. It's crazy, but it was the silence that made me think there was a problem. You know how loud the cats are at night."

She nodded. "If they were all quiet, there was someone or something out there."

"Whatever it was, it's gone now." He took another sip. "I checked the gate. No one had touched it. Maybe it was just some camper who got lost. He took one look at the jaguars in those end cages and headed back for the hills."

"I'm sure you're right."

"Am I?" He set his mug down and leaned toward her. "I still can't remember everything. It's driving me crazy. I know forcing my memory only makes it harder to recall exactly what happened, but I'm tired of waiting."

A strand of gold-blond hair fell over his forehead. She wanted to push it back into place. It was difficult to sit here and carry on a conversation while he was half-naked. She glanced down at her thin nightgown and smiled. She wasn't much more dressed than he was, but Cort didn't seem to be noticing.

"You don't want to hear this," he muttered, staring at the Formica table.

"Of course I do." He looked at her. The haunted expression in his eyes made her want to cry out in pain. Instinctively, she reached for his hand and covered it with hers. "Tell me anything you want. It won't go past these walls. I promise."

He turned his wrist until their fingers entwined. She squeezed tightly, trying to tell him she would hold on as long as he needed.

"I still don't know how the mission ended. I only have Jeff's word that I didn't kill my friend." He shook his head. "It doesn't matter if you know his first name. Dan. His name was Dan."

"Why do you doubt Jeff?"

"He may think I'm not ready for the truth." He leaned toward her. "I didn't have to pull the trigger to have killed him. There are a lot of ways to die on an assignment. A misspoken word. A route not changed quickly enough. Did I do or say something to tip the bad guys off?"

"Stop making yourself crazy," she said. "You have to put it behind you and go forward."

"I can't."

He stared out the window into the black night. She felt his pain as surely as if it were her own. She looked at his strong profile, at his straight nose and firm jaw. The pang inside her shifted and she realized it wasn't all about his hurting. She had a few wounds of her own to wrestle with.

He made her lonely. As they sat here in the quiet, baring souls, he made her ache with a wanting that would never be eased. She'd convinced herself she would never find a man who could understand her life-style and love her enough to stay. But being with Cort, sharing things with him that she'd always done alone, caring about him, made her vulnerable to hope. It was futile, she knew. But that didn't stop her from dreaming.

When the mission was over and the cubs were in their new home, he would leave her. His good fight required that he travel without excess baggage. He wouldn't have the room or the desire to carry her heart along. Even if she tried to tuck it in his pocket unnoticed, he would figure out the truth and cast it aside.

She listened as he spoke haltingly about Dan and their first meeting at the academy. He mentioned Jeff and the good times they'd shared. She could resist the warrior. He intrigued her, but didn't call to her innermost self. But this man, the one who exposed his wounds, swept through her barriers. She could not resist his vulnerability. His strength had first attracted her. His weakness made her care too much.

"The hell of it was," he was saying, "Jeff went ahead and asked me to be best man at his wedding." He shook his head. "At first, I didn't understand why he got married. Then I saw him with Jeanne. I don't know." He rubbed the bridge of his nose. "Loving that woman almost killed him." He shook his head. "That's not right. Losing her almost killed him. Loving her..." He trailed off. "It was all a waste of time, if you ask me."

Loving her made him strong, Faith thought, silently finishing Cort's sentence. She stared at their clasped hands, at his long, powerful fingers curling around hers. The truth swept through her, with all the power of a hurricane.

She understood Cort's reluctance to get involved. She knew he believed emotions weighed a man down. She recognized his confusion about love and duty because she shared it. For days she'd thought she felt attracted to him because he reminded her of the cats. All wild, unholy beauty with an amoral heart. Now she knew the truth. She'd seen more than the cats in Cort. She'd seen herself. They were, in the most basic of terms, soul mates.

"I need to go back," he said.

"Why?" she asked, trying to keep her voice from shaking. Her discovery shocked her to the core of her being.

"I have to know I can make a difference. It's all that matters." He looked at her. "Does that make sense? You—" he swept his arm across the table "—you make a difference every day. Every time you save a cougar or send a snow leopard back into the wild, it changes the future."

She ached for him, for herself and what she had to say. "If fighting your battles makes the world better, then go back and fight."

"Does it matter a damn?"

"I don't know. Does it?"

He drained his mug and squeezed her hand. "Sometimes," he admitted. He hunched over as if the weight of his responsibilities were too heavy to bear. "When I know who the bad guys are, like now, yes, it matters. Other times—"

"You mean, when the enemy might be your best friend?"

"You see too much." He looked at her. His lips curved up in a faint smile. With his free hand, he stroked her cheek. "You are so beautiful."

The compliment surprised her. She knew what she looked like, and while she didn't have to run around with a bag over her head, she wasn't anyone's idea of a beauty. She covered the hand on her cheek with her own and pressed his large palm against her skin.

She saw it deep in his gold-flecked eyes. He wanted to forget. And she was the easiest road to oblivion. He didn't love her; he never would. His heart had been given away long ago to a woman who hadn't bothered to appreciate the gift. Faith wanted to find the woman and demand she return Cort's heart so that someone else—someone like her— could have it.

Not likely. She knew her failings as well as her looks. She wasn't the kind of woman that men stuck around for. But the wanting in his eyes was a temptation. It would be easy to allow him to forget, if only for a night. She didn't give her body lightly, but this was Cort, and she could deny him very little.

Cort didn't regret the compliment. He'd spoken without thinking, but now, looking at Faith, he knew his words to be true. In the evening light, with compassion filling her eyes and her hair down on her shoulders, she was beautiful. It wasn't about the shape of her face, or her breasts almost visible under her gown. It was about the woman herself. All cats were gray in the dark, he'd told himself. But with Faith, he wanted to keep the lights on and know he was with her.

The itch that needed scratching, the desire to get lost, required a specific cure. It wasn't about any woman. It wasn't about the heat in his groin. It was about her. He needed *her*.

The realization scared him more than any sniper's bullet. He pulled away from her and stood up.

"Cort?" she asked quietly from her place at the table.

"This doesn't make sense," he grumbled. He walked over to the counter and leaned against it. "I'm sorry."

"Don't be." She rose to her feet. "I understand completely."

"I wish *I* did." He looked at her, at the shape of her body, at her honest face. "Go back to bed, Faith."

"I don't mind talking." She hovered beside her chair, not moving closer, but not going away, either.

"Maybe I don't want to talk."

She took a deep breath and moved to stand in front of him. "Maybe I don't mind that, either."

Her calm statement made his mouth water. His gaze swept over her. He told himself she couldn't possibly mean it. It was just the night or the circumstances. She was Jeff's friend and he'd promised his boss he would take care of her. Sex wasn't part of the package. Still, that didn't stop him from wanting her. He deliberately tortured himself by examining the shape of her generous breasts and watching her nipples pucker under the thin fabric of her gown. He felt the heat of her body so close to his. When he looked down at her feet, he almost groaned aloud.

She painted her toenails. Bright red. A completely, uselessly feminine flaunt in an otherwise utilitarian life. How the hell was he supposed to resist that?

He grabbed her by the arms and hauled her close. Her soft curves flattened against him, making his ache harden. "I need you," he said. "You're all I have to keep me sane."

She stared up at him and licked her lips. Deep inside, a powerful hunger snowballed through him, blocking out all rational thought, all pretense, leaving only the need.

"Cort, I—" She reached up to touch his face. Her fingers slipped against the stubble on his cheek, making a rasping sound. Her thumb brushed across his mouth. He touched her sensitive pad with the tip of his tongue and made her gasp. She tasted salty and sweet. Her blue eyes darkened, and she nodded as if coming to a decision.

"I feel it, too," she murmured. "And I don't mind if you pretend. I know it's about her."

He jerked his head away from her touch. "What are you talking about?"

"The woman. The one who broke your heart. I know you're remembering her. You can pretend she's the one—" She broke off and glanced down. She seemed to gather her strength together. She shook her hair away from her face and smiled faintly. "You can turn the light off."

Passion turned bitter and made him sick to his stomach. He'd told himself he'd lied so he wouldn't make Faith feel badly, but the truth was he'd lied to hide the blackness of his soul. Now it was coming back to haunt him.

He stared at her. She was the most open, honest person he'd ever known. He had, through the twisted hollowness of his life, turned her into a replica of himself. She was willing to let him pretend. But a woman like her wouldn't give herself lightly. He would go to a special place in hell for having reduced her to thinking she could only be a substitute when, in fact, she would have been the best thing that had ever happened to him.

"I'm so sorry," he said, knowing the words weren't enough.

She smiled. "Don't be. I couldn't help but notice how you were feeling. It makes perfect sense."

"No, it doesn't. I'm not the right one for you."

She flinched as if he'd slapped her. Her eyes flashed with the pain of rejection. "You don't want me." It wasn't a question.

"It's not that."

"Never mind. I understand." She stepped back and folded her arms over her chest. He recognized the protective gesture and wished he'd never started this particular game. There was no woman for her to remind him of. *She* would assume he was thinking of someone else, while he would only be thinking of her. But he couldn't tell her the truth without hurting her more.

"You can do better than me," he said, trying to ease her discomfort.

"Funny, that's what they all say."

"Faith." He reached out to her. She took another step back. "I'm just some guy who can't remember his past. You need to look beyond this to something better."

She walked over to the table and braced her arms against one of the chairs. "You mean *someone* better."

That one stung. "Yes."

God, he wanted to tell her the truth. He wanted to explain there never had been another woman, never would be. He didn't have relationships, didn't know how. Faith was the closest he'd come to caring. But telling her would mean admitting the lie, and the blackness in his soul.

"Faith, I—" He ran his hands through his hair. "Good night." He walked out of the room.

He was willing to admit he cared about Faith. But that wasn't his job. He was supposed to protect her. Better for him to remember that and not try to be her friend. Dan had been his friend, and look what had happened to him.

In the hallway he paused long enough to wonder when he'd changed. He wasn't the man he used to be. If only he could figure out if that was good or bad.

Cort blinked at the bright sunlight and bit back a groan. Last night, after Faith had gone back to bed, he'd taken the bottle of rum and finished almost half of it. Not only hadn't he been able to forget the accusing look in her eyes, he'd woken up with the mother of all hangovers.

By the time he fed the cubs and cleaned their cage, the pounding had subsided to the rhythm and volume of a jackhammer. His stomach lurched every time he thought about food, and he wondered if he could ask Faith to simply shoot him and put him out of his misery.

Just the thought of her made him feel worse. After last night, she would probably enjoy taking a shot at him, but she wasn't likely to make the end merciful. He slumped down against the building and shaded his eyes from the sun. He would sit here another minute, then he would crawl back to his room.

Sparky appeared at his side. The black leopard sniffed his face, gave him a rough lick on the cheek, then settled down next to him, laying his massive head on his thighs.

"Just don't purr loudly," Cort muttered, stroking his large, rounded ears.

"Hey, Cort!"

Cort flinched at the call. Ken jogged over and squatted in front of him. "You feeling all right?"

"No," Cort answered, being careful not to shake his head.

"Can I talk to you for a minute?"

There was something in the kid's voice that sounded a warning bell. Cort straightened. "What is it?"

Ken shifted and sat on the ground. "It's probably nothing, but I got to wondering, and what with the cubs and all—"

"The point," Cort said, then rubbed his head.

"I met a guy at the fund-raiser. He asked me about the cats and offered to interview me for a job." Ken looked up at him. "It's tough to get any work with big cats. The zoos don't have a lot of openings, and private facilities like this don't usually hire."

Faith had told him much the same thing. "So you're leaving?"

"No. Not yet." Ken shrugged. "I met with him yesterday and gave him my résumé. Only last night I realized I'd left out a letter of recommendation. So I called the hotel where he was staying. They didn't have anyone under that name registered there. Bowmund only has two hotels. I called the other one, then phoned around a few of the local motels on the mountain."

"And?" Cort asked, but he already knew the answer.

"Nothing."

"What's the guy's name?"

Ken flushed. "John Smith."

"You have a business card?"

The kid shook his head. "Guess he wasn't offering me a job, was he?"

Cort pushed Sparky out of the way and stood up. He ignored the pain in his head and looked at Ken. "Doesn't sound like it. Did he ask about the cubs?"

"I think so." Ken rose and shoved his big hands into his jeans pockets. "I know he asked about security. Cort, I'm sorry. I didn't mean—"

"I know you didn't. These people are pros. There's no way you could see what was happening. You were just looking for a job. Did you recognize the guy? Has he been at other fund-raisers?"

"He didn't look familiar, but I don't spend that much time with the guests."

"We'd better go talk to Faith." Cort led the way into the building.

Faith sat at her desk poring over official-looking forms. She glanced up as they entered the room.

"We may have trouble," Cort said.

She looked from him to Ken. "You'd better both sit down."

Ten minutes later she was going over the guest list. "I know most of the people personally," she said. "The description could fit a couple, I suppose, but there were about thirty guests I'd never seen before. There was no John Smith at the party, which means he probably used a false name to get in. You've seen the tape of everyone who came in the building the night of the party. Did you recognize him, Ken?"

Ken looked miserable. "I don't think so. It's dark and the tape only shows people from the back. Maybe. Oh, I don't know."

"Don't sweat it, kid," Cort said. "You did the right thing by telling us. If this guy approaches you again, be polite, but keep your distance. Tell him you can't talk now, and let me know right away. Whatever you do, don't play the hero."

Ken nodded.

Faith smiled at him. "Try not to think about this. Why don't you exercise Tigger for a while?"

"Okay, thanks." He left.

Faith closed the folder in front of her and sighed. "Was it one of the men after the cubs?" She didn't dare glance up at Cort. He looked awful and she didn't want to know why.

"Yes. I'm going to put a call in to Jeff. Apparently they've found out we're holding the cubs here. We need extra security around, and I want him to get those tigers moved as soon as possible."

"I don't like the idea of strangers—"

He cut her off. "You don't get a vote. I'm the security expert. I wasn't kidding when I warned Ken not to play the hero. Don't you be one, either. We need a team of at least six guys."

"Six!" She made the mistake of really looking at him. He hadn't shaved. The dark stubble made him appear even more dangerous. His eyes were red and had dark circles under them. "You look like hell."

"I feel like hell." He picked up the phone and punched in the number.

While he spoke with his boss, she toyed with her pencil. She would have to say it. Last night she'd lain awake and stared at the ceiling. The words had circled around and around in her head. She had to thank him.

He hung up the phone. "All set." He perched on the corner of her desk. "They'll be here by tonight."

"Thank you," she said.

"Just doing my job."

"No." She bit her lip. "Thank you for last night."

"Faith, I didn't mean—"

"I really appreciate your not taking advantage of me. I'm not promiscuous, and I might have regretted it later."

He stared at her oddly for a moment, then nodded. "You're welcome."

That was it? That was all he was going to say? She felt as deflated as a popped balloon. Somehow she'd hoped for a little more from him. Something about how *he'd* lain awake wishing he were in his bed. Even a flicker of regret. She tossed her pencil on the desk and glared at him. He didn't seem impressed. As she studied him, she felt her body start to quiver. Despite his rejection and the other woman in his life and everything that was happening with the cubs, she still wanted him.

"You're a brave woman," he said.

"What does that have to do with anything?"

"It doesn't. The thought just occurred to me."

Great. She didn't want to be brave. She wanted to be irresistible and feminine and all those things she would never be. She laced her fingers together on the desk and allowed herself to think the truth. For once in her life, she wanted to be enough.

He rose and walked to the door. Before leaving, he turned back to face her. "Courage is a learned behavior, Faith. Who taught you yours?"

She frowned. "I'm not especially brave."

"That's the whole point. It's facing the fear that makes you strong."

Chapter 11

Thomas eased his dark sedan to a stop in front of the entrance to the university parking lot. He was not having a good day. He'd been awakened by a phone call informing him he had one week to complete his mission.

"Or we will be forced to discontinue our association."

Thomas grimaced. He knew what that meant. Association, hell. It was *him* they would be discontinuing. Damn.

He stared at the college students walking toward their cars. A quick call to the registrar's office had given him Ken's schedule. He knew what time his classes ended and had decided to wait by the entrance to the parking lot and intercept the student as he was leaving for the day.

He needed a way into the compound. Last night had been a complete failure. The gate had been too sturdy for his car to break through, and a study of the equipment used to open and close it had convinced him any tampering would result in an alarm sounding somewhere up at the compound. He'd been forced to drive up the mountain and hike into the facility.

Thomas grimaced as he shifted in the seat. His arms and legs were a mass of scratches from the underbrush and trees. With only a quarter moon and a flashlight to illuminate the way, it had taken him almost two hours to get near the place. Before he'd even gotten close to the main building, the security guy had been out walking around. Thomas would have taken him out, but then he'd seen the black leopard patrolling the cages. Jesus. A shiver rippled through him. What kind of crazies kept something like that for a watchdog?

To add insult to injury, his car had gotten a flat. He'd had to roll it down the mountain in neutral. He'd barely made it back to his room by dawn. He had to find a better way inside.

He was going to get the kid to let him in the gate. It was the only approach that made sense. If the kid didn't want to cooperate, he would force him.

The flow of students had subsided some, but now a large group of young people were making their way toward the parking lot. Thomas watched intently. There. Behind the blonde with the big chest. Thomas eased the sedan forward until he blocked the main path. Kids moved around the car, giving him dirty looks.

When Ken passed in front of him, Thomas opened the door and stepped out.

"Ken," he called, forcing himself to smile. "How are you?"

Ken froze in his tracks. He looked startled, then scared. "You? What are you doing here?"

Thomas didn't like the expression in his eyes. He had a bad feeling about this. He casually reached under his jacket for his gun. "I had a few more questions. You got a minute?"

The last of the students walked toward their cars, leaving Thomas and Ken alone at the edge of the parking lot. Ken shook his head. "Leave me alone." He started to walk away.

Thomas sprinted two steps and caught him by the arm. "Not so fast, buddy."

Ken jerked free. "Don't 'buddy' me. We're on to you, man. You're not going to get away with it."

Thomas felt the fury build up inside him. This little piece of trash had ratted on him. He grabbed Ken again and pulled him close. They were almost the same height. Thomas eased the gun out of its holster and pressed the barrel against Ken's stomach.

"Don't make a sound," he growled. "You hear me?"

Ken glanced down at the gun and caught his breath. He made a strangled noise in his throat. "Don't hurt me."

Thomas pushed him toward the door. "Get in."

Ken's face paled. "What are you going to do with me?"

"Just ask you a few questions."

The kid had nailed him, he thought with disgust. The whole facility was probably on alert. He cursed. Could it get any worse? He shoved Ken in the back seat, then reached in the glove box for a pair of handcuffs. When the kid was secure, Thomas started the car and drove off around the parking lot.

"Where's your truck?" he asked.

"Over there." Ken nodded in the direction.

Thomas stopped behind the truck. The kid would have a remote control device to control the gate. He could make use of that. It would take a couple of days to come up with a foolproof plan to get the tiger cubs. Before he made another attempt, he had a lot of work to do.

First he was going to find out everything Ken knew. Then he was going to get rid of his problem.

Faith slammed down the phone. Two days. Ken hadn't shown up for two days. She'd put a call in to his dorm room but no one had seen him. Any worry she'd felt disappeared when Ken's roommate informed her that Nancy, Ken's girlfriend, had gotten an assignment in Las Vegas. No doubt Ken had taken off with her and was currently having the time of his life.

She slowly turned her chair until she was facing the window and could see out into the compound. For the last few months, Ken had been completely irresponsible. The incident with the reporter had been the final straw. But since she'd warned him to straighten up, he'd been doing a good job. What had happened? When she got her hands on him...

She clutched the arms of her chair as a cold ribbon of fear curled up her spine. John Smith, or whatever his name was, had approached Ken and talked to him. Was it possible something had happened to the young man?

She watched Beth playing with Samson. The bobcat chased after her, catching her easily and gently taking her arm in his mouth. No, not that, she told herself. Ken *had* to be fine.

"You look pensive," Cort said.

She turned her chair until she could see him. He held the smaller of the tiger cubs in his arms. Little crawled up his chest and nuzzled his neck.

"I'm just cranky," Faith said, wondering why on earth she envied the cub's place in Cort's arms. She'd put her desire behind her the night he'd turned her down. She wasn't interested in him. She didn't care about Cort Hollenbeck at all. She sighed. Yeah, right.

"One of those days?" he asked.

She shrugged.

He came into the office and sat on the chair in front of her desk. The cub sat in his lap and blinked at her. Sparky trailed in, took one look at the cub and walked over to Faith, deliberately turning his back on the younger animal.

"You're jealous, aren't you?" she asked softly, scratching his ears. He humphed at her. She pointed at the cub. "How are they doing?"

"Eating, playing." He held up his arm, showing her a long red scratch from his elbow to his wrist. "Learning to wrestle."

She shook her head. "I told you to wear gloves when you play with them. They do require social interaction, but there's no need for you to pay for it with a pound of flesh."

He grinned. "Social interaction? Faith, these are tiger cubs, not children."

"They still have needs. As the surrogate parents, we have responsibilities that can't be ignored. If we don't take care of their social needs, they won't be well adjusted enough to spend time with other tigers and breed.''

He scratched Little under the chin but stared at Faith. There was something about the expression in the gold-flecked eyes that made her want to squirm.

"Why are you looking at me like that?" she asked.

"I was thinking that the snow leopards are very lucky cats."

She busied herself adjusting Sparky's collar. "Don't be maudlin."

"I'm very serious. You're a dedicated woman."

"I'm still not sure I'm going to be able to pull this off."

He dismissed her with a shrug. "You'll open your center. You'll find a way to get the money and handle the permits. I have every confidence in you." Little nibbled on the buttons of his shirt. He pushed her away. She wiggled to get comfortable on his lap and shifted onto her back, exposing her white belly. Cort rubbed her soft fur and skin, making her squirm with pleasure. Bright blue eyes blinked sleepily. She grabbed his hand in her front paws and gnawed on his thumb.

Faith stared at the small cub and fought down fierce jealousy. Cort handled the baby and her needs with a combination of competence and affection that left her breathless. She wouldn't have thought one of Jeff's warriors would so easily adapt to the ways of the real world.

She smiled and glanced around at her dilapidated office, at the compound visible through the window and the black leopard sitting at her feet. Okay, so maybe this wasn't a normal situation, but it was much more domestic than he was used to. Perhaps his ability to adapt was what made him so good at his job. To think about tying him down would be as cruel and inhuman as caging a wild panther or snow leopard. Only domesticated creatures belonged in polite society. Even if he had been emotionally available to her, she couldn't, in good conscience, chain him to a life of mortgage payments and dinner at six.

Foolish dreams. He wasn't available to her. And she wasn't the kind of woman who could hold a man. Her own father hadn't loved her enough to stick around, and she'd been his only child.

Sparky flicked his tail and stared into her eyes. "You love me, don't you, baby," she said softly. He rumbled deep in his throat and shot the cub a malicious stare.

"Where's Ken?" Cort asked. "I haven't seen him in a couple of days."

She hesitated. "It's probably nothing, but I just got off the phone with his roommate. They haven't seen him, either."

Cort straightened in his chair. The quick movement caused the cub to roll onto her side. She mewed her protest, but he didn't notice. "What do you mean they haven't seen him? He's missing?"

Faith shook her head. "No. Nancy, his girlfriend, had an assignment in Las Vegas. His roommates think Ken went with her, and I agree. It's not the first time he's taken off without saying anything to me."

Cort reached forward and grabbed the phone from her desk. He pulled it toward him.

"What are you doing?" she asked.

"Calling the police."

She bit her lower lip. "Jeff had already checked out the guest list, and everyone was cleared. The guards checked ID at the gate. No one tried anything funny. I find it hard to believe one of the guests is involved with stealing the cubs."

"Maybe one of your guests wasn't who he pretended to be. There was no John Smith at the party, but we don't know the guy's real name. Or if he used a stolen invitation to get in."

She hadn't thought of that. "Is Ken in danger?"

Cort's call connected and he didn't answer her. He spoke to the local police and explained Ken might be missing. They agreed to contact the authorities in Las Vegas and try to locate Ken's girlfriend.

"Now what?" Faith asked when he hung up.

"Now we wait. I want—"

A knock on the door interrupted him. One of the security guards stuck his head in her office. "Cort, Andy told me to let you know the trailer's arrived. They're setting it up beside the Big House."

"That's fine." He motioned for the man to come in the room and handed him his walkie-talkie. "I want to change the frequency on these today. Tell Andy when he's done, I want to see him. We may have a missing employee."

The man stepped forward cautiously. He was in his late twenties, shorter than Cort by several inches and not nearly as muscular. He kept his pale eyes fixed on Sparky. When he reached out to take the equipment, the leopard raised his nose and sniffed. Before Faith could grab him, he spun on his huge paws and roared at the security guard. The man turned white and started to run. The tiger cub jumped at the sound and tried to bury herself in Cort's belly.

"Freeze," Cort commanded.

The man froze.

Sparky flinched slightly, and Faith cuffed him on the shoulder. "Mind yourself," she told the leopard.

The cub stared up at Cort, not sure which way to run. He picked her up in one hand and pulled her against his chest. "Sorry, Little," he said, petting her reassuringly. After studying him for several seconds, she mewed and nestled against this chin.

The guard stood trembling by the door. Cort rose and faced him. "Never run from the leopard. He won't hurt you unless you provoke him."

The guard nodded, looking unconvinced. Cort handed him the walkie-talkie. "You can go now."

The man left without saying a word.

Cort took his seat and shook his head. "You're going to have to keep Sparky chained up."

"I won't."

"Faith, if I hadn't been here, the guard would have shot him."

She touched Sparky's back protectively. "How do you know?"

"His hand was resting on his holster. It's an instinct. The men here are trained to react to danger. They perceive a large black leopard as danger. If nothing else, letting him roam free distracts them.''

"I can't keep him chained up twenty-four hours a day. That's cruel.''

"Let him roam this building at night, if you want. But other than that, he can only go out on a leash.''

"I hate these changes,'' she said. ''There are too many strangers here. There are cars running around the compound. The cats are restless. It's not good for them. This morning when I spoke to Jeff, he said he'd have the cubs moved by the end of the week. That's only four more days. What can happen between now and then? Is all this necessary?''

Cort leaned forward and placed the cub on her desk. "I didn't question you about your instructions regarding the cubs. Trust me to know my job and to do it right. I'm going to keep you and them safe.''

She sat back in her chair and drew one leg to her chest. "But six men? Is that necessary?''

"Two men per eight-hour shift isn't excessive.''

The cub sniffed at the papers on her desk, then batted at a pen. It went flying off onto the floor. Little raced to the edge and looked down. Sparky turned toward the kitten. Their eyes met. Little arched her back, her hair raising on end, and spit wildly at the leopard, then ran to the In-basket and dove into a pile of papers.

Cort moved around the desk and stood in front of Faith. He held out his hand and pulled her to her feet. "What's really the problem?'' he asked.

She shrugged. "I'm out of sorts. Don't *I* get to have a bad day?''

But it wasn't the day at all, she thought glumly. It was the man. Time was ticking away. Her phone conversation with Jeff had upset her more than she'd realized. Only four more days until the cubs were gone, and Cort with them. He was healthy now. He'd remembered most of his last mission. It was probably enough to get him cleared to go back to the field and do what he loved. But inside, deep in the place where dreams hid, she felt a restless longing. It was about more than being with him physically, although she wanted that, too. It was about caring for someone and having him care back.

"Are you sure there's nothing wrong?" he asked, staring into her eyes.

She reached out and touched the scar on his chin. The cut had healed completely, but the line from the corner of his mouth down across his chin still looked raw. He'd gained weight since he'd arrived and the hollows in his cheeks didn't look so gaunt. He walked without a limp. Truly there was nothing to keep him with her.

"Faith?" His gold-flecked brown eyes filled with concern. A lock of hair tumbled onto his forehead. Broad shoulders blocked out most of the overhead light. He was every inch a powerful alpha male, and she wanted to be his mate.

"What are you thinking?" he asked.

Something incredibly foolish, she told herself.

A loud squawk cut through the silence and drew her attention away from him. The tiger cub had jumped from the desk onto Sparky's back. She clung tenuously, digging her claws into his fur. Sparky shook like a wet dog, trying to dislodge her, but every jerk of his body made her dig in more.

Faith started to laugh. Sparky glared at her and growled. Cort leapt toward the pair. Little howled. Cort accidentally snagged the chair with his foot and started to go down. Faith grabbed his arm with one hand and the chair back with the other. She felt herself being pulled forward, but couldn't stop laughing. Sparky jumped toward them, knocking over the trash can in his haste. The metal container fell right where Cort stepped.

"Dammit, cat, get out of my way," he grunted, jerking sideways to avoid the container and losing his balance. Sparky spun in a circle, trying to pull the cub from his back. Faith released her grip on Cort and fought to hold on to her balance. The chair fell to the ground. Sparky's rear caught her behind her left knee and she went down, hitting her leg on the trash can and landing across Cort's midsection.

The "ooph" of his sharply exhaled air whistled by her ear. As Sparky circled by, desperately trying to pull the tiger off by grabbing her tail, Faith reached for the cub. Little dug in one more time, then released her claws and scrambled against Faith. Sparky made a beeline for the corner and curled up in a tight ball beside the file cabinets.

Faith was still laughing. She pushed herself into a sitting position, using Cort's stomach for leverage. He groaned as she pressed down against him. The cub slipped from her grasp and fell on Cort's chest. There she promptly collapsed and mewed in his face.

"You okay?" Faith asked, gasping for breath. She moved off his legs and onto the floor.

"No."

He sat up slowly, grabbing the cub by the scruff of her neck. Little instinctively curled up her back paws and looked expectantly at him as if saying, "Where are we going, Mom?"

Cort shook her gently. "You're a pest." Little meowed happily, and he dropped her onto his lap.

Faith leaned against her desk and surveyed the damage. Only the chair and the trash can had hit the floor. Not bad.

"Feeling better?" Cort asked.

"Yeah, I am. Are you going to tell me you planned that just to make me feel better?"

He shook his head. "No, but I'm glad you're smiling again."

She stared self-consciously at her lap. Cort leaned forward and placed his hand on the back of her neck. "Forget about all this," he said. "Ken, the cubs, the security. You've done all you can. I'm going to put this monster in with her brother, then take Sparky for a leisurely walk around the compound. You head up to the Big House for a long, hot bath. I don't want to see you back here for at least a couple of hours."

He kneaded the tense muscles in her neck, and she leaned into the relaxing pressure. "Is that a direct order?"

"You bet. And I expect it to be obeyed."

She told herself not to, but she couldn't help looking at him mouth. Those firm lips had once claimed hers with an amazing passion. She still remembered the fiery need that had raced through her at the first touch of his tongue. Her fingers curled toward her palms as she recalled the feel of his hot skin and the tight curve of his buttocks. Would he join her in her bath?

Before she even thought about collecting the courage to issue an invitation, she pushed the fantasy aside. He'd already turned her down once. She wasn't going to be foolish enough to ask a second time.

She stood up and reached for the cub. "I'll put her away. You see to Sparky. Can you check his back and make sure she didn't break the skin?"

"Not a problem." He looked at the black leopard glaring at the tiger cub. "We're buddies."

She held Little close to her chest as she left. The small bundle of fur wasn't enough to fill the ache she had inside. It would take a man in her life to make that need go away.

"Life is never fair," she murmured to the kitten before tucking her into her cage. "And loving someone can be very dangerous."

It was past midnight when Sparky padded into Cort's room. Cort sensed more than heard the animal as he silently slipped through the blackness. Cort raised up on one elbow.

"What is it, boy? What do you hear?"

The leopard grunted low in his throat and left the room. For the second time in a week, Cort pulled on jeans and boots, then reached for his gun. After making sure the cubs were in their cage, he backed out of the room and locked it behind him. Sparky hovered close by, following when he went to wake Faith.

He pushed open her door. "Faith, I think I—" He stared at the empty bed. Where had she gone? He glanced down at the leopard, but Sparky simply stared back. After checking the other rooms in the building and making sure they were empty, he verified that the front door was locked, then stepped to the rear door leading out to the compound. Sparky butted his knee.

"No you don't," he told the leopard. "You're staying in here. It would be too easy for one of the guards to accidentally shoot you."

The leopard growled and tried to slip past him. Cort dragged him back to the office and secured him to the chain. Sparky glared his anger. Cort ignored him. "Nobody's dying while I'm in charge," he muttered. He collected his walkie-talkie as he moved past his room.

At the rear door, he looked through the glass before stepping into the night. As they had before, the cats paced silently in their cages.

He scanned the compound. The jeep wasn't where it had been parked when he went to bed. One of the guards must have taken it on patrol. The rule was that the two guards on duty were never to leave the area together. Someone was to stay by the main building at all times. But he couldn't see the second guard, or Faith. Yet someone was out there. He could feel it.

He spoke softly into the radio. The unit crackled, but there was no response. Low in his gut, a sense of unease grew. He spoke again. Still nothing. Cort chambered a round into the gun and put his thumb on the safety. He began moving toward the cages on the far side of the road to the Big House. He crouched low as he walked, constantly looking for signs of the intruder.

He was almost to the first cage when a flash of white caught his eye. He glanced up and saw Faith coming out from behind the habitat at the end, the one that housed the first of the two wild jaguars. He inched toward her and spoke her name. She turned toward him.

She wore black jeans and boots, but her white T-shirt made her visible in the night. He motioned for her to get down. She didn't see the gesture and continued walking toward him. The hairs on the back of his neck bristled. He didn't dare call out his instructions and alert whoever was out there.

Cort broke into a jog. A sixth sense caused him to look up ahead, where the compound bled into the trees. A glint of something metal made his heart pound in his chest.

"Get down," he called, not caring that the man behind her could hear him.

Faith stopped walking toward him and stared. "Down," he yelled as he jumped toward her. She hesitated a second, then hit the ground. He landed on top of her, just as he heard the distinctive *pop* of a silenced gun firing. He didn't bother waiting to catch his breath; he simply got to his feet, grabbed her arms and pulled her along with him, between the second and third habitats.

He counted six more shots fired at them as he and Faith came to a stop between an empty cage and one of the jaguars. The flat-faced cat growled and stuck its paw out by the front corner. Cort pulled Faith out of the way. He scrambled on his belly toward the walkway and fired into the bushes where the intruder had been.

The sound of his Beretta cut through the night. In the distance, he heard the trailer door bang open and the four other security guards run out toward the compound. Nothing stirred in the brush, and he knew the man was gone. Only then did he realize Faith hadn't said a word to him. He returned to her side and touched her face. "Faith. Are you hurt?"

She didn't answer. He pulled a penlight from his jeans pocket and shone it on her body. Blood seeped from her arm and collected in a pool on the ground.

Chapter 12

Faith's eyes fluttered open. She blinked several times, then raised her hand to push the light away.

"Don't move," Cort said, grateful she was conscious. "I think you've been shot."

"What?" She glanced down at her left arm. "Oh my God, I'm bleeding."

"Is that the only place that hurts?" He began to feel along her legs, then moved up to her torso.

While he was running his hands along her thighs, she raised herself up to a sitting position and stared at her arm. "I can't be shot. It doesn't hurt that badly."

"Shock," he muttered, slipping his hands under her T-shirt. When his palm brushed her bare midsection, their eyes locked. Despite the danger, electricity raced between them. He forced himself to ignore the sensations and quickly explored her chest and back. "Seems to be the only injury," he said, sitting back on his heels. "The bleeding is slowing."

The guards ran into the compound. "What happened?" Andy asked. "The Jeep is gone and neither of my men are answering."

"I know." Cort stood up. "Have Mike take her inside and stay with her. Tell Ralph to take a truck down to the gate and stay there. Don't let anyone out. You and Tom, come with me. I want to catch the bastard who did the shooting." He looked down at Faith. "Are you going to be all right?"

One of the guards stepped forward and gave her a hand up. "I'm fine. Go." She waved Cort off.

He drilled her with one more hard look, then gave directions to the men and jogged toward the bushes.

Once in the forest, it was difficult to find a path. He paused to listen. The two guards with him fanned out. Within five minutes he knew they didn't have a prayer of finding anyone tonight. Not unless the shooter tried to make a break for it. With only a quarter moon for light, and all the trees and leaves blocking that faint glow, he could barely see two feet in front of him. He pulled out his radio and told the two security men to head back to the main building. One of them was to guard the structure, the other was to join Ralph down at the gate. Cort turned around and took a step forward.

Time bent and ripped with an almost audible wrenching sound as he was flung into the past. An explosion roared through the night. He felt it lift him up and toss him aside like a rag doll. He hit the floor of the warehouse. Smoke and heat filled his lungs. And something else. Salt air. He could smell the ocean.

He tried to move, tried to escape, but his body refused to obey his commands. His head throbbed. Someone tugged on his arms, pulling him away from the flames. He was dragged from the burning building and tossed into the back seat of a car. He blacked out for several minutes and regained consciousness on a bumpy dirt road. The vehicle drove on, speeding through the night without even headlights to show the way.

Who was driving? Where were they going? Who had saved him? He forced himself to sit up and lean forward. There was only one other man in the car. The driver. He squinted his eyes and peered into the darkness. "Dan?"

His friend didn't turn around. "I'm glad you're awake. There's a nasty bump on your head, buddy. I was afraid you were out for good."

"What the hell happened?"

"Someone blew up the warehouse."

He had a hard time concentrating through the pain. "Was it you?"

Dan didn't answer for a long time. "Why are you here, Cort? Have you come to take me back?"

Now it was Cort's turn to be silent.

"I get it," Dan said at last. "I'm not supposed to come back. Don't worry, buddy. Going home to the good old U.S. of A. wasn't part of my plan, either."

He turned into a long, narrow field and cut the engine. Cort gingerly stepped out of the car and stared around him at the familiar landing sight. "What are we doing here?"

"Getting you home. The gentlemen I'm doing business with are onto you." Dan came and stood beside him. "Have been since the day you arrived. You're lucky to be alive."

Cort sure didn't feel lucky. With one hand, he held on to the car for balance. He had moments of clear vision, followed by sensations of vertigo. With his other hand, he reached under his sports coat and pulled out his gun. The metal finish gleamed in the light of the full moon.

"You sold out," Cort said. "Why?"

"I would tell you it was for the money, but you wouldn't believe me."

"You got that right. What happened? Blackmail?"

Dan turned toward him. Cort slowly raised his gaze and stared at the familiar crooked smile of his friend.

"That would be easiest, wouldn't it?" Dan asked. He lit a cigarette, then blew out the match and dropped it on the ground. "You would like to think I was being forced into this. Anything else would upset your tidy ideas of right and wrong."

"Damn you." Cort raised the gun toward his friend. "I'm taking you back with me."

Dan shook his head. "That's not what your boss told you to do, Cort. You're supposed to get the proof, then make sure I'm never a problem again." He waved his cigarette toward the heavens. "Here comes your ride."

Cort turned and looked up. A fast-moving plane seemed to drop from the sky like a rock. It dove down toward the narrow field, the sound of its engine growing as it approached. When it was seconds from landing, Cort jabbed Dan in the side with his pistol. "Move."

"No." Dan took one last drag on the cigarette and dropped it to the ground. After stepping on it, he looked at Cort and smiled. "You can kill me, or you can let me go, but I'm not coming back to the States. I wouldn't like prison."

From behind them, headlights swept across the field and focused on the car. A low, dark four-door car raced toward them. Cort recognized the vehicle and the men inside.

"Looks like your friends found us," he said.

Dan surprised him by laughing. "Nothing goes right in this country. Come on." He started toward the plane, which was bumping its way across the rough field.

Cort ran after him, keeping low to the ground. He was about ten feet away from the wing when a bullet caught him in the leg. He went down.

Instantly Dan backtracked and crouched at his side. "You're not having a good stay here, are you?"

Cort grinned, despite the pain. "Hell of a vacation. Get me on board that plane, you lazy bastard."

Dan hoisted him up over his shoulder and carried him to the open door. From inside, someone reached out to pull him to safety. Cort grabbed Dan, but his friend jerked free.

"I meant what I said. I'm not coming back." Dan had to yell to be heard above the plane's engine. The men on the ground started shooting at the plane.

"They'll kill you," Cort shouted.

"Better them than you. I'm not coming back." The plane started moving forward, gathering speed for takeoff.

"No! You can't stay. Stop!" Cort screamed to the pilot. "We've left one on the ground." But no one listened. He tried to jump out, but the men inside started hauling him away from the door. He leaned out and stared back at Dan.

His friend gave him a jaunty salute, then spun to face the men racing toward the plane. They were all firing at the small craft. Dan pulled out his gun and shot at them. Two went down. The remaining three turned their weapons on him. Cort stared in disbelief as they pumped Dan's body full of bullets. His friend hit the ground without a single scream of pain.

The plane rose above the field and the surrounding trees, then angled north for the trip home. Cort let himself be pulled inside, and the door was secured. The pain in his head increased with each heartbeat, and he felt the blood flowing out his leg. Then he closed his eyes and willed himself to forget.

The sounds of the past receded slowly, the plane engine fading until all Cort could hear were the night creatures and an owl in a nearby tree. He sank to the damp ground just outside the way station compound. He'd remembered it all. The hell of it was he just wanted to forget the whole damn thing.

Dan had known Cort had been sent to verify that he'd betrayed his country—and if Dan had, Cort was to keep him from being a problem again. Yet Dan had saved Cort, sacrificing his own life in the process.

Why? It didn't make any sense. Why had Dan sold out in the first place? It wasn't about the money. Dan had never cared about that. He'd claimed it wasn't blackmail. Cort fought the memories. He'd gotten what he'd wanted most—he was fit to return to duty. But for what? Did any of it matter anymore?

He stood up and started walking back to the compound. Every step made him more aware of what he'd almost done. He'd accepted a mission that meant killing his friend. What kind of man had he become?

He stepped into the clearing. One of the guards rushed up to him. "We've heard from the missing two men."

"What happened?"

"The Jeep's tires were slashed. When the second guard on went to go get help, he was knocked out and left tied up."

"Anyone hurt?"

"No. Andy put a call in to the police. We have to report the intruder and the shooting."

"Good." Cort shook off the memories clinging to him and jogged toward the main building. He needed to make sure Faith was going to be all right.

Thomas pounded on the steering wheel of the sedan and cursed out loud. Every damn thing that could go wrong had. If he'd believed in luck, he would swear his was all bad.

He eased up on the gas as he negotiated a rough patch of ground and headed for the paved driveway leading out of the compound. He'd left the gate open when he'd come through two hours before, in case he had to leave in a hurry. He reached over and grabbed the remote-control device he'd stolen from Ken's truck, fingering the open button. Someone might have closed it.

He hadn't even gotten close, he thought with disgust. Even going up the driveway and parking a couple hundred yards downwind of the compound hadn't helped him get in without being seen. Those damn cats had begun acting funny, spooking him with their silent appraisal. He hated animals. He'd have to come up with a better plan. Time was—

He rounded the last bend and cursed when he saw the two trucks parked in front of the closed gate. Two men took up positions on either side of their vehicles and pulled out guns. One reached for something. Thomas punched the "open" button on the gate remote at the same time he hit the gas. The dark sedan jumped forward. Just in time, he remembered the asphalt gave way to a bumpy dirt road that would destroy the underside of his car. He jerked the steering wheel hard to the left and bounced off the road.

The rear end fishtailed on the soft ground, but he didn't ease up on the gas.

One guard raised a gun in his direction. Thomas ignored him. The gate continued to swing open. Tree branches scratched against his windows. He smiled. The jerks had parked their trucks too far away from the gate. They hadn't planned on anyone going around. He would be able to slip through easily.

A bullet hit the passenger door.

"Amateurs," Thomas muttered. He jammed on the brakes as the car rolled onto the bumpy road. Turning sharply to the right, then left, he drove between the gate post and the trucks. The rear of his car just grazed the smaller vehicle. Two more bullets hit his car. One popped through the rear windshield and stopped in the passenger seat.

Sweat popped out on Thomas's back. Maybe he'd been too quick to dismiss them. Then his front wheels rolled onto smooth public road. He floored the gas pedal and went screaming down the highway without looking back.

Fifteen minutes later he pulled into an abandoned barn and turned off the engine. If the guards had followed, he'd lost them when he'd left the highway and turned onto the backroads. But he couldn't keep playing around like this. Obviously he wasn't going to be able to steal the cubs without someone seeing, so why worry about subtlety? It was time to bring in reinforcements.

"Anything else you can add, ma'am?" the police officer asked.

Faith shook her head. "No. I'm sure they were after the white tiger cubs, but I don't know the name of the people interested in them. I've given your detective the phone number of the man in charge of this case." She reached up and rubbed her eyes. They, along with almost every other part of her body, hurt. "Jeff didn't bother to tell me names, and quite frankly, I didn't want to know who they were."

"Thank you." The officer smiled politely and left.

Faith leaned forward and rested her arms on her desk. It was almost two in the morning. The police had arrived an hour before and had combed the compound, searching for clues and asking everyone questions that couldn't be answered. Of course the man had been after the tiger cubs. But Cort and his team had handled the situation. She just wanted the police gone.

"How are you holding up?" Cort asked.

She raised her head and saw him standing in the doorway of her office. Sometime in the last hour he'd pulled on a sweatshirt. But his hair was still rumpled from sleep, and he needed a shave. He looked wonderful.

"I'm surviving," she said. "Are they almost done?"

"Yeah. Look at this." He moved into the room and held out a small plastic bag. A flattened slug rested in one corner.

"What is it?"

"A bullet. They found three altogether."

For the first time since Sparky had awakened her with his restless pacing, she smiled. "You'll have to forgive me if I don't share your enthusiasm. Finding bullets is rarely the highlight of my day."

"I'm having the police forward Jeff one of the bullets."

"What does he make of all this?"

"He's out of the country for the next two days. Nobody knows where he is. I can't get ahold of him."

"Don't look so grim. We'll be fine."

He settled on the corner of her desk. "I would like to pack you and the cubs up and get the three of you out of here until Jeff gets back and can make other arrangements."

She shook her head. "Don't even think about it. I can't leave the other cats. If it makes you feel any better, I'm going to call the kids and tell them not to come in to work until Saturday. That way there are fewer of us to guard. It's only a couple more days until Jeff moves the cubs. With you and your security team here, we'll make it."

"I wish I had your optimism." He shook his head. "Because this isn't an official operation, I'm going to have trouble getting more security. In the morning I can call in a few favors and see what happens. I just wish I knew where Jeff was."

"There's nothing you can do about it now." She reached up to touch him, then winced as pain shot through her arm.

Cort glanced down at the blood on her T-shirt. "You get anyone to look at that?"

"It's just a scratch. I think a piece of wood or something caught me. I'm fine."

He grabbed her good arm and pulled her to her feet.

"Where are we going?" she asked.

Instead of answering, he led her into the examining room, placed his hands on her waist and lifted her onto the high metal table. "Wait right here," he told her, then disappeared.

She heard him ushering the police out of the building and giving instructions to the security guards. The back door closed, and she heard the sound of a lock clicking into place.

"Is everything all right?" she asked.

"Yes. I've left two men on for the rest of tonight. Nothing is going to happen for the next few hours." He frowned. "I'd feel better if I knew where Jeff had run off to."

After washing his hands and collecting supplies, he stood next to her and gently tried to push up her T-shirt sleeve. Pain shot through her as the dried blood peeled off her skin. She flinched.

"We'd better take this off," he said, fingering the T-shirt. "One way or the other, you're going to have to pull it over the wound. Might as well be now."

She fought the instinct to cross her arms over her chest to protect herself. With the rush to figure out what Sparky was so upset about, she hadn't bothered to put on a bra. Was this how Cort had felt when she'd told him to take his shirt off? She bit back a smile. No, she didn't think he'd had quite the same reservations.

She pulled up the hem and slipped her good arm out of its sleeve, then tugged the shirt over her head. He took it from her and gently peeled it down the wound and dropped the T-shirt on her lap. The air felt cool on her breasts and she knew her nipples were puckering.

She glanced at Cort, but he was looking at her with all the interest of a vet looking at a sick cat. He stared at her wound and nothing else. She'd really impressed him with her feminine charms. Casually, she drew the shirt up in front of her and covered her bare chest. He didn't notice that, either.

"I don't see any fragments," he said. "Looks like a deep cut. I'll clean it up and bandage it."

He reached for the cleaning fluid and thoroughly doused her arm. She studied his familiar face and the focused look in his eyes. There was something about the set of his jaw. Lines of pain straightened his mouth. He looked like a man who had gone ten rounds with the devil and lost.

"Is something wrong?" she asked.

"No, why?"

"You look—" She paused, not sure how to explain it. "Did something else happen tonight? Something you're not telling me?"

Cort moistened sterile cotton with antiseptic. She took a deep breath and nodded. The flare of pain in her arm caused her muscles to stiffen. She forced herself to relax.

"Nothing to worry about," he said. "Whoever was out there made a run for the gates."

"Andy told me. I'm glad no one was hurt."

Cort peeled the protective covering off the bandage and pressed the dressing firmly against her wound. "Good as new."

She glanced down. "First you get hurt in the arm, then it happens to me. Does that mean I'm going to take a bullet in the leg next?" He didn't smile at her attempt at humor. There *was* something bothering him. "What is it?"

"Nothing." He collected the medicines and put them away.

"Cort, what's going on?" She slipped off the table, clutching her shirt in front of her.

"I told you everything is fine. Go to bed, Faith."

He stood with his back to her. She could practically see the pain radiating from him, but she didn't know how to make him talk to her. What had happened to him tonight?

"I'm going to take a shower," she said at last. "If you need me, I'm—"

He cut her off. "Good night."

She left because she couldn't think of any reason to stay. She took a quick shower, careful to keep her bandage dry, and changed back into the oversize T-shirt she was sleeping in. Then she turned off the light and crawled into bed. But instead of lying down and trying to sleep, she leaned against the headboard and stared into the dark.

She could hear Cort pacing restlessly up and down the hall. It stopped long enough for him to take a shower as well, then resumed. She heard him speak softly to Sparky, then a grunting "humph" as the big cat settled down in her office. The minutes ticked by.

Ten minutes, she thought. She would give him ten minutes, and if he didn't stop pacing and go to bed, she was going to demand he tell her what was going on.

She actually waited fifteen because she chickened out twice before finally throwing back the covers on the queen-size bed and stepping onto the floor. Her bare toes curled against the cold wood. She opened her door and stepped into the hall.

She found Cort in her small kitchen. He stood beside the Formica table, leaning against the window, staring out into the dark forest.

He'd brushed his hair away from his face, and the dampness made the gold-blond strands look darker. Jeans covered the lower half of his body, but his chest and back were bare. His muscles bunched under his skin as if he was steeling himself against whatever troubled him. He hadn't bothered to shave, and stubble outlined his jaw. He braced one arm up high on the window frame, the other hung at his side. Both hands were clenched into fists.

"Why aren't you asleep?" he asked without turning toward her.

He didn't sound angry. That gave her hope. She risked moving closer to him. She hovered by the counter before stepping toward the table and chairs. "Do you want to talk about it?" she asked softly.

Slowly he lowered his arm and turned to look at her. She almost cried out at the raw anguish in his eyes. "You don't want to know, Faith. Go back to bed and leave me alone."

"I can't," she said.

"I'm still just like one of your cats, aren't I? You can't bear to see any of us suffering." He shrugged. "I'm not bleeding anywhere for you to patch me up. Sorry."

He wasn't like one of her cats. He was far more dangerous. A man like him could leave her battered and broken, without ever touching her. That's because it was more than her body that was at risk; it was her heart. But he was right about one thing—she couldn't turn her back on his pain.

"Don't apologize," she said. "I heard you pacing and I want to do whatever I can. Would you like a drink?"

"I still haven't recovered from the rum."

"Oh." She twisted her hands together, not sure if she should leave. Obviously he didn't want to tell her what was wrong. "If you're sure I can't..." He didn't say anything. She drew in a breath. "Good night." She turned toward the hallway.

"Wait."

He'd spoken the words so softly, she wasn't sure she'd heard him. "What did you say?"

He pulled a chair back and invited her to sit down. "Don't go. Please. You're right. Something did happen."

She walked over to the chair and sat. He took the seat next to her. His elbows rested on his knees as he clasped his hands together. Cort studied his white knuckles and rubbed a scar at the base of his thumb.

"I remembered the rest of it," he said abruptly. "I got my memory back."

It took her a minute to figure out what he was talking about. "Your last mission? That's terrific. Now you can—"

"No." He cut her off. "It's not like that. I—" He swore. "I told you I was sent in to take care of a rogue agent? That he'd turned?"

Faith shifted in the hard-backed chair and pulled her T-shirt down until it reached her knees. "Yes, but you didn't kill him. You told me that, too."

"I was prepared to. When he refused to come back with me, I had my gun out and was ready to get it over with."

She swallowed the sudden bitter taste in her mouth. She was sorry now that she'd pried. She knew whatever he said was going to haunt her for a long time.

He raised his head and looked at her. Despair and self-loathing swirled in his brown eyes. Pain deepened the lines by his mouth. "He died for me. To save my useless butt. And I don't know why."

"Why he turned in the first place, or why he saved you?"

"Both. Either. I don't care. I want answers and I can't get any."

"How did it happen?" she asked.

"The bad guys showed up just as our rescue plane landed. I took a bullet in the leg." He jerked his head toward his healed wound. "Dan hauled me out to the plane, but refused to come on board. He stood there like some hell-bent hero and shot at them. While they pumped his body full of lead, we got away."

She leaned toward him and gently touched his cheek. He didn't pull back. She stroked the warm skin, her palm rasping against the stubble. "Maybe he knew he had nowhere to go. If he came back here, he would have been tried and sent to prison."

Cort laughed without humor. "Dan would rather have died than go there." He stopped suddenly. "That bastard. He died anyway."

"But this way, he gave his life for something good. He saved you."

He looked up at her. "Hardly a fair exchange." He straightened up. Her hand fell away and she clutched her arms to her chest.

"It used to be easy," he said. "We knew who the enemies were. Now the lines are blurring. Jeff keeps telling me to come in. Maybe I should. Maybe it's clearer if you have the big picture. Maybe it's too late for any of it. All the good guys are dead."

"Was Dan one of the good guys?"

He leaned back in his chair. "You like asking the tough questions, don't you?"

She shrugged. "Just trying to be a friend."

"Are we friends, Faith?"

"I hoped so."

"I'm not sure you need a friend like me."

She wanted to tell him that she needed a friend *exactly* like him. More than that, she needed a man like him. This night, the trouble with the cubs, the passage of time, Cort's leaving getting closer and closer, all reminded her how tenuous everything had become. In a few short days, her life would revert to normal. Cort would be nothing but a memory.

His pain was as tangible as the man himself. It radiated out from him and surrounded her, seeping inside until she wanted to weep for his suffering. It wasn't because he reminded her of her cats and she wanted to heal his wounds. It was more than that. She had come to care for this man. More than was safe.

She wanted to blurt out that fact, but knew he wouldn't take comfort in her feelings. Instead she risked speaking a smaller truth.

"I do need a friend like you," she whispered.

His brown eyes glowed as if lit with a fire. "Not as much as I need you."

The flame of his desire stirred her own to life. His uncharacteristic admission gave her courage. Without giving herself time to think, she rose to her feet and held out her hand.

He stared at her. "I don't think this is a good idea."

"Don't think anymore," she told him. She bent down, took his hand in hers and tugged him to his feet. He rose slowly, towering over her.

"You tempt me," he said, his gaze locking with hers.

Her knees trembled; he made her weak and yet at the same time, incredibly strong. "Good. I want—"

She never got to say what she wanted.

Chapter 13

Even as his mouth came down on hers, she clutched at his shoulders for balance. His skin was hot beneath her fingers. The anticipation of their kiss left her dizzy. She remembered the passion that had flared between them before.

The moment his lips pressed against hers, she felt as if her bones were slowly melting. Firm lips, soft pressure and hard, hard heat molded to her. Instantly, she parted to admit him. His tongue swept inside. She tasted the faint mint of toothpaste and something else. Something heady and sweet that could only be Cort himself. She met his caresses with slow sweeping strokes of her own. His stubble prickled her skin, adding to the deluge of sensation. She clung to him as her world narrowed to this moment. Her muscles quivered, and she feared she might collapse right there on the kitchen floor.

His hands moved up and down her sides, each pass raising her oversize T-shirt higher and higher until her midriff was exposed. He caressed her bare stomach down to her panties, then moved behind and cupped the curve of her buttocks.

She angled her head to deepen the kiss, and at the same time pressed her hips against him. His jeans felt rough against her belly, and his hardness strained against his button fly.

She moved her hands up his neck to the silk of his gold-blond hair. The short strands slipped through her fingers, their coolness a delicious contrast to the heat flaring between them.

He raised his head slightly and gazed down at her. Passion drew the lines of his face taut. His mouth was moist from her kiss, his lips slightly parted. His bare chest rose and fell with each breath he took.

"Faith." He spoke her name softly.

The sound whispered against her skin. She lowered her hands until they rested on his arms. Beneath her fingers, his muscles tightened, the sinewy length defined and powerful. Their eyes met. She saw the wanting there, and the affection. In his way, he cared for her. It was enough.

He squeezed her derriere. The need between them rose to an unbearable pitch. She could hear it filling the room, pressing against her until she could barely breathe. She felt as if she had wanted him forever. She'd needed him for even longer. She had been waiting for the right moment, the right man, to risk sharing her heart and her body again. And now she wanted to be a part of him, joining in the ancient ritual of love.

At the exact moment he bent down to kiss her again, she reached up to pull him close. Their mouths joined in a conflagration of tastes and pressures. She licked his lips frantically as if he were her only source of sustenance. He grasped the hem of her T-shirt and pulled. They parted long enough for him to draw it over her head. He paused to slide it gently over the bandage on her arm. When he'd freed the garment, he tossed it aside and reached for her breasts.

She swelled under the onslaught of his tender touch. Strong hands cupped her curves, weighing them in his palms, moving across her hard nipples. She moaned her pleasure as he swept his fingers over and around her breasts. He bent down to take her in his mouth. Sensation shot through her, reaching to her fingertips and toes, then collecting between her thighs.

He stepped back enough to pull her panties down to the floor, then grabbed her by the waist and lifted her onto the kitchen table. The tabletop felt cold on her bare derriere. She gasped at the contact. He grinned, then moved between her legs and urged her to lie back. His strong arms protected her from the table, while her position raised her exposed chest to him and thrust her breasts forward. He nibbled at her jaw and neck, moving lower, leaving a wet trail across her throat and her chest. His stubble rasped delightfully. His hands supported her head as he took first one, then the other nipple in his mouth. He dueled with the puckered tips, sucked them deeply and raised up far enough to blow on the trembling, damp skin. He rubbed his fingers through her long hair, massaging her scalp, easing tension even as his mouth sought to increase it.

She arched against him. Her bare femininity brushed against his jeans and his hardness. She rocked her hips gently, teasing him as well as herself, but it wasn't enough. The wanting grew. She stretched her arms out to undo the first button, but couldn't reach it, so she brushed her hands on his arms and continued to move herself against him, trying frantically to ease the ache. He groaned softly with each flexing of her body.

He pulled her upright and kissed her hard. Their lips pressed together. Her heart pounded and her lungs burned for more air, as her blood surged through her body. Pressure and hunger built inside her. There was no time to think or analyze. She could only feel. Spreading her legs wide, she urged him closer. His jeans stood between them. She reached for the buttons and quickly popped them open. His hands clutched at her shoulders. His fingers bit into her as she freed him. She pushed the jeans to the floor and touched him.

He filled her hand. All long, hot maleness. So ready. She stared up at his face. He stood with his eyes closed, his expression savage. There was no pretense in their mating. It was primal and necessary. If she didn't have this man, if he didn't ease the ache within her, she would perish.

She stroked his length. He groaned, then opened his eyes and looked at her. His gaze dropped to her hands holding him. Immediately she started to become aware of herself and began to pull away. He put his hand over hers and refused to let her go. Their eyes met. He kept his hand over hers and urged her to move back and forth. Beneath her hand, he felt hot and smooth and hard. Above her hand, the calluses of his palm rubbed her knuckles, and his fingers slipped between hers.

With each stroke, the fire in his eyes grew brighter. The pulse at the base of his throat thundered in time with her own. Between her thighs, moisture collected in anticipation of her release. She rocked her hips, wanting to ease the ache. At last he pushed her hand away and moved closer to her. He probed her moist center, rubbing his tip against her most sensitive place. She arched her back and let her eyes drift shut.

Up and down, yet barely moving at all, he teased her until she could do little but writhe at his command. She strained forward, toward her peak. At last, when the release was as inevitable as the tide, he plunged inside of her. Her breath escaped with an audible sound. He pulled her legs tightly around his hips and began to plunge back and forth. Her hands clutched at him; his reached for her breasts and touched her hard nipples. She became lost in the journey, focusing on nothing but the sensation of him driving in and out of her. Deep inside, the pressure built and built until she had to give herself up to his rhythm.

He let go of her breasts and hauled her up against him. As his mouth claimed her, as she touched his tongue with hers, she plunged into the madness. It swept her along, rippling her muscles around him, as he surged deeper and his release joined hers.

The fires faded slowly, and she returned to normal. The night was silent except for the sound of their ragged breathing. When Cort tried to ease her back, she clung to him, burying her face in his chest. Now that she'd been sated, sanity returned. She didn't want to look at him and see what he must think of her. She'd acted like an animal, mating with him like that. She'd had no time to question her actions, she'd simply reacted. She squeezed her eyes shut. They'd done it on the kitchen table!

But he refused to be put off. He drew her arms from around his neck and brought her hands to his mouth. After kissing each of her palms, he slipped out from between her legs.

She kept her eyes tightly closed. "Cort, I—"

"Hush," he murmured. She felt him reach under her thighs and behind her back, then he was lifting her.

Her eyes opened. "What are you doing?"

"Taking you to bed." He smiled down at her. "It's a little more civilized, don't you think?"

He didn't look shocked by what they had done, she saw with some relief. Maybe, just maybe, he'd felt the incredible passion, too.

When he placed her in the center of her mattress, she tensed, waiting to see if he would leave her. She need not have worried. He slipped in next to her and pulled the covers up over both of them. She turned on her side, and he snuggled up behind her, fitting his body around hers. One of his arms rested on her waist. She pulled it between her breasts and laced his fingers through hers. She felt soft kisses on her shoulder.

"Thank you," she whispered.

"You're welcome. Thank *you*."

She smiled. "It's never been that...that wild before." She bit her lip. "You probably think I'm silly."

"Never." He raised up on one elbow and pressed on her shoulder until she half turned to look at him. His gold-flecked eyes still glowed from their inner fire. He touched her swollen mouth with his finger. "It was extraordinary and extremely powerful." He gave her a rueful grin. "Too powerful. I never thought to ask about protection. I know it's a little like closing the barn door after the horse has left, but were you protected?"

"Yes."

"Good."

Cort lowered himself back down onto the bed. He waited for the tidal wave of relief to sweep over him. It had been stupid as hell to make love with Faith without checking to see if she could get pregnant. For once, though, the thought of being tied down with a relationship and a child didn't send him reaching for his jeans and car keys.

It was just exhaustion, he told himself. That and the fact that Faith's bed was a lot more comfortable than his cot. Or maybe it was the scent of her body. He leaned close to her back and sniffed. She smelled of sex and French perfume.

The lights he'd set up in front of the building shone through the window blinds. He could just make out the four parallel scars on her shoulder and down her arm. He touched his mouth to those puckered lines. She wiggled against him. Her round derriere brushed against his groin, stirring him back to life. Slowly, he traced the scars with his tongue. The contrast of textures, rough and bumpy on the scars, smooth and silky on her skin, intrigued him. He licked them again.

"I knew it would be like this," she murmured.

"Why?"

"The alpha male always makes the best mate."

He smiled against her. "Am I the alpha male?" he asked, then trailed kisses down her back.

"Uh-huh." She sounded distracted.

He ran his tongue up every bump in her spine, then pushed her long hair aside and nibbled on the back of her neck. She moved her hips back toward him. Need surged between his legs and he felt himself growing harder.

"What makes me the alpha male?" he asked.

"Size, courage. The a-ah—"

He sucked on her earlobe. "Go on."

"The ability to lead the pack. Acceptance by others."

"Including the female?"

He leaned over and kissed her throat. She tilted her head to expose herself more. "Especially the female."

Her eyes were closed. She looked as relaxed and pliable as a cat getting her ears scratched. But he wasn't interested in her ears.

He trailed more kisses down her spine, then tossed back the covers exposing her bare buttocks and legs to view. She gasped when he nibbled the sensitive skin behind her knees. She parted her thighs when he slipped his hand between them and stroked her damp center. She raised her hips back toward him when he nibbled the round curves of her rear. He was already hard and throbbing. He could feel her moistness.

He bent over her back and kissed her neck. Then he bit her, hard enough to make her jump. A shiver ran through her. With one hand, he reached between her thighs and found her waiting wetness. He touched her sensitive core, and she spread her legs farther. He bit her again, then pressed his hardness against her and plunged inside.

She moaned and pushed against him, until the backs of her thighs pressed against the front of his. He continued to rub her center, matching the rhythm of his strokes. With his other hand, he reached around to feel her breasts. They bounced with each thrust, the hard nipples brushing against his hand. He squeezed gently. She cried out, and he felt the quick pulsing of her orgasm.

When her contractions had stopped, he withdrew, turned her onto her back and thrust into her again. Her eyes were wide and unfocused. She grabbed at his shoulders, pulling him down close, then kissing him hungrily. She bit his lower lip, sucked it in her mouth and soothed the hurt. She grabbed his buttocks and pulled him so close he thought he might explode inside of her. She clawed at his back and tossed her head from side to side.

He felt the pressure building inside him. She moved her hips faster and faster. As all his energy collected between his legs in preparation for that moment of release, he felt her contractions begin again. She lifted off the bed and clutched at him. Her eyes met his. He saw the pleasure in her face even as he felt her body quiver around his.

And then he couldn't think at all. He could only feel and stare at her, knowing she saw the same ecstacy in his expression. The climax went on and on, draining him of all thought, all coherency, until he could only collapse on the bed and pull her down next to him. Tremors shook their bodies. Sweat-slicked skin slid on the cotton sheets.

She touched his face, then leaned close and kissed the bullet wound on his arm. He touched his lips to the scars on her arm. They stared at each other in silent understanding. He had never felt this contentment, this connection, and it scared him to death. He pulled her close and shifted so she could rest her head on his shoulder. He didn't want her to see the fear in his eyes.

Cort held her in his arms until she fell asleep. He brushed her hair from her brow and stroked her cheek. Unfamiliar tenderness welled up inside of him, stretching his heart into new and painful vulnerability.

When Faith sighed and rolled away from him, he slipped out of the bed and looked down at her. The light from outside illuminated her long hair which flowed over her bare shoulders. He could make out the four scars across the back of her arm. The scent of her perfume mingled with the pleasing aroma of sex and animal heat. He pulled the covers up around her and walked silently out of the room.

In the kitchen he found his jeans and slipped them on. While he made coffee, he put on boots and a sweatshirt. Then he filled a mug and carried it to his bedroom, where he collected his gun and made his way to the foyer. He sat on the worn vinyl couch by the door and waited.

His muscles ached pleasurably from their lovemaking. He was tired, but he wouldn't sleep. Not until he knew Faith was safe. Pictures filled his mind. Pictures of her and the way she gave herself completely to him. Of naked female flesh, full breasts, long legs. Of the expression on her face as she lost herself to pleasure and forced him to do the same.

He smiled slightly and sipped his coffee. The smile faded as the pictures changed, mingling past and present, and he remembered how Dan had died in a field, shot down by arms dealers in the dead of a South American night.

He would never know why Dan had decided to go to the other side. Just as he would never know if he could have killed his friend. He'd been so sure at first, confident he could have done what was asked of him. He'd told himself it was just another mission. Now he knew better.

The comfort of a job done well mattered little in the cold hours before dawn. He suspected blackness had filled his soul many years ago. It was a price of his occupation, one he'd paid without question. The state of his soul had never mattered before. But Faith had reminded him to look past the obvious to what was important.

Cort chambered a round into his Beretta and checked to make sure the safety was on. Sparky padded down the hall and sat down beside him. The large black leopard rested his head on Cort's thigh. Cort scratched the animal's ears and listened to the sounds of the night. The big cats outside paced and called out; all was well in their world, if not in his.

Yet, if given the chance to do it all again, he would change nothing. Not the suffering he'd seen, not the questions, not even what he had tried to forget. Sparky leaned heavily against him and huffed out a sigh. Cort rested his hand on the animal's powerful shoulders.

Better to have seen hell and survived, he told himself, better to have a dark, empty soul, because he knew what he was capable of. He knew all the variations of the game, and he trusted his ability to keep Faith and the cubs safe. In the past, his missions had been a battle of wits—him against the enemy. This time the stakes were much higher.

Sparky stretched out and rested his head on his paws. Cort welcomed the company on his vigil. He knew the leopard shared his desire to protect. Whatever it took, Cort would pay the price. He was the best at what he did, and he would give his life before he would let anything happen to Faith.

* * *

At first light, Thomas backed the car out of the abandoned barn and returned to the main road. He drove past Bowmund and on to the next town. There he left the rental parked on a side street, walked to another car rental agency and got a good-sized van using one of his false IDs. The police would find the black sedan and notify the other rental company, but Thomas didn't care. He hadn't used his real name there, either.

He drove back to Bowmund, collected his belongings and checked out of the motel, paying the bill with cash. He got in the van and started driving.

He'd had a lot of time to think about what went wrong last night. His goal had been to collect the cubs without anyone knowing. But why was that necessary? All the stealth was getting in his way. Last night, those damn cats had spooked him. So much so, his shots aimed at the woman had gone wide.

He was no closer to getting the cubs than he'd been a week ago. Time was running out. The people guarding the cubs weren't stupid. Now that he'd shown himself, they were probably making plans to move the cubs. He had to get the job done tonight. But he couldn't do it alone.

He drove to a liquor store next to an alley. The store was closed. Parking the van close to the building, he went to the public phone on the outside wall and dialed a number.

"Yes?" a man answered.

"It's Thomas."

"You have the cubs?"

"No."

The man on the other end was silent. Thomas would have preferred him to get angry. Despite the cool morning, sweat collected on his back and his upper lip.

"I need men and supplies," he said quickly. "I want to take the cubs tonight."

"I'll send what you need," the man said. "But this plan must work the first time. Our mutual employer returns tomorrow."

Thomas fought down a flash of panic. "He's early."

"He would have arrived today, but there has been some unpleasantness with the federal government. It will be straightened out by the end of the day. You must get the cubs."

"I understand." Thomas quickly explained his needs and made arrangements for a meeting at four o'clock that afternoon. By the time he drove up the mountain it would be dark. He would wait until around ten, and then go in and take the cubs.

"Do not fail," the man told him.

"I won't," Thomas promised, and prayed he wasn't lying.

Chapter 14

Faith shifted in her bed. Her hand bumped something hard and flat, and she heard the rattle of silverware. She opened her eyes and saw Sparky leaning over the bed, eating off a tray beside her.

"What on earth...?"

The leopard looked up briefly, then reached over and lapped up a pile of scrambled eggs with a single swipe of his tongue. The toast followed in a quick gulp.

Faith grinned and pushed herself into a sitting position. She leaned against the headboard and brushed her hair out of her face.

"I don't think that's for you," she told the cat. He didn't look chastised.

Faith heard footsteps in the hallway. She pulled the sheet up to her shoulders. Sparky grabbed all three strips of bacon and made a beeline for the door.

"What the hell?" Cort said as the leopard sprinted past him. He entered the room, took one look at the tray and spun around to chase the animal. "You bring that back here." His voice faded as he jogged down the hall.

Faith giggled and used the moment to duck into the bathroom. With every move, unfamiliar muscles reminded her of what had gone on the previous night. She didn't regret what had happened. How could she? Cort had shown her things, made her feel sensations, she'd never imagined. Their bodies had reacted as if they'd been specially formed to bring each other pleasure. The trick was going to be whether or not she could keep Cort from figuring out she'd given him more than a night of pleasure. Sometime between hot hungry kisses and sweat-slicked thrusts, she'd also handed over her heart.

She stared at her face in the mirror. She didn't look especially different. Her eyes seemed a little brighter this morning, her mouth smiled easily. Her lips were still swollen from his kisses and the abrasion from his stubble, but other than that, she had no outward evidence that she was in love.

Love. She leaned against the sink. A big mistake. Cort was like all the other men she had known: He would leave her. This time however, she had only herself to blame for her heartbreak. She'd known from the beginning that his stay in her life was temporary. So why had she let herself care?

She heard him enter her bedroom and knew she couldn't hide out in the bathroom forever. Better to face him and get it over with. When she'd washed her face and brushed her teeth, she pulled her robe from the back of the bathroom door and slipped it on. She paused with her hand on the doorknob and reminded herself Cort had admired her for her courage. She couldn't let him down.

She drew in a deep breath and opened the door, then breezed across the hall to her bedroom. Cort was stretched out on the bed, on top of the covers, his arms folded behind his head. Worn jeans and a white shirt outlined his lean body. His tanned skin accentuated the gold flecks in his brown eyes. One lock of hair tumbled onto his forehead. After last night, she probably had the right to sit on the edge of the bed and brush it back with her fingers. No doubt he wouldn't even blink if she then leaned forward and kissed him. He might even respond.

But as she hovered by the foot of the bed, shyness gripped her. It had been a long time since she'd had to face the awkwardness of the morning after. It hadn't gotten any easier with time.

"I meant to surprise you," he said, pulling back the covers and patting the bed. "That cat ate your breakfast. I'm sorry."

"Don't be." She smiled hesitantly. "I appreciate the thought."

"Come here." He motioned for her to come closer.

She took a step in his direction.

"No, here." He touched the sheet. "I want to say good morning."

She moved forward and gingerly sat on the edge of the mattress.

He raised himself up on one elbow. "Don't," he said, taking her arm and pulling her close to him. "Don't regret last night."

"I don't. It's just—"

He didn't let her finish. He drew her closer and then claimed her mouth with his. The kisses demanded little from her. He pressed his lips fully on hers, then slid them back and forth until she parted to admit him.

His tongue swept over hers, gently, slowly, as if this sweet contact had nothing to do with the tempest from the night before. Without breaking contact, he lowered her onto the bed. She let her eyes drift shut and gave herself up to the feel of him.

It was different this morning. In the light of day, after admitting her feelings to herself, she felt raw and exposed in his presence. And yet she needed to be with him, to be held by him. The one man who would cause her heartache was the only man who could comfort her.

But it was more than comfort. He moved closer to her and loosened her short cotton robe. He tugged on the belt until it gave way, then parted the edges. She felt the cool morning air on her bare skin. Before she could open her eyes or even think about protesting, he cupped one breast in his hand.

She moaned. Their loving last night had left her tender. He seemed to know that instinctively, for he cupped her curves with the gentleness of a man handling priceless crystal. He barely grazed her nipples with his fingertips, yet electricity shot through her.

She reached up to slip her fingers through his hair, then moved down to grip his shoulders. He kissed her lips once more before moving to her neck, then lower to her breasts, where he sweetly sucked her into mindless passion, then lower across her belly. His fingers led the way, seeking her most sensitive spots. His mouth followed, loving the places that made her tighten and writhe and toss her head from side to side. Closer and closer, until he kissed her most secret place. He touched her with the tip of his tongue, making her jump. She drew her knees up and parted her thighs. He tasted her fully, then cupped her buttocks and gently assaulted her center, moving in a slow rhythm that threatened to drive her mad with passion before allowing her to seek her release.

It built slowly at first, like a single spark beginning a fire. The embers caught and grew, glowing hotter and hotter. Her skin burned as if lit from within. Her breasts swelled, and between her legs the flames enveloped her. Her heart pounded in her ears. From outside, she could hear the guards talking, the cats as they played and called to each other. Yet that world wasn't real. All that mattered was Cort and the magic he plied between her thighs. The flames grew and grew, pushing her higher with each flick of his tongue, yet the explosion surprised her.

She found herself tossed to the wind, carried aloft by the heat, then brought back to the real world, caught safely in Cort's arms. He held her tightly in his embrace as her body quivered in aftermath. Oddly, her eyes burned and she fought the need to cry. She wasn't sad or in pain. It wasn't her nature to give in to tears. She wondered why he was able to reduce her to such raw, exposed need.

He shifted until her head rested on his shoulder. "That was because Sparky ate your breakfast," he said as he stroked her hair.

She sighed in contentment. "What do I get if he eats my dinner?"

He chuckled. She heard the sound and felt the vibration in his chest. "You'll just have to wait and see."

She reached down and cupped the hardness straining at the button fly of his jeans. "You deserve a reward for going to all the trouble of cooking my breakfast."

He lifted her hand and brought it to his lips. "Later," he promised and kissed her fingers one by one.

She pulled her arm back and gazed at him. "Cort?"

"It's all right." He smiled. "I pleased you. That's all I want right now."

"But you, ah—" she glanced at his crotch "—obviously—"

He cupped her chin in his hand. "Yes, I am aroused. Yes, I could make love to you right now and it would be great. This was a different kind of pleasure. Let me enjoy it."

The tears she'd fought moments before threatened again. She blinked several times, then nodded and rested her head back on his shoulder.

"Thank you," she whispered.

"You're welcome. How do you feel?"

"Are you fishing for compliments?"

"I don't have to," he said smugly. "How's the arm?"

She rotated her shoulder. "I'd almost forgotten. It feels fine."

"Maybe you should try take to it easy. You didn't get a lot of sleep last night."

"Neither did you."

He shrugged. "With everything that's going on, you need your rest."

Something in his tone caused a vague feeling of discomfort to steal over her, dissipating the lingering glow of their lovemaking. She raised herself on one elbow and looked down at him. "If I didn't know better, I'd say you were trying to keep me in bed this morning."

"Is that so bad?"

Yes, because it was completely unlike him. "What's wrong?"

Cort hesitated long enough for her stomach to lurch. "Nothing specific," he said at last. "I don't like the fact that Ken is still missing and I can't get ahold of Jeff. I've called a couple of friends and we'll have a few more security people here by nightfall."

"Are the cats all right?"

"Fine. I fed them earlier and I was about to start on their cages."

"I can do that," she said, sitting up and reaching for her robe. "They're my cats. I'm responsible for them."

"I wish you'd consider spending a couple of days in L.A. or San Francisco."

"No." She rose to her feet and tied the belt at her waist. "This is where I belong. I'm not afraid."

Cort shrugged as if to say he'd done the best he could, then he stood up and started toward the door.

"Is that—" She stopped talking long enough to clear her throat. She didn't want to ask, but she had to know. When she spoke again, she forced her voice to come out level, so he wouldn't know she was trembling. "Is that what this was about?" she asked, glancing at the bed. "Were you trying to distract me?"

"Faith, no." He crossed the room in three strides and gathered her close to him.

She hated herself for the weakness that invaded her body, knew she would regret clinging to him as if she was drowning and he was her lifeline, but she couldn't help herself.

"Never," he murmured, touching her hair, her back, her arms, then cupping her face and tenderly kissing her mouth. "I'd never hurt you."

Deliberately, she thought, mentally voicing the unspoken word. Because he would hurt her—he would leave.

"And I'll never abandon my cats," she said, disentangling herself from his embrace. "Go on, get out of here so

I can get dressed. I'll meet you at Tigger's cage in ten minutes."

He kissed her once more, then left the room. She stood there, alone. By the end of the week, the cubs would be gone and Cort along with them. She touched her fingers to her mouth. She could almost taste the heartbreak.

Faith stared at the pile of forms on her desk. She'd sorted them by category, dividing them into federal, state and local agencies. Several had to be sent off to her attorney. About a third of them were finished. Those she slipped into envelopes and put in an empty box. The rest still had to be filled out. She fingered the two-inch-high pile. Could she do it? Could she not?

Sparky strolled into her office, followed by Cort. Despite spending the morning helping her muck out cages, he still looked good, she thought, staring at his face. His hair had grown since he'd been here, and reached about a half inch past his collar. She liked it longer. Faith shook her head. Who was she trying to kid? She liked everything about him.

"Now what are you working on?" he asked, plopping down in the chair in front of her desk.

"More forms."

"So you've decided to go ahead with the snow-leopard project?"

"I guess."

He grinned. "That doesn't sound too enthusiastic."

"I'm not convinced I'm going to make it, but I've realized I have to try."

His gold-flecked eyes flickered with something that might have been respect. "I always knew you would."

She leaned forward and grabbed the top form. "While you're expounding on your precognitive powers, why not give me a little peek into the future and tell me how it's all going to turn out? You could save me dozens of sleepless nights."

"I have every confidence in you."

She tossed the form into the air and watched it flutter back to her desk. Sparky settled in the corner and yawned. She envied the big cat his simple, boring life. Right now, boring looked pretty appealing.

"Why are you so sure it's going to happen?" she asked.

He crossed his ankle over his opposite knee. "Because I know you. I know what you're capable of. Remember when we went shooting?"

She nodded.

"You told me you used to be afraid of guns, but you learned how to handle a rifle. Now you're a marksman. You're the best kind of team player, Faith. You're not afraid to get the job done."

His compliments made her want to do something foolish, like blush and stammer. Or worse, tell him how she felt about him. She took a deep breath and did neither.

"I'm still afraid," she said.

"What do you need that you don't have?"

"Aside from these forms and permits, I need—" She stood up and walked over to a map she'd pinned up on the wall. It showed the northeast section of North Dakota reduced to a two-foot square. She'd highlighted the land she'd bought. "I need a road from the state highway up to where I want the breeding center to be. I need to find a vet who wants to learn all he or she can about snow leopards. I need habitats and buildings and a source of food. I need six breeding pairs, but I'd settle for two. I need employees." She touched the map, trying to remember how beautiful and rugged the land had been when she'd visited it last year. "I need a house to live in and a room of some kind, big enough for fund-raising parties." She looked back at Cort and smiled. "Not much, huh?"

He raised his eyebrows. "What's your bottom line?"

"How much money?" She shrugged. "Interesting. I'd need enough for all that I've mentioned, plus the snow leopards. Of course, getting them is a lot more about government forms and legalities than it is about money. Altogether?" She did a couple of mental calculations. "Five million dollars. That would keep me up and running for a year."

Cort let out a low whistle. "I was going to offer to float you a loan, but the spy business doesn't pay *that* well."

"Thanks for the offer, but I wouldn't have accepted, anyway."

"Why? I thought we were friends."

"We are, it's just—" She paused. "What *do* spies spend their money on?"

He stood up and grinned. "Life insurance." He walked over to the map. "How much have you already raised?"

Faith leaned against the wall. "Once I set up my own foundation, the way station will give me a million and a half."

"So you're a third of the way there."

"If I get it all together." She looked at him. "I only have a two-year college degree. I know cats, but I don't know business."

"That's what lawyers are for, Faith. And business managers. Hire someone."

"Edwina always did it herself."

"You're not Edwina. You have other goals."

"I know you're right. I'm just—"

"Scared." He reached out and touched her cheek.

"Yeah. See, I'm not the strong woman you thought I was." She tried to smile, but she could feel her lips quivering and she let it die. Cort stared at her with an intensity that made her uncomfortable. She wanted to lean on him and let him tell her that she could do it, but she knew she would be foolish to start that particular habit.

"What about you?" she asked brightly, stepping away from him and returning to her desk. She perched on the corner. "When Jeff has the cubs moved on Friday, are you going back in the field? Fight the good fight and all that?"

He surprised her by shaking his head. "I'm not sure I can go back."

"Why?"

"What's waiting for me there? Another situation like the one with Dan? How many more friends am I going to be asked to kill?" He laughed harshly and without humor. "Who am I kidding? Except for Jeff, I don't have any friends."

"I'm your friend," she said softly.

"It's a risky proposition. You might want to rethink it, Faith. I could be after you next." He walked across the room, turned and paced back.

"I don't plan on doing anything illegal."

His slight smile gave her hope. She had always been so good at reading her cats when they were in pain. She concentrated and tried to do the same with Cort.

"I belong out in the field," he told her, shoving his hands in his pockets.

"There are other options."

"Come in, you mean? Take that promotion Jeff's been offering me? You think I haven't considered that? But I'm a field man. Jeff had a reason for coming in. I don't."

Jeff's reason had been his wife. Cort had no one. Faith told herself she was foolish to hope, and yet she remembered how tenderly Cort had held her and made love to her last night and this morning. He might still be in love with that other woman, the one who had stolen his heart, but maybe, just maybe, he was starting to care about her, too.

"Maybe you don't have to have a reason to come in," she said. "Maybe it's just the best thing for you to do. You can't punish yourself forever. You have to let go of the past and try to recover. It's been long enough for you to forget." If only he *would* forget.

He came to stop in front of her. "Long enough? It's been less than a month."

"A month? You said it had happened years ago."

Cort's eyebrows drew together. "Dan died on my last mission."

"Dan? I was talking about that woman you loved. The one who broke your heart."

Cort turned away and swore.

"I'm sorry," she said quickly. "I didn't mean to bring up the past. I respect the feelings you had for her. She was a big part of your life, and it's never easy to let something like that go. It's just that I was thinking, you and I . . .''

He started to walk out of the room. Faith swallowed and told herself she'd made a huge mistake. Of course he hadn't recovered from his past. Of course he wasn't interested in a woman like her. It was stupid to imagine otherwise. She wasn't the kind of woman who made men want to stay. She wasn't the kind of woman men loved.

"I shouldn't have said anything." She stared at her hands and twisted her fingers together. "I'm sorry."

Cort slammed his hand against the half-open door. Faith jumped and Sparky half rose to his feet before peering around the room, then settling back down.

"Why do women do this?" he asked, turning to face her. She could see the rage in his eyes. "Why? Can you explain it? I respect you. I care about what happens to you. I had a hell of a good time in bed with you. Why isn't that enough?"

Embarrassment flooded her body, and her cheeks flushed. "I didn't mean—"

"Yes, you did. You want to know about my past, Faith? You want to hear every detail?" He walked over and stood directly in front of her. "I met this girl in college. A few laughs, nothing long lasting. I knew what I wanted, and it wasn't a wife. So one day she says she's pregnant." He planted his hands on his hips. "Great way to mess up a life. Turns out she was just late. As soon as I found out she wasn't pregnant, I took off." He shrugged. "No mess, no broken heart."

Her horror grew with each word of his story. Dear God, she'd ached for him, for a heartbreak that had never existed. "Why did you lie to me?"

"Because you wanted me to. You said you wanted to hear the *real* reason why I wasn't married or involved, but you didn't *really*. You wanted the female fantasy. The truth is, Faith, love is a lie. I never cared about that woman or any woman."

"You never cared about me," she said numbly.

"You're a job. I do my job damn well."

"Especially in bed. I'll have to mention that in my thank-you note to Jeff," she said, then pushed past him. She ran down the hall and out into the compound. Once in the bright sunshine, she paused to catch her breath. Her chest felt tight, as if she'd been running for miles.

Funny how he'd almost made her cry this morning. His tender words and gentle embrace had left her exposed. But this ugly truth didn't make her want to cry. It hurt too much for tears. The hole inside, the place that had been formed by years of her father's abandonment, and later by the man who had left her in college, doubled, then tripled in size in the face of Cort's betrayal.

It was worse this time, because she had known better. Life had taught her the reality of relationships. She'd stopped believing. But Cort had caused her to hope. He'd laid it all out for her to see, all the ugly scars of his past. By spinning his convincing tale, he'd made her think he'd truly loved before. And knowing he had loved once had made her hope he could love again. That was the irony of the situation. He had reminded her of how much she had to give. But it was a gift he didn't want.

She stumbled along the path in front of the cages. Behind her, she heard Cort call her name. She couldn't face him now. She ducked between the two wild jaguars in their cages, narrowly missing being clawed by one of them, and doubled back through the trees. She came out behind Cort, ran into the building and locked herself in her office.

Sparky looked curiously at her as she took Cort's place pacing the room. She wanted to lash out at someone—at the man who had caused this ache. It felt as if her insides were twisting together into a tight knot. She wanted to be comforted and held, but the only person who could make it all go away was the one person who had caused the problem in the first place.

As she approached the wall, she saw her map and the shaded area of her land. She saw the carefully sketched drawing of the habitats and the house. She glanced at the forms piled up on her desk.

With a cry of despair, she picked up her metal trash can, and with one long sweep of her arm, she pulled the forms into the trash. Then she jerked the map from the wall and balled it up. It would never happen. She didn't have the experience or the education. She had nothing but a stupid dream.

She collapsed to the floor and pulled her legs up to her chest.

"Faith!" Cort pounded on the door. "Let me in."

She rested her head on her knees and ignored him. Sparky walked over and nosed her. She ignored the black leopard, too. He bumped her on the shoulder, as if telling her he would always be there, then he laid down next to her and began to purr.

It hurt, she thought, barely able to breathe through the pain. It hurt more than she'd imagined anything could. It wasn't just knowing she'd lost Cort. It was that he wasn't the man she'd thought him to be. She'd lost something that had never existed. The death of a dream. Of hope. He'd played her for a fool, handing her a line he used on all his women. That's what she was, just another woman in a long line of broken hearts. Nothing special at all.

Sparky sniffed her arm. She leaned down and cuddled the big cat, listening to his heartbeat. Cort continued pounding for a few more minutes, then he went away. When the ache in her chest became manageable, she let her gaze drift over the small room. She could be happy here, she told herself. She had been in the past. She could go on with what she was doing, keep the way station successfully. No one expected more.

She looked up at the photos on the wall and saw the two of the snow leopards. She remembered her joy when she'd found out they'd survived after she'd rescued them. She shifted and pulled the trash can close and stared at the forms.

No. She couldn't give up and walk away just because her heart was broken. She couldn't take the coward's way out. She was stronger than that. Due to God or fate or whatever controlled the world, she was in a unique position to make a difference. She might fail, but she had to do her best first. She had to try.

Faith collected the forms and stacked them back on her desk. She smoothed the map flat and pinned it on the wall. Then she took her seat and picked up the top paper. For a second, she couldn't figure out why the lines and words seemed to be blurring, then she touched her cheek and felt the tears. She blinked them away and bent over to complete what she had begun.

Chapter 15

Cort stood beside the police car and watched the entrance of the main building. Faith followed the security guard out into the parking lot. She glanced around at the two police cruisers, searching through the small crowd collected next to the vehicles, until she found him. Their eyes met briefly. She stopped in midstride.

She'd pulled her hair back in a ponytail, exposing her face to view. The blue T-shirt she wore clung to her torso, outlining her breasts, breasts that he had touched and tasted. The haunted look in her eyes and the quick steeling of her backbone was the only sign she gave that not two hours before he'd behaved like the worst kind of bastard and had deliberately hurt her.

If it had been in his power to do so, he would have called the words back. He would gladly have paid whatever price to forever erase the look of pained humiliation on her face as he'd blurted out the ugly truth of his past. He had no right to treat her that way. Not just because Faith was his responsibility or because he respected her, but because no one deserved that kind of slap in the face. In a moment of anger, he'd selfishly allowed himself to lose his temper.

He'd wanted to lash out at her specifically because she was the one who had made him question the very fabric of his existence. She was the one who asked about the good fight and his role in it. She was the one who made him wonder if doing his job well was enough to show for his life.

He was no better than her father and the other men who had hurt her. He shook his head. That wasn't right. He was worse, because he'd known what he was doing as he'd spoken the deadly words, and he'd gone ahead and said them, anyway.

His only excuse was that in the moment of her confession, when she'd hinted that their relationship didn't have to end just because his assignment was over, he'd wanted to stay. The need to put down roots scared the hell out of him. Sometime when he wasn't looking, Faith had burrowed her way into him. Cutting her out would leave a hole inside. Fear of the pain had made him lash out to scare her away. The excuse was meaningless in the face of what he'd done, but it was all he had.

Cort walked around the uniformed officers to where Faith hovered on the edge of the crowd. He saw her swallow as he approached. She glanced at the ground, then tossed her head back and stared straight at him.

"What's going on?" she asked, her voice calm and even.

She looked pale. He couldn't tell if she'd been crying, and the knot in his stomach jerked tighter. He hated knowing he might have made her cry. Not Faith. Not because of him. He'd always loved her strength best. Damn his sorry soul to hell.

"I'm sorry," he said.

She glared up at him, her blue eyes flashing rage. She motioned to the police officers around them. "This is hardly the time. What are they doing here?"

"I am sorry about before," he said. "But that isn't what I meant. Faith—" He took her arm. She tried to pull away from him, but he wouldn't release her. "Ken is dead."

Her eyes grew wide. She made a strangled noise in her throat and covered her mouth with her hand. He started to pull her close to him, but she jerked away and stood alone.

"What happened?" she asked.

He tilted his head toward the officers talking together. "They found his body earlier today. He'd been shot. They're checking, but they think it's the same gun that was used here last night."

"Someone killed Ken because of the cubs?"

He nodded.

"Oh, no." She folded her arms over her chest as if to ward off the bad news. "That poor boy. Not Ken. He was finally getting it all together." She glanced around wildly. "He has no family. And now he's gone? That's not fair."

"Faith, I'm sorry." He reached for her.

"Don't touch me."

He shoved his hands in his pockets and fought to ignore the bitter taste on his tongue. "The police have a few questions."

"Are they sure?" she asked. "Maybe it's not really him. Maybe it's a guy who looks like him."

"His girlfriend, Nancy, identified the body."

She seemed to fold in on herself. Her hands clutched at her arms and her shoulders bent forward. He wanted to comfort her, but she didn't want to have anything to do with him. He couldn't blame her.

She turned away and walked over to the police officers. The detective in charge pulled out a notebook and began asking questions. Cort had already told them what he knew. He'd asked the cops for extra protection for the way station, but they didn't have the manpower to do more than patrol the area.

He looked at Faith one more time. She stood with her back to him, speaking softly. The detective asked another question, and she nodded. Cort hovered nearby for several minutes. When it became obvious she wasn't going to acknowledge him or accept his offer of help, he went into the building to try and contact Jeff.

He entered her office and was greeted by an irritated Sparky. With all the activity around the compound, the leopard was chained up during the day. Sparky walked to the end of the chain and tugged, then sat down and humphed in disgust. Cort scratched the cat's ears and turned toward Faith's desk. A flat white box sat on the chair he normally used. It was stacked with mail. He picked up the top letter and stared at the address. Then he looked at the second and the third. He felt the weight of the envelopes. Every piece of correspondence was addressed to a government agency. He saw the stack of forms on her desk had been reduced considerably. There was a large pile rubber-banded together with a big note reading "Ask Attorney." A notepad contained a list of contractors. The area code next to the phone numbers was unfamiliar to him, but he would bet money it was for North Dakota. She was going to do it. She was going to open the snow-leopard breeding center.

Pride welled up inside of him. Pride for her and her gutsy nature. There weren't many people, male or female, who would be willing to risk it all for an endangered species. It wasn't just that she might face difficulties in handling red tape and funding and the unique problems of raising the leopards themselves. She was giving up so much. A normal life. Home, family, things most women wanted. She was willing to put her needs aside for the greater good.

He cursed under his breath. He had to forget about what had happened with Faith and get on with his job. He sat in her chair and picked up the phone. After punching in the familiar number, he waited.

It was answered after the first ring. "Markum."

"Where the hell have you been?"

"Hello to you, too, buddy," Jeff said, sounding weary. "I've been chasing the bad guys."

"Did you catch them?"

"No. He slipped through our fingers at the last minute." Jeff exhaled wearily. "What can I do for you?"

"We've had a shooting up here. Faith was injured. And one of the kids working here turned up dead."

Jeff was quiet for a minute, then he said, "Start from the beginning."

Cort brought him up to date. He finished his story by
telling him about the police showing up that afternoon with
news of Ken's murder.

"The men after the cubs will make their move soon,"
Jeff said.

"I know. That's why I was trying to get ahold of you.
You have to get the cubs out of here. We can't wait until
Friday."

"You're right. Ironically, I was chasing the guy responsible for buying the cubs in the first place. That's why I
took off. I didn't have time to let you know, but I knew you
would handle it. How's Faith doing?"

For a second, Cort thought he meant because of what
had happened that morning. "She seems fine, but Ken's
death shook her up."

He heard Jeff tapping his pen on his desk. His boss
cleared his throat. "I'll have a team in there first thing in
the morning. The cubs will be moved, but I'll leave the security in place to protect Faith. Can you hold out for the
night?"

"Yeah. I made a few phone calls of my own while you
were gone and called in some markers. I've already got four
extra guys here."

"That's why you're the best, Cort," Jeff said. "I
couldn't have left Faith in better hands."

Cort didn't bother responding. His boss had that one a
hundred and eighty degrees wrong, but there was no point
in bringing it up now. Jeff would find out the truth soon
enough.

"I'd feel better if Faith wasn't at the compound tonight," Jeff said. "Why don't you send her into town?"

"I've tried. She refuses to budge."

"Try again."

"I'll do my best. You think *I* want her here when the
bullets fly?"

"I know she can be a very stubborn lady."

"You got that right."

"Anything else?" Jeff asked. "Are you and your men
armed?"

For the first time since that morning, Cort smiled. "We have enough guns and claw power to hold off an invasion from a third-world country." His smile faded when he remembered that Faith had been the one to use that example. It had been his first morning at the way station. Funny, he would never have guessed it would turn out this way.

"What about the rest of it?" Jeff asked. "What about you?"

With all that had been happening, it took Cort a second to figure out what his boss meant. "I remembered everything," he said flatly, fighting the anger inside.

Jeff didn't answer.

"You didn't think I would, did you?"

"I knew you'd remember," his boss said finally.

"You don't sound very happy, Jeff. Can't say as I blame you." He thought about the moment when he'd come face-to-face with Dan and pulled a gun on his friend because that was his job. "When this business with the cubs is over, you and I are going to have a talk about what happened down there."

"I look forward to it," Jeff said quietly. "You deserve some answers."

It wasn't the fight he'd been hoping for, but it would have to do. "Get the men here as quickly as you can," Cort said. "We'll hold down the fort until then." He hung up without saying goodbye.

He left Faith's office and headed toward the foyer. Once there, he pushed open the front door and stepped out into the parking lot. The police cars were pulling out. Faith stood watching them.

"Faith?"

She didn't bother turning around. "He's going to come here, isn't he? The man who killed Ken. He's going to come for the cubs and he doesn't care who stands in his way."

"Yes."

She nodded once. "At least you have the decency to tell me the truth about that. I appreciate it. We better get ready." She spun on her heel and started toward the building. As she brushed past him, he grabbed her arm. Immediately, she jerked away from him. "Don't touch me."

Something hot and wild flared from her eyes, but it had nothing to do with passion and everything to do with betrayal. Intellectually he'd known he'd hurt her, but until this moment, until he saw the raw emotion in her eyes, he hadn't known how much. Her agony caught him like a bullet to the gut.

"I'm sorry," he said.

"'Sorry' doesn't cut it."

"I know. For what it's worth, I never meant to hurt you."

She looked at him for a long moment. "It's not worth a damn." She pulled open the door and stepped inside.

He followed her. "Faith, wait. We have to talk. Not about this morning, if you'd rather not, but about what's going to happen tonight."

She stopped so quickly, he almost plowed into her. She balled her hands into fists and looked at him. "How dare you?"

"Stop it. I'm not talking about sex." This time when he grabbed her arms, he held on tight enough to bruise. She twisted away from him, but couldn't break free. "Listen to me. That man *will* come back. He's already proved himself a killer."

She stopped struggling. Fear invaded her eyes. "What are you going to do?"

"My job."

Faith flinched, but didn't look away. "What can I do to help?"

"Leave." He shook off her attempt to interrupt him. "I mean it, Faith. It would be a hell of a lot safer for all of us if you weren't here. You're not a pro. I don't want you to get hurt. I spoke to Jeff, and he's going to move the cubs, but he can't do that until morning. I want you to drive to town and check into a hotel. Two of the security guards will go with you and make sure you're safe."

"No."

She gave one last pull and he released her. He saw a red mark on each of her arms. It darkened into the shape of a man's hand.

"I won't go," she said. "Beth and Rob can't come to work. Who's going to take care of the cats? You're going to be busy. Someone has to look out for the animals. The guards are terrified, and if you sent one of them in to clean a cage, you would be asking for a bloodbath. You're the best. Jeff told me. So keep me alive. It should be easy enough."

She pushed past him and walked down the hall, stopping at the small room used to hold supplies. By the time he'd joined her, she'd unlocked the weapons locker and had pulled out a .22 rifle. She reached in and removed a small revolver and two boxes of ammunition.

She looked up at him and smiled faintly. "As you can see, I'm perfectly capable of taking care of myself."

"I never doubted it for a minute." A single strand of hair floated against her cheek. He wanted to tuck it behind her ear and stroke her soft skin. He wanted to taste her lips and love her into a passionate frenzy until she remembered nothing except the magic they'd shared with their bodies.

She wore no makeup. Her T-shirt wasn't particularly new or stylish. Her jeans had a rip above one knee. Sensible work boots covered her feet. There was nothing glamorous about Faith. Yet he'd never seen her look more beautiful. Her plain clothes, her lack of artifice, made him ache. She'd never pretended to be more than what she was. He was beginning to see he'd destroyed something very precious.

He remembered the addressed envelopes in her office. "You made up your mind," he said. "You're going ahead with the snow-leopard project."

She tilted her chin up. "Yes. There's nothing to keep me here."

He wondered if that was a jab at him, but he didn't ask. Better not to know. "You'll be a success."

She didn't answer. Some of her pain had faded, along with the fear. Strength and determination shielded her emotions. She tucked the pistol into her waistband at the small of her back, closed the locker and picked up the rifle.

"Make sure no one gets trigger-happy and shoots one of the cats," she said, brushing past him. "And stay out of my way."

He couldn't let it end like this. "I know there's nothing I can say to excuse what I did."

She froze in the doorway, her back to him. "You're right about that."

"I never meant to mislead you. I don't know why I lied, except that it was easier than telling the truth. You're right. I *was* treating you like all the other women in my life. But by the time I figured out you were different, I didn't know how to fix it. I'm sorry."

She looked at the ground. "What are you sorry for, Cort? That you never loved that woman? That you said things to hurt me? Are you sorry I'm upset?"

"Yes." He stepped up behind her and took the rifle from her. Slowly, so she wouldn't run away, he turned her until he could look at her face. "All those things."

But he knew something was terribly wrong. She didn't look any happier. Her mouth trembled slightly. The knot in his gut gave another twist.

"You still don't get it," she said. "That's not what matters. Why did you take your last assignment?"

What did that have to do with anything? "It was my job."

"Dan was your friend. Someone else could have gone to bring him back. Someone else could have handled the situation. But you agreed. Why?"

"I'm the best."

She nodded slowly. "And that's all you'll ever be. Damn good at your job." She closed her eyes and drew in a deep breath, obviously struggling for control. It didn't help. A single tear escaped and rolled down her cheek.

He couldn't have been more surprised if she'd pulled out her pistol and shot him. Faith wasn't the type who cried. Cort touched his index finger to her cheek and swept the tear away. The moisture clung to his skin. He curled his hand into a fist, but he could still feel that tiny spot of salty moisture.

She opened her eyes and blinked away the tears. "Fight your fight, Cort. Be the best. Make it enough. Hold on to that, because everything else in your life is meaningless. You want to know why I think you went to South America?"

More than anything, he wanted to disappear and forget the entire conversation. This wasn't what he'd planned. But it was like a car-accident scene. As much as he wanted to, he couldn't make himself look away. "Why?"

"You went because you didn't care about Dan. What kind of man voluntarily puts himself through that kind of hell? I don't think you've cared about anyone, ever. Not even yourself."

"That's not true. Dan was my friend."

"I'm supposed to be your friend, too. Were you as kind to him as you were to me?"

Her verbal blow landed right in the center of his soul and knocked his facade askew. There was nowhere to hide from her words. He could run to the other side of the world, but her voice would follow, screaming out from his mind.

"That's not—"

"Fair?" she asked, staring at him. "Don't talk to me about fair. Were you fair when you let me believe you were the kind of man who knew how to love? I'd just confessed my heart's desire to you. No one ever loved me, no matter what I did. You rewarded that confidence with a lie. You let me believe and hope you were different." Another tear slipped down her cheek, but this time she was the one to brush it away. "You let me believe you might be the one."

She took the rifle from him and rested the butt on the ground. "You have taught me one thing. I'm a strong and determined woman. I'm going to start that breeding program and I'm going to make it work. I'm going to pour my whole being into it, and it's going to be a success. You know why?"

He sensed she was about to deliver the death blow. He stiffened to prepare himself. "Why?"

"Because I was ready to give you my heart, but you weren't interested."

She picked up the rifle and walked away.

He watched her go and knew in a blinding flash of truth that he'd lost her forever. Worse, he'd never known he had the chance to have her. He'd been too caught up in his war against faceless enemies to realize there was more to life than battles. Even warriors needed a home to return to.

He had found the one thing he'd been searching for all his life, and now she was gone. He had killed her love for him, as surely as he'd killed Dan.

Faith spent the rest of the afternoon making phones calls to potential donors to the way station. She spoke to Jeff to see if he could help her with her application for two breeding pairs of snow leopards. By tacit agreement, neither mentioned the cubs, the danger they faced, or Cort. If Jeff heard the catch in her voice, he didn't say anything. He promised to contact several friends he had in Washington and gave her a few more names of possible donors. For minutes, even tens of minutes, she was able to forget what had happened. Then it would all come crashing in on her. Ken, the cubs, Cort. Her mouth would grow dry and the hole inside her would get bigger.

As dusk settled on the compound, she told herself she couldn't hide out in her office forever. She had to face Cort. Of course he would leave in the morning, along with the cubs. In theory, she *could* avoid him until then.

She straightened the papers on her desk. It was so easy to be a coward, but it wasn't *her* way. She might be shaking in her boots, but she would face down the fear and do the right thing. She would go out there and deal with Cort and the cats and the danger.

But what about the things they'd both said? She remembered how she'd angrily told Cort everything that was wrong with him. She'd lashed out like a wounded animal, seeking to inflict as much or more pain on her tormentor.

She sighed. That wasn't fair. Cort hadn't tormented her. He'd hurt her, but she was as much to blame. She'd known from the beginning how it all would end. If the truth be told, she respected his life-style choice. After all, compared with the battle of good versus evil, how important was her heart?

She glanced at Sparky. The leopard looked bored after being chained up all day. "Come on, boy," she said, going over and unhooking him. "Let's go scare the guards."

Sparky leapt to his feet and followed her to the door. He made a beeline for her apartment, rushing with a haste that told her Cort must have already put out his dinner.

The small living room was empty, but a light shone from the kitchen. Dear God, she didn't want to face him in there. Not with the memories of their lovemaking so fresh in her mind. But there wasn't any escape. She drew in a deep breath and forced herself to walk in calmly.

Cort stood at the stove. Two pots and a pan sat on lit burners. The table was set.

"I thought you might be hungry," he said without turning around. "I've made chicken curry."

So they were going to pretend it never happened. She could do that, too, even though it felt dishonest. "It smells great. Can I help?"

"Why don't you go tell the guards we're letting Sparky out." He jerked his head toward the pantry. She could see the leopard's long tail flicking back and forth as he consumed his dinner.

"Sure," she said, wondering how she would get through this last evening. She would almost rather fight with him than pretend they were strangers.

But she didn't get her wish. The meal was long and awkward, with starts and stops of conversation, avoided glances and unspoken feelings hovering like unwelcome guests. It was as if they'd never laughed and talked together. Too much pain, she realized. Too many truths. As soon as they'd finished, she shooed him out of the room and took her time doing the dishes. When the last pot was clean, she wiped the counters, then carefully folded the dishcloth over the edge of the sink. She turned to leave and saw Cort standing in the doorway.

He had his arms folded over his chest. "A truce," he said. "For tonight."

"Why? Is something going to happen?" With all the emotional upheavals, she'd been able to put aside her fear, but now it returned.

"I don't know."

She nodded slowly. "All right, Cort. A truce."

He walked over to her and placed his hands on her shoulders. "I didn't mean to—"

"Hush." She looked up at him. "We both have regrets." His fingers felt warm and comforting as he touched her. "This has been hard on us. You have to worry about security. I feel responsible for what happened to Ken."

"You're not responsible. If anyone's to blame—"

"It's not your fault, either."

He studied her solemnly. "You're a hell of a woman, Faith Newlin."

"You have your moments, as well."

"Gee, thanks." He put his arm around her shoulders and led her out of the room. "What are the chances of you quietly going to bed and sleeping until morning?"

She told herself to step away from him. The casual contact was exquisite torture, reminding her of all the things that would never be. "What are *you* going to do?"

"Sit guard."

"I thought the expression was 'stand guard.'"

"Only if there's no chair."

She gently punched him in the side. "Then I'm going to sit guard with you."

"Somehow I figured you'd say that." He stopped in front of her bedroom door and looked down at her shirt. "You need to dress in dark colors. Long sleeves would be best. Get changed, then meet me in the foyer." He grinned. "You any good at poker?"

"I've never played much."

His grin got broader. "Good."

* * *

Somewhere close to midnight, Cort picked up his radio and made a routine call to the two men down at the gate. Faith listened to the crackling static and stifled a yawn. The spy business was pretty boring. They'd spent the evening sitting on the vinyl couch in the foyer of the main building, playing cards. So far she'd learned how to play blackjack and *Siguiendo la Reina*. The latter consisted of a series of changing wild cards that made the outcome of each game a surprise. She and Cort had avoided mention of anything personal, which left very little to talk about, so they'd concentrated on the game.

He spoke into the walkie-talkie again, this time louder. She looked up. "Anything wrong?" she asked.

"They're not answering." He stood up, walked over to the light switch and flipped it off. The room plunged into darkness with only the outside light filtering through the windows to ease the gloom. He tried to raise the other men.

Faith's boredom vanished and apprehension took its place. She wiped her suddenly damp hands against her black jeans. As Cort had requested, she'd changed into a long-sleeved dark shirt. He wore black pants, sweatshirt and athletic shoes.

After several seconds of static, she heard a man speak. She reached for the guns positioned next to them on the floor. She tucked her revolver in her waistband at the small of her back, and handed Cort his Beretta. He spoke for a minute, listened to the reply, then issued instructions and clicked off the equipment.

"None of the six men on duty are answering," he told her, his expression grim. "There were two guards at the gate and four positioned around the perimeter. Andy and three others were sleeping. They're going to surround the compound and start looking for the missing men."

"What are you going to do?"

His answer was cut off by a low whistle. Faith wasn't even sure she'd heard it, but Cort instantly sprang into action and headed for the door. "Stay here and lock the door behind me," he told her as he slipped out into the darkness.

"Wait a minute," she said, about to complain, but she was talking to herself. As she debated whether or not she should follow Cort, she locked the door. But before she could make up her mind, someone or something bumped against the back door.

Her heart leapt to her throat and her palms grew damp. She drew her gun and held the weapon out in front of her.

"Who is it?" she called quietly.

"Cort. I've got an injured man. Open up."

She stuffed the pistol back in her waistband and pulled the door open. Cort stood in the shadows, holding one of the guards.

"Oh my God." She helped him carry Ralph into the examining room. While Cort slid him onto the metal table, she made sure the blinds were pulled tight, then clicked on a single light directly above the wounded man.

Blood coated the upper half of his body and stained his khaki pants. Faith swallowed hard. She'd seen lots of wounded cats before, but never a person this badly hurt. She washed her hands and grabbed the tray of antiseptic and bandages that she'd set up earlier.

As she unbuttoned Ralph's shirt, Cort checked his eyes. "They're dilating," he said.

She pushed the shirt aside and saw a wound in his left shoulder and another in his right arm. Cort glanced at the holes. "Small-caliber bullets," he said. "Doesn't look fatal."

"Glad to hear that," Ralph mumbled, shaking his head.

Faith pressed gauze to the wounds to stop the bleeding. "How do you feel?"

Ralph started to sit up, then dropped back with a groan. "Like I'm going to pass out."

"What happened?" Cort asked.

She reached for wide tape and secured the dressing on the guard's arm, then started to work on his shoulder. Having something to do took her mind off her fear.

"They came out of nowhere."

"You were posted by the gate?"

"Yeah. I thought I heard something. A truck or a van. I stepped out into the road, then bang, they shot me. Never saw where they were hiding. Next thing I know, I'm eating asphalt." Faith wrapped tape around his shoulder. When she was done, he gave her a shaky smile. "Thanks. When I came to, there wasn't any sign of intruders or the other guard on duty. I'd dropped my radio, but the Jeep was still sitting there. I drove up here right away."

"Where's the Jeep?"

"In the bushes."

Cort gave a curt nod. "Good work." He looked at Faith. "Call the police and get an ambulance up here."

She hurried to the extension on the wall and picked up the receiver. It was dead. She tapped the button several times, but nothing happened.

"There's no dial tone."

Cort swore. "They've cut the lines. The trailer has a two-way radio." He pulled his walkie-talkie from his pocket and spoke into it. He instructed Andy to have one of the men call for help and informed him of the guard's condition.

When he was finished, he looked at Faith. "Unless there's a patrol car already on its way out in this direction, it'll be about a half hour until help arrives. You lock yourself in here and—"

"No! I'm not staying here. I'm a good shot, Cort. I can help."

"You've never been in a combat situation. Stay here with him."

Ralph raised himself up on his elbow. "I'm fine."

"They're my cats," she said, determined to make him listen. "My responsibility. You're going to need all the help you can get. I'll just follow you, anyway. Unless you plan on tying me up, you're stuck with me." With that, she covered the wounded man with a blanket, gave him a quick smile and doused the light. "Let's go."

Cort hesitated. "Damn fool woman."

"Yell at me later."

He stepped into the hall, paused, then went back and gave his walkie-talkie to the guard. "Call if you get into trouble."

"Right."

Cort closed the door behind him, locked it and motioned for Faith to follow. "Do exactly as I say," he told her, his voice quiet.

"I will."

"If you don't, you'll die."

The fear returned, but she refused to give in. "I understand."

He went first, leading the way out the back door and around the right to the underbrush. She kept low to the ground, imitating his crouching run. When they stopped in the cover of several bushes, she pulled out her revolver.

"We can't see the front from here," she said. "How will we know when they get here?"

"They won't come up the front."

"How do you know?"

Cort grabbed her arm and pulled her farther back into the brush. The bushes rustled with each movement. Small branches scratched at her arms, and she was grateful for the long sleeves of her shirt.

"If they were coming up the driveway, they would already have arrived. They're probably going around the long way, up by the Big House."

She glanced to her right. The narrow road from the Big House to the compound was barely visible through the leaves.

"That means they'll come out right here."

"Exactly."

It was as if her questions had conjured up their enemy. First she heard the muffled sound of an engine. It grew louder, then there was silence. Seconds later a large dark van moved along the road and rolled to a stop just before entering the compound. The driver's door opened, and a man stepped out. Faith caught her breath in her throat. They were so close, she could smell the sweat of his body and see the gleaming black leather of his boots.

In front of her, Cort motioned for silence. She nodded her assent; she had no intention of making a sound. She placed her hand on her chest and prayed they couldn't hear the pounding of her heart.

The men collected on the opposite side of the van. She heard the door slide open and the distinctive clinking of rifles banging together. Then the men stepped out in front of the van and fanned out. There were four altogether. Three went toward the building, and the fourth moved up the compound, keeping close to the cages.

Cort leaned close to her. "Stay here. If they try to get away, wait until they're in the van, then shoot the tires. But don't leave the cover of the forest."

"Don't be crazy," she whispered heatedly. "You can't go out there alone. It's four against one."

In the blackness of the night, with only the moon to light his face, she saw him smile. His eyes glinted with the knowing confidence of a born predator. "Even odds," he said, and he disappeared behind the van.

Faith shifted until she was sitting on the ground. The dirt was still warm from the heat of the day, and although she was scared, her nerves were finally settling down. Cort could handle it, she told herself, hoping her belief made it true. He had four guards of his own out there. He would simply call and tell them that—

She rose to her knees. He couldn't call for help; he'd given the wounded man his walkie-talkie. She started to stand, then remembered he'd told her to stay put.

"Now what?" she muttered, torn by indecision.

Then she recalled something that made the fear return. Her stomach clenched tight and her palms grew damp. After dinner, she'd never bothered to chain Sparky. He was loose in the building, and armed men were about to invade his territory.

Chapter 16

Cort stepped across the narrow road, then slipped behind the van and into the forest. For a split second he wondered if he should have brought Faith along with him. She would have slowed him down, but he didn't trust her to follow directions.

Damn. He should have tied her up and left her locked in a closet in the main building while he had the chance. At least there he would know where she was. Concern weighed on him. She would follow instructions as long as it was convenient, and there wasn't anything he could do about it.

He paused by an old maple tree and faded into the shadows. Closing his eyes, he drew in a breath and pushed all thoughts of Faith from his mind. He couldn't afford the distraction, not if they were both going to make it out of this situation alive. He concentrated on his prey, focusing until his hunter instincts hummed with readiness. He heard a low growl from one of the jaguars and began moving in that direction.

When Cort was behind the last cage, he peered around it toward the main compound. He saw the stranger staring warily at the jaguars in their separate cages. He stood about three feet away, just inside the protective chain. The cats paced angrily, eyeing him, resenting the intrusion. But they hadn't lashed out yet. Cort allowed himself a slight smile.

He bent down. Never taking his eyes off the man, he felt for small rocks and clumps of dirt on the ground. When he had a handful, he moved behind the cage, slipping silently, until he was between the two wild cats' cages. He tossed two pebbles at the metal base of the cage. They made a small pinging sound.

As Cort stepped back to fade into the darkness of the forest, he saw the other man lean toward the sound. One of the jaguars came to investigate the noise, the other stayed at the front of the cage.

Come on, Cort mouthed silently. *Just a little closer.*

Thomas stopped in front of the main building and motioned for his two men to wait. He listened, but there was only the quiet restlessness of the cats.

So far the mission was progressing well. They'd taken out a total of six guards. Two had been shot, another four tied up. If only he knew how many were left. So far there'd been no sign of the woman. He could only pray the cubs were still here.

He stepped forward; the two men with him followed close behind. No lights shone out from the building. Thomas gripped his pistol tighter. His assistants carried rifles, but he preferred a smaller weapon. Tucked in his jacket pocket were two bottles of tranquilizer and a needle. The cubs had been difficult to handle when he'd tried to smuggle them into the country.

"Stay here," he said softly to one of the men. "Don't let anyone in."

The man took up position beside the door. Thomas reached for the knob and pulled. The door opened slowly. He motioned for the second man to go in first, then followed him into the building. His heart was pounding with excitement and fear. He couldn't afford to fail.

As he stepped into the foyer, the glow from the lights out front illuminated the shabby furniture and part of the hallway. He knew the room the cubs had been in before. He turned and headed in that direction. He paused and sniffed. Mint? He inhaled again. What the hell ... ?

Cort held his breath as the man stepped closer to the cages. He willed the jaguars not to lash out at their prey, but to let him get close enough to step between the cages. He tossed another rock and it bounced off the cage.

The jaguar closest to him growled low in its throat. Cort ignored the cat and watched the man. A rifle gleamed in the faint moonlight. Cort didn't want any of the cats getting hurt. He lifted his pistol and took aim. He would rather take prisoners, but if that wasn't an option, he would kill him before risking the jaguars, or any of the cats.

When he had the stranger in his sights, Cort stepped back and deliberately snapped a twig. The man started at the sound, then took the last step that put him in between the two cages. Cort ducked down, raced toward the cage and banged into it hard. The jaguar by him roared and lashed out with a huge paw. Cort rolled out of the way and came up on his feet.

The second cat reached through the front of the cage and caught the man's arm with a swipe of its paw. The man screamed and dropped his rifle. It slipped between the bars and into one of the cages. The stranger clutched his arm and ran toward the rear of the cages. The jaguar by Cort snarled, stuck its paw out of the corner and clawed at the air. The man froze. He spun, but there was no escape. A large cat waited at each end of the narrow corridor. He moaned softly, then sank to his knees. Cort turned and jogged toward the main building.

Faith stopped in her tracks when she heard a man scream. Please, God, let Cort be all right. Her stomach lurched. She listened again, but there was only the sound of the cats pacing restlessly. One of the jaguars howled its frustration.

Faith wasn't sure which way to go. She would never catch up to Cort in the undergrowth. The moon provided some light, but not enough. Outdoor lamps illuminated the front of the building, but little of their glow spilled into the back. She peered into the darkness and bit her lip. She had to make up her mind; she couldn't just stand here forever.

She clutched her pistol tighter in her hand and turned toward the main building. Keeping close to the ground, she circled in front of the bushes, ducked behind the van and came out fifty feet from the man on guard. She moved slowly, cautiously, never taking her eyes from his dark form. He paced restlessly, like one of the cats; but unlike them, he was afraid. She could smell his fear. It made her feel better. When she was twenty feet away, she stepped up onto the porch. Her work boots scraped against the wood, and the man spun in her direction. She thrust her arms up in front of her, her pistol aimed.

"Freeze," she called. "And drop it."

The man stared at her as if he'd seen a ghost. Then he took a step toward her. "Lady, you're going to hurt yourself." He eased his rifle off his shoulder.

"I'll shoot," she said, and in that second, wondered if she could. She started shaking. The gun in her hand wobbled slightly.

"Come on," he said, taking another step. "No one is going to hurt you."

"I mean it," Faith said. She drew in a calming breath. He wasn't giving her a choice.

He started to raise the rifle, then he jerked his head and looked behind her. Faith resisted the instinct to turn around.

"Drop it," she said again.

He ignored her. She took aim, held her breath and pulled the trigger.

The gunshot echoed loudly in the compound. Several of the cats roared at the noise. Faith stared as the man slumped to the ground. His rifle went spinning on the porch. As she reached down to pick it up, someone grabbed her arm.

She turned to fight, then drew in a gasp of relief when she recognized Cort.

"I thought I told you to stay put," he growled, taking the rifle from her and opening the breech. The ammunition spilled onto the ground.

"I couldn't," she said. "I remembered that Sparky isn't chained up. They might hurt him."

"They might *kill* you."

"I couldn't leave him."

"That bitch shot me," the man on the ground spat out. He cursed several times.

Cort thrust her the rifle, then went forward and bent over the man. "You got him right through the knee. What were you aiming at?"

"His knee."

He looked up at her and grinned. "Good shot."

She smiled back, then felt the adrenaline begin to leave her body. Her legs wobbled as her muscles threatened to give way. She leaned against the building.

Suddenly the lights on the other side of the building went out. Then she heard a thumping noise from inside.

"Cort?"

Cort reached in the pocket of his black jeans and pulled out a thin rope. "One of them cut the power to make it harder for us. The other one is breaking open the doors we left locked. We don't have much time." He secured the bleeding man's hands behind his back.

"You can't leave me here," the man protested.

Cort didn't answer. He pulled a cloth out of his other pocket and used it to gag the man, then he dragged him to the far end of the porch and into the brush.

"Stand near him," Cort said. "Make sure he doesn't try anything. And stay out of trouble."

Another man came running across the compound. Cort raised his gun up toward him, then lowered it to his side. "Andy, what's going on?"

"I heard a shot. Are you—"

"We're fine. How are the other men?"

"We've found three of the six missing guards. They were tied up."

Cort jerked his head toward the building. "One is inside. Wounded, but he'll make it. I'm going in the building. Stay out here with Faith." He glanced at her. "Don't let her do anything foolish."

"Fine." Andy reached for her arm to draw her away from the building.

Faith hesitated, then allowed herself to be led toward the cages. "Don't forget about Sparky," she said. "I don't want anything to happen to him."

"I won't." Cort moved toward the building and paused by the door. He listened intently, then pulled it open and disappeared inside.

"And take care of yourself," Faith whispered when he was gone.

Cort let his eyes adjust to the gloom. Here, in the building, there wasn't even the faint light of the moon to guide him.

When he could make out the shape of the couch by the front door, he knew it was time to move. He listened to the silence and tasted the air, waiting to see where his enemy hid. His senses became hypersensitive. Every muscle tensed in readiness. At last he felt it—a crawling sensation on the back of his neck. He turned and started down the hallway on his right, away from the cubs.

The first three doors stood open. The fourth was shut, but not locked. He waited two heartbeats, then pushed it open and ducked inside.

Immediately, he hit the floor and rolled silently to a crouched position. A single gunshot pierced the wall inches from where his head had been. He scanned the darkness, waiting for a sign of movement. There. Under the window. The shape of a man. Cort crept forward until he was inches from him, then he reached out and pulled his left arm hard against the guy's throat.

The man struggled, but Cort hung on. The man fought to bring up his gun. Cort raised the Beretta and pressed it against the man's temple.

Instantly his prisoner went limp and dropped his weapon to the floor. It landed with a thud.

"I thought you'd see it my way," Cort said, tucking his gun in the waistband at the small of his back. He reached in his pocket for the rest of his rope.

He was tying the last knot when he heard a sound from outside in the compound. He froze. The sound came again. It was Faith calling his name.

No! He grabbed his prisoner's gun and jogged down the hall toward the foyer. No, not Faith. Panic threatened, and was doused by rage. If that bastard tried anything—

He pushed opened the door and stepped outside. The glow of the moon illuminated the tableau in front of him. Andy lay on the ground unconscious. Blood poured from a cut on his head. A medium-sized man stood holding Faith as a shield in front of him. He had a gun pressed to her cheek.

Cort forced himself to ignore her and stare only at the man.

"Throw down your weapon," the man said quietly. "You try anything and I'll blow off her pretty face."

Cort did as he was asked. He still had his Beretta, but the man couldn't see it. Patience, he told himself. He'd get this bastard yet.

"I want the cubs," the stranger said. "Bring them out."

"I told him," Faith said desperately. "They've already been moved."

Cort allowed himself a quick glance at her. Her wide eyes showed fear, but she didn't plead for help. The determined set of her mouth and her squared shoulders told him she wanted to play this game out. Even now, with her life on the line, she was able to think on her feet. He felt a flash of admiration.

The man jabbed her cheek with the barrel of the weapon and she cried out. "Don't lie to me. I know they're here. Bring them out."

"They're not here," Cort said evenly, stalling for time.

"Don't play with me," the man warned.

"They're up at the Big House."

Faith stared at him as if he'd lost his mind, then she got it. She wiggled against the man holding her. "Don't tell him. I won't let them take the cubs back."

She was convincing, he thought, realizing in that moment exactly what he'd lost when he'd turned his back on what she offered.

"Okay, lady, let's go. You—" he jerked the gun at Cort "—lead the way. Don't mess with me. I'm not squeamish about killing women."

Cort started to turn when he saw a low black shadow moving around the side of the compound. He glanced over his shoulder. When he'd come outside, he'd left the door open.

"Move," the man said, not noticing the menacing shape silently slipping closer.

Cort took another step and prepared himself to lunge toward the man. He looked at Faith, trying to communicate with her. She followed his gaze, looked surprised, then nodded faintly.

"Now," the man ordered, tightening his hold on her waist.

She cried out, louder than necessary, then twisted in his hold. "Let me go," she demanded.

The shadow froze, then leapt up toward the struggling pair. Cort jumped toward them, too. Sparky landed on the man's back and sank his claws through the layers of shirt and jacket down to the skin. The man screamed and dropped his gun. Cort grabbed Faith and pulled her behind him, then pulled out the Beretta.

Sparky held the man's shoulder and bit hard. The man screamed again.

"Let him go, Sparky," Faith said shakily. The leopard raised its head and looked at her. "Sparky, come," she said, and collapsed to her knees.

Sparky bent down, gave the man a shake, then padded over to her. Cort moved next to her and held his gun on the intruder. In the distance, he heard the faint wail of a police siren.

* * *

Two weeks later, Faith was at her desk when she saw the sleek sports car stop just outside her office window. She ran down the hall and out into the compound.

Jeff had driven in the back way, and he parked by the narrow road. He got out and grinned at her. "You don't look too bad for a lady who faced down armed bad guys."

She gave him a quick hug. "I've had time to recover from the shakes." She smiled. "It's good to see you."

He looked around the compound. "I meant to get here sooner, but work got in the way. Here, I brought you these." He reached in the car and pulled out several photos. "They're doing great."

She glanced at the snapshot of the tiger cubs. "I can't believe they've grown that much in two weeks."

"They miss you."

"No." She shook her head. "They miss Cort. He was the one who took care of them."

She glanced over to where Cort was playing tug-of-war with Sparky. He'd barely looked up when his boss arrived, but she sensed his tension. She knew he wanted to talk to Jeff about Dan. Not that he'd bothered to tell her. In the last two weeks they'd done little more than work long days and stay out of each other's way.

Behind him, most of the habitats stood empty. The California zoo people would take possession at the end of the week. The jaguars had been returned to their zoo. Samson and Tigger had been moved to a way station in the high desert of Southern California, and the other cats had been shipped off to different facilities across the country. The last two cougars were leaving in the morning, but she wouldn't be here to see them go. She would already be on her way.

She handed Jeff back the pictures. "Thanks for all your help."

"Hey, you did the hard part." He draped an arm around her shoulders and led her toward the main building. "I'm sorry about all the trouble."

"You've apologized about fifty times. It's okay. None of us expected those men to show up like that to take the cubs."

"I'm just glad it's all over. Once we arrested him, William Thomas spilled his guts, and we've finally got his boss indicted."

"When did that happen?"

Jeff held open the door for her. "Last week."

"So why did you leave Cort here?"

"He was still on medical leave, and I wasn't sure one or two of his men might not try to get a little payback. The security couldn't hurt. But we've rounded up the last of them."

She led the way into her office. As she moved to go around her desk, she stepped out of his casual embrace. Her feelings for her friend were warm and pleasant, but nothing like the sweeping passion and heart-stopping love she felt for Cort. It was like comparing a house cat to a tiger. She glanced at the bare walls of her office. Or a snow leopard.

Jeff took the seat on the other side of her desk, in the chair she thought of as Cort's. Cort would be leaving, as well. But not with her. Jeff would give him a lift into the city, and then he would go back to wherever spies went in between assignments.

"So you're really going to do it," Jeff said.

She glanced around at the packed boxes stacked at the side of the room. "Sure looks that way. Edwina's foundation has assured me I'll get the promised funding. They even came through with a little extra money. I have an attorney in Washington and another in North Dakota working with the necessary government agencies. It'll take months to get the final approval. In the meantime, I have meetings with contractors scheduled the week after I arrive. I should be up and running by the end of the year."

"This may help with those start-up costs." Jeff reached into his suit jacket pocket and pulled out an envelope. He handed it to her.

She glanced at it, then at him, taking in his blond surfer good looks and the haunted expression that never left his eyes. She wished there was something she could say to take away his pain, but she knew words wouldn't help at all. She felt that same emptiness herself. Her chest tightened every time she thought about Cort leaving.

Since the cubs had been taken away, she'd thought of little else. What was she going to say? How could she tell him what he meant to her without embarrassing him or making him feel he owed her something? Maybe it would be better to say nothing at all. She should simply let him go. Fancy last words wouldn't make a difference. His leaving was going to devastate her.

She opened the envelope. The first piece of paper was a check for one million dollars. She glanced up at Jeff and raised her eyebrows. "You've been saving your pennies."

He smiled. "I did get a raise with my promotion. Actually, it's from an environmental group. Not one of the ones doing the calendars and mailings, but a smaller organization, funded by a handful of very wealthy patrons. I gave them a copy of your proposal and a list of your credentials. They were quite impressed."

"You didn't have to do that."

"I wanted to."

She felt herself getting weepy, so she scanned the other sheets. They contained names and addresses.

"Potential donors," he told her. "I've met a few people."

"Oh, Jeff." She stood up and came around the desk. He rose, and she stepped into his embrace.

As his arms pulled her close, she fought an overwhelming sense of sadness. If only they could have cared about each other the way they had cared about their respective soul mates. But it wasn't to be.

She looked up at him. "You're the best friend I've ever had."

"You're some lady yourself." He tapped her nose and smiled. "When are you leaving?"

"Right after you. The movers are coming tomorrow, and Beth is going to oversee all of that. I'm just taking some personal things."

"And Sparky."

"Of course. What else could I do with him? He's my family."

Jeff's blue eyes met and held hers. "What about Cort?" She tried to pull out of his embrace, but he wouldn't let her go. "I thought something had happened between the two of you."

"You thought wrong. Cort's healed completely and ready to go back to fighting his wars."

Jeff cupped her face in his hand. He studied her, then slowly nodded. "I'm so sorry," he said softly, and kissed her cheek.

"I'll be fine."

He stepped back. "You know what, Faith? I believe you will be. I admire that."

"You don't have to mourn forever, either," she said.

"I don't know how to do anything else." He turned toward the door. "I'll try to get up to visit in the next couple of months."

"I'd like that," she said, then watched him go.

When Cort saw his boss leave the main building, he released his grip on the thick towel. Sparky immediately took off for the telephone poles and climbed up, holding his prize in his massive jaws.

As Jeff approached, he pulled several photos out of his jacket pocket and held them out. "I thought you might like to see how the cubs are getting along. Faith says they've really grown."

Cort folded his arms over his chest. "You've got a hell of a lot of nerve."

"Oh? Something tells me you don't mean the extra time you've spent up here."

"Not quite. What the hell were you thinking of, sending me after Dan? Jesus, Jeff, he was my friend. You sent me to kill him."

Jeff tucked the pictures away. "I didn't see any other way."

Cort narrowed his eyes. "The hell you didn't."

"The director wanted Dan taken care of. I disagreed. I thought Dan deserved a chance. So I sent you in to solve the problem. You were my ace in the hole. I knew you couldn't kill your friend."

Cort stared at him, dumbfounded.

Jeff gave him a slight smile. "I trusted you to find another solution."

"Yeah, I got him killed by his new associates." Cort leaned against the telephone pole.

Jeff's smile faded. "That wasn't your fault. If you hadn't been shot, you would have forced him onto the plane. Once he was here, the director couldn't have done anything about it. Dan would have been alive."

"And in prison. Not much better than being dead," he muttered, but most of his anger had faded. Jeff's plan might even have worked.

"He would have had a chance," Jeff said. "Everybody deserves that."

"You could have clued me in on this."

"I didn't want to interfere. If I told you the plan, it would be my decision, not yours. You were the one going out in the field. What if Dan had to be killed? Only you could make that determination. Plus, I was breaking all the rules. If it all hit the fan, I didn't want you to take the fall with me."

Cort stared past him to the empty habitats. Once it had been easy to know the bad guys. Now the lines blurred. "Why did he do it?"

"I don't know. Maybe for the challenge of seeing if he could. We'll never know for sure."

"Hell of a way to make a living."

"So do something else."

"Like what? This is all I know."

Jeff started toward his car. "We're starting a task force with the Canadians to help deter terrorism in both countries. I don't have anyone to run it yet. It's a promotion. Interested?''

For the first time, he was tempted by one of Jeff's offers. Cort shoved his hands in his pockets. "Maybe."

"You would have to travel a lot, but you wouldn't need to live in D.C." Jeff pulled open his car door. "I have to make a decision by the first of the month. Let me know." He stepped into the car and shut the door. Then he rolled down the window. "You can still fight the war from the inside, Cort. Sometimes it helps to see the big picture. Think about it."

Cort watched him drive away. It was only when the dust settled and the sound of the engine faded that he realized he'd meant to bum a ride with Jeff. Cort looked up at the main building. Who was he kidding? He couldn't leave without saying goodbye. The problem was, he should have left here days ago. He just couldn't find the right words to let Faith go.

He'd hung around for two weeks pretending to handle security, when the truth was that he couldn't bear to leave. He'd been hoping she would say something, or even walk into his room naked one night. Any hint would have been enough. But she'd been all business, and he'd been— scared. He wanted her to know that he'd finally figured it all out. He cared about her. But would she believe him? Had he left it too long or hurt her too much?

The door opened, and Faith stepped out. She stared at him. "I thought you were gone. Wasn't Jeff going to take you to town?"

"I guess he forgot."

Faith held a leash in her hand. She started past him and called for Sparky.

"Wait," he said, touching her arm.

She stopped. Now. He had to tell her now. Only, the words stuck in his throat. They would all sound stupid, anyway, and she was so tough, she probably didn't need him at all.

"I'll be happy to take you into town," she said, clenching the leash tightly in her hands. "You can rent a car and drive wherever it is you're going." She didn't look quite as in control.

"Where are *you* going?" he asked.

"North Dakota. I told you."

"Alone?"

She drew in a breath and glanced at him. "With Sparky."

He could practically feel the tight grip she had on herself. The effort it took her to act normal gave him courage.

"What is this all about, Cort? What do you want from me? A tearful goodbye? I'm not like your other women. I can't cry on command."

"You're so damn feisty," he said, and smiled. "No, don't cry. I couldn't stand it if you did that. I *would* like you to tell me you love me, though. Just once."

She stared at him as if he'd told her to shoot one of her cats. "Are you crazy?"

"No." He shrugged. "I'm scared as hell. Jeff offered me a job."

Her eyes narrowed. She wasn't going to make this easy on him. "You *have* a job."

"This one would be inside. I'd have to travel, but—"

Her anger faded. The lines of pain around her mouth softened. A few strands of hair escaped from her braid and drifted around her face. He reached out and tucked them behind her ear. She didn't flinch from him.

"But what?" she asked softly.

"I could live anywhere."

In her worn jeans and pale yellow work shirt, she wasn't anyone's idea of a beauty. He smiled. That wasn't true. She was his idea of the perfect woman. Strong and faithful, and incredibly sexy. She drew herself up to her full height, then nodded as if she'd come to a decision.

"All right. What have I got to lose? I love you, Cort."

He was surprised the words affected him. His throat tightened, and deep in his chest he felt an answering flood of emotion. "Just like that. Doesn't anything scare you?" he asked.

"You scare me. Here's my heart. Are you going to trample it again?"

He thought he saw her tremble, but he wasn't sure. He thought about the price he'd paid to fight his good fight and about how few times anyone got a second chance.

"No, Faith," he said. "I'm going to keep your heart with me always."

She looked hopeful, but wary. "Why?"

"That's easy. I love you, too."

She stared at him, then flung herself into his arms. He held her tightly against him, and the cold darkness around his soul cracked, allowing a little light to creep in. It hurt, but in a good way. Nothing had ever felt this right.

"Think I'll be the only spy living in North Dakota?" he asked.

"I'm almost sure of it."

"Think we can make this thing work?"

"Absolutely."

"Good, because I'm not letting you go."

He cupped her face and bent down to kiss her. She met him more than halfway, and passion flared between them. The rightness of their embrace, the feel of her body pressing against him, that damn French perfume, all called him home.

He felt something nudging his leg. He tried to ignore it, but the next nudge practically knocked him off balance.

Faith stepped away and laughed. He petted the black leopard. "Yes, Sparky, I care about you, too." Sparky rumbled deep in his throat. The purring sound floated out into the afternoon.

"Come on," he said, taking the leash from her and attaching it to the leopard's collar. "Let's get going. We've got a long drive ahead of us."

"But don't you have to report to work?"

He took her hand and started toward the building. "Jeff said he didn't need an answer until the first of the month. That gives us enough time to stop off in Las Vegas and get married." He glanced at her. "Unless you want a big wedding?"

"Married?" She stared at him. "We're getting married?"

"Don't you want to?"

She grinned. "Of course. I'm just surprised. Next thing you'll be telling me you want kids."

"Why not?" He held open the door for her and followed her through the foyer and out to the front. A large truck sat in the driveway. In back was a special cage for Sparky. Cort loaded him in and secured the latch. "I mean to do this thing right. I want a whole litter of kids. What is that—maybe five?"

"Five?"

He held open his arms and hugged her close. "One, five, whatever you want." He stared down into her blue eyes. "I'll love you forever. I swear."

"I believe you," she whispered, drawing his head down closer to hers. This time she *could* believe. He would cherish her with the same unswerving loyalty with which he'd fought his battles. She trusted his honor and his love. Cort was the most special of creatures—a man who mated for life.

* * * * *

COMING NEXT MONTH

#559 KEEPER—Patricia Gardner Evans

American Hero

From the moment American Hero Cleese Starrett encountered
Laurel Drew fishing in his river, he was hooked. But this alluring woman
had a tortured past and a threatened future, a future that Cleese wanted to
share—at any cost.

#560 TRY TO REMEMBER—Carla Cassidy

Romantic Traditions

"Jane Smith's" memory had vanished, so when Frank Longford offered
her a safe haven and a strong shoulder, she accepted. Then the nightmares
began, with remembrance proving scarier than amnesia, and Jane feared
losing the one man she truly loved.

#561 FULL OF SURPRISES—Maura Seger

Chas Howell's life changed irrevocably the day he laid eyes on
Annalise Johannsen. This feisty lady rancher needed help and protection,
and Chas knew the job would suit him just fine—and so would
the employer....

#562 STRANGER IN TOWN—Laura Parker

Jo Spencer thought she'd seen a ghost, so strongly did Gus Thornton
resemble the forbidden love of her past. But even though Gus claimed to
be new to town, Jo swore she glimpsed familiar desire—and haunted
memories—in this stranger's eyes.

#563 LAWYERS, GUNS AND MONEY—Rebecca Daniels

With the conviction of a major crime boss to her credit, federal prosecu-
tor Gillian Hughes became a red-hot target. Undercover agent Ash Cain
vowed to keep her safe. Yet soon he found himself in over his head,
because tough-guy Ash had fallen head over heels....

#564 HARD EVIDENCE—Laurie Walker

Pursuing the evidence that would clear her of a manslaughter charge,
Sergeant Laurel Tanner found herself with an unlikely ally, the dead
man's brother. But she soon feared that Scott Delany's helpful intentions
stemmed not from desire—but from double cross.

ROMANTIC TRADITIONS continues in April with Carla Cassidy's sexy spin on the amnesia plot line in TRY TO REMEMBER (IM #560).

"Jane Smith's" memory had vanished, so when Frank Longford offered her a safe haven and a strong shoulder, she accepted. Then the nightmares began, with memory proving scarier than amnesia, as Jane began to fear losing the one man she truly loved.

As always, **ROMANTIC TRADITIONS** doesn't stop there! July will feature Barbara Faith's DESERT MAN, which spotlights the sheikh story line. And future months hold more exciting twists on classic plot lines from some of your favorite authors, so don't miss them— only in

INTIMATE MOMENTS
Silhouette®

by Linda Turner

Out in **The Wild West**, life is rough, tough and dangerous, but the Rawlings family can handle anything that comes their way—well, *almost* anything!

American Hero Cooper Rawlings didn't know what hit him when he met Susannah Patterson, daughter of the man who'd shot his brother in the back. He *should* have hated her on sight. But he didn't. Instead he found himself saddling up and riding to her rescue when someone began sabotaging her ranch and threatening her life. Suddenly lassoing this beautiful but stubborn little lady into his arms was the only thing he could think about.

Don't miss COOPER (IM #553), available in March. And look for the rest of the clan's stories—Flynn and Kat's—as Linda Turner's exciting saga continues in

THE WILD WEST

Coming to you throughout 1994...only from Silhouette Intimate Moments.

SPRING fancy '94

They're sexy, single...
and about to get snagged!

Passion is in full bloom as love catches
the fancy of three brash bachelors. You won't
want to miss these stories by three of
Silhouette's hottest authors:

CAIT LONDON
DIXIE BROWNING
PEPPER ADAMS

Spring fever is in the air this March—
and there's no avoiding it!

Only from

Silhouette®

where passion lives.

As seen on TV!
Free Gift Offer

With a Free Gift proof-of-purchase from any Silhouette® book,
you can receive a beautiful cubic zirconia pendant.

This gorgeous marquise-shaped stone is a genuine cubic
zirconia—accented by an 18" gold tone necklace.
(Approximate retail value $19.95)

Send for yours today...
compliments of ▼ *Silhouette*®

To receive your free gift, a cubic zirconia pendant, send us one original proof-of-purchase, photocopies not accepted, from the back of any Silhouette Romance™, Silhouette Desire®, Silhouette Special Edition®, Silhouette Intimate Moments® or Silhouette Shadows™ title for January, February or March 1994 at your favorite retail outlet, together with the Free Gift Certificate, plus a check or money order for $2.50 (do not send cash) to cover postage and handling, payable to Silhouette Free Gift Offer. We will send you the specified gift. Allow 6 to 8 weeks for delivery. Offer good until March 31st, 1994 or while quantities last. Offer valid in the U.S. and Canada only.

Free Gift Certificate

Name: _____

Address: _____

City: _____ State/Province: _____ Zip/Postal Code: _____

Mail this certificate, one proof-of-purchase and a check or money order for postage and handling to: SILHOUETTE FREE GIFT OFFER 1994. In the U.S.: 3010 Walden Avenue, P.O. Box 9057, Buffalo NY 14269-9057. In Canada: P.O. Box 622, Fort Erie, Ontario L2Z 5X3

FREE GIFT OFFER   079-KBZ
ONE PROOF-OF-PURCHASE
To collect your fabulous FREE GIFT, a cubic zirconia pendant, you must include this
original proof-of-purchase for each gift with the properly completed Free Gift Certificate.

079-KBZ